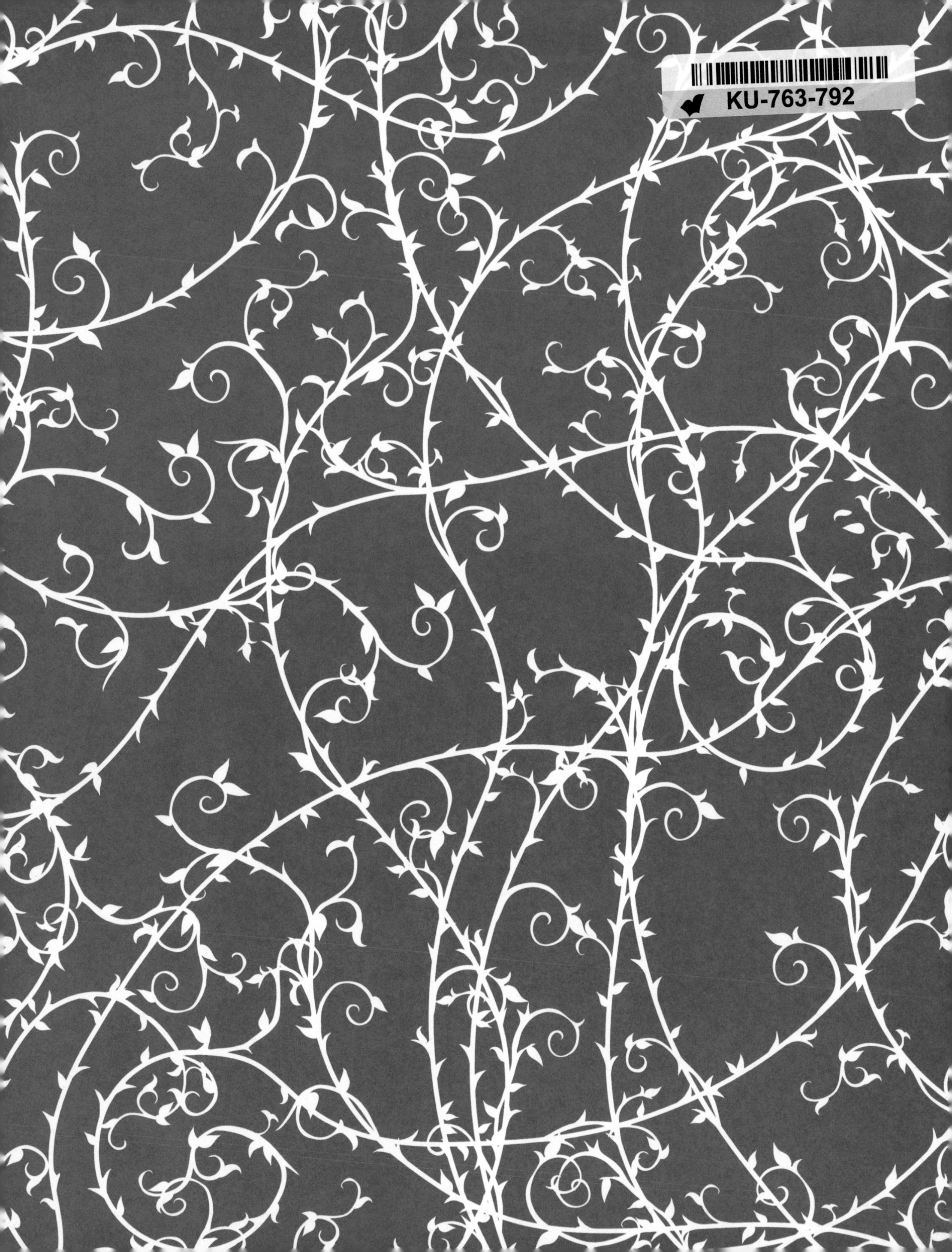
KU-763-792

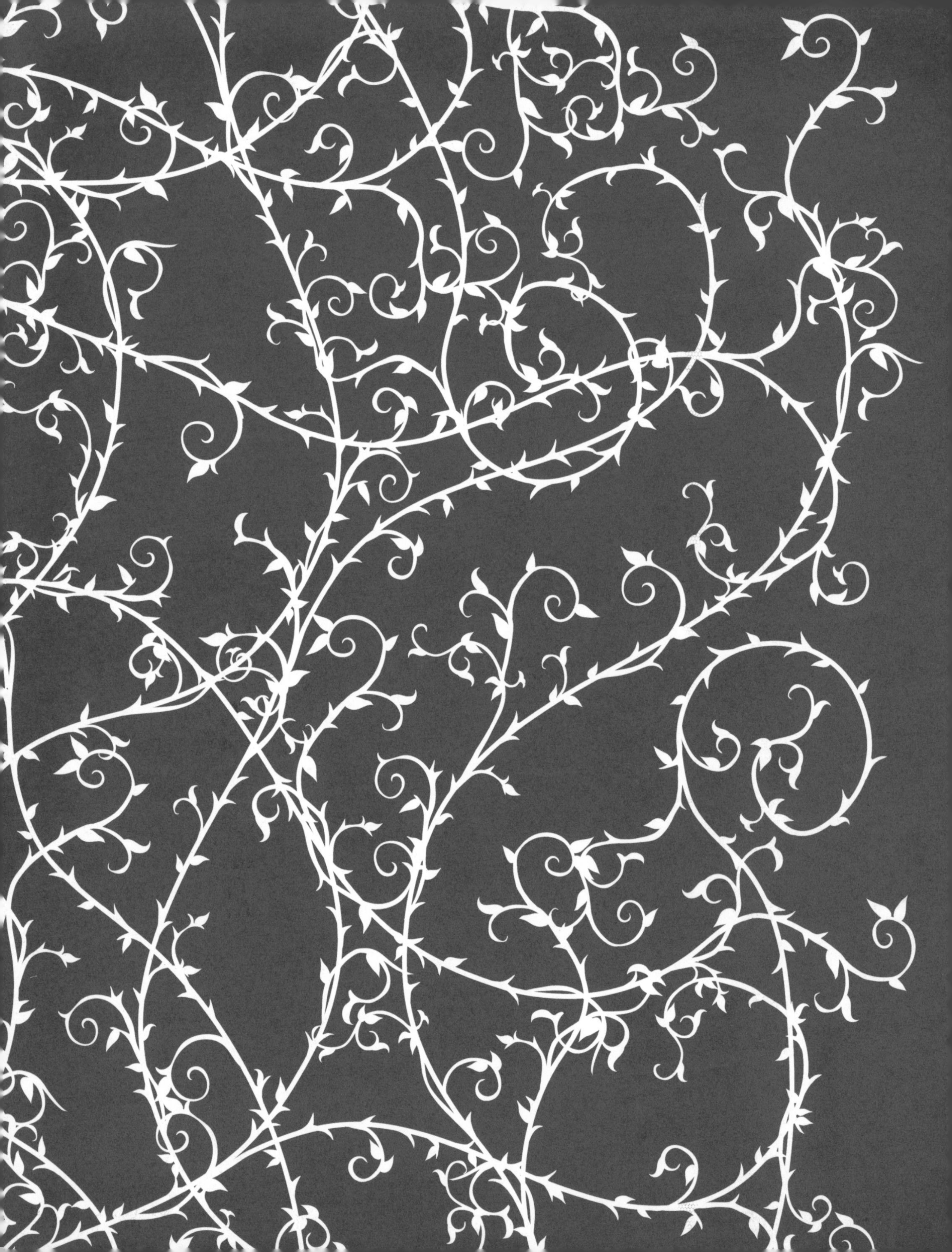

The FAIRY TALES of the BROTHERS GRIMM

Edited by
Noel Daniel

Newly translated by
Matthew P. Price
with Noel Daniel

TASCHEN

—CONTENTS—

—CONTENTS—

More Than Words Can Say: The Grimms' Enduring Legacy and the Art It Inspired

by Noel Daniel

More Than Words Can Say:
The Grimms' Enduring Legacy and the Art It Inspired

t has been two hundred years since two brothers from Kassel, Germany, first published, in 1812, "Hansel and Gretel," "Sleeping Beauty," "Rapunzel," "Snow White," and many other fairy tales that have since become classics. Jacob and Wilhelm Grimm kept adding colorful stories they found, and by the time they released their seventh edition forty-five years later, in 1857, the collection had ballooned to a staggering two hundred tales and ten children's legends. Today, the collection contains many of the most famous tales in the world and has been translated into many languages. What began as an attempt to collect German tales for posterity has become a cultural treasure belonging to all of us, and a potent, ceaseless source of inspiration for generations of writers, artists, and filmmakers around the world.

The Poetry of the People

Initially, the Grimms set about collecting tales as cultural anthropologists and linguists, not as children's authors, and by embarking on this undertaking they joined the ranks of others before them who began publishing tales for adults as early as the eighteenth century. For instance, French writer Charles Perrault became the toast of Louis XIV's Versailles upon the publication of his collection of fairy tales for well-heeled courtiers in 1697. But the Grimms were not interested in fame. Trained as scholars, librarians, and lawyers, their ambition lay elsewhere. The most important thing to them was to gather evidence of a people's poetry—what they perceived as a collective consciousness embedded in a vernacular oral tradition of storytelling—and to permanently secure it in writing for future generations.

Collecting and editing the tales, and even rewriting some, was a Herculean task, and it took time for the Grimms to find their audience. Initially, their adherence to their mission blinded them to the diverse tastes of a growing literate middle class that emerged with the Industrial Revolution and that expected the tales to be entertaining. Despite the title that the Grimms gave their collection, *Children's and Household Tales*, they did not initially intend the book to be primarily for children. It was only after the publication of their early editions that they realized that they straddled two markets: scholars on one hand, and general readers, including children, on the other. The Grimms began to edit out the more adult content to tailor their book for younger readers. It is from their last and most child-friendly edition, published in 1857, that the twenty-seven tales in this book are drawn, as this edition includes all of the changes they made to create a volume that would appeal to children and adults alike.

PAGE 2 AND 8 *The Brothers Grimm made tales such as "Sleeping Beauty" (page 2) and "Hansel and Gretel" (page 8) famous around the world. Danish legend Kay Nielsen created these mysterious, exotic watercolors for his 1925 book of the Grimms' tales.*

LEFT *In 1855 German artist Gustav Süs illustrated "The Hare and the Hedgehog" in a style that appears very modern today (pages 268–274). This book is a striking example of an early children's book that featured multiple large, color images. Economical color printing was still many years off, so each image was colored by hand.*

A World Without Fairy Tales?

It is nearly impossible today to imagine a time when the world—from children's books to literature to movies to everyday quips—was not saturated in the persistent, robust legacy of these classic tales. They have become pervasive code words in popular culture, where "Beware the wolf," or "You have to kiss a lot of frogs to find a prince," or even simply "Cinderella" delivers meaning everyone understands. For this reason alone, the tales are a worthy addition to everyone's library. But the Grimms' influence has been not only literary, but also visual. The Grimms' tales were a vital engine for a whole new caliber of artistic activity, not only in Germany, but across Europe and North America. When the tales were published, they caught the attention of those in society who were already primed and sensitive to fantasy, craft, and creating imaginary worlds: visual artists. The partnership between artists and publishers of the Grimms' tales helped change the way children's books were made and marketed, and this, in turn, had a profound impact on the history of illustrated books. With the rise of professional art schools beginning in the seventeenth century, scores of rigorously trained visual artists were ready to work for hire; publishers, emboldened by a growing book market, employed these artists and harnessed new printing technologies to great effect and, by the end of the nineteenth century, for wide distribution. There were painters, engravers, bookmakers, watercolorists, graphic designers, architects, stage designers, and draftsmen adept at the new nineteenth-century printing technique of stone lithography, and many of the artists were talented in a range of media. Suddenly, artists across the Western world could make a living illustrating books, and they found a solid foundation for new work in the heroes and princesses, talking animals, dwarfs, and witches of fairy tales. The tales were an important part of each technological advancement along the way, and the best of this visual iconography still influences artists, art directors, filmmakers, and animators today. As an added feature, we have provided extended biographies in the appendix of this book that offer more information about the lives and works of the illustrators represented. Even as our modes of reading continue to change with new technologies, taking a measure of the interactivity of text and image in these past treasures helps us understand the changing landscape of reading in the future.

Popular Visual Culture Takes Root

As more and more books were published to meet the expanding needs of a literate public, and as these books began to include illustrations, the nineteenth century saw the dawn of a mass visual culture on a scale not seen before. Fairy tales and folktales helped ignite the intense conflagration

RIGHT *British artist Walter Crane emerged as one of the most popular illustrators of his day, integrating text, image, and design in new ways. He illustrated many children's books, including the Grimms' classic tale "The Frog Prince" in 1874 (pages 23–30).*

FAR RIGHT Ins Märchenland *(*Into the Fairy-Tale Land*) by sisters Fanny and Cécile Hensel is a book of silhouettes of the Grimms' tales, some of which are shown on pages 20 and 200. With their strong characters and mythical landscapes, fairy tales were a perfect subject for the art of paper cutting.*

of art and commerce that set in, as they expanded the field of book illustration and changed how books were made and marketed. Thus the Grimms' tales and their many adaptations, along with the tales of Charles Perrault, with whom there was some crossover of tales (although with differences in the retelling), became critical ingredients that ignited the combustible kindling of widespread literacy, prolific artistic talent, and advances in affordable printing technology. It was this perfect storm of factors that laid the foundation for what we now take for granted as "children's books." Children's literature had existed in the centuries before, but it was generally pedagogical, morally safe, not illustrated, and available only to the upper classes. The new children's books that began to emerge provided innovative artists opportunities to experiment with the relationship between text and image, and this, in turn, put an indelible mark on the history of illustrated books.

This book offers a new approach to understanding the Grimms' important place in this history by pairing twenty-seven of their most famous tales in the order they originally appeared, such as "Little Red Riding Hood," "Sleeping Beauty," and "Snow White," as well as lesser-known gems such as "The Fisherman and His Wife" and "Tom Thumb's Travels," with a carefully chosen selection of fairy-tale illustrations. Some of the most influential artists of the 1820s to the 1950s (when the trend turned away from traditional fairy tales toward fictional tales by author-illustrators and author-illustrator teams) are represented. Other contemporary compilations of the original tales either are not illustrated or they relegate the illustrations to a minor role with poor, sparse reproductions. This book, however, generously illustrates the original tales as never before, so that they can be not only enjoyed as works of art accessible to the whole family, but also appreciated for their part in the international legacy of the Grimms' tales. By bringing together tendencies ranging from Romanticism to protocartoons to Art Deco and beyond, we gain an understanding of artistic developments whose influence can still very much be seen today, whether in books, movies, animation, or video games.

The DNA of All Fairy-Tale Scholarship

Although the Grimms' influence on visual culture was widespread and formidable, this legacy has received less attention than the well-documented and thunderous influence of their prolific study of language and history. The Grimms helped standardize the German language in their books *German Grammar* and *The History of the German Language*, and in the comprehensive German dictionary they initiated. In their *German Legends* and *German Mythology* they gathered pre-Christian tales from the region. With regard to their fairy tales, the Grimms were the first to annotate their

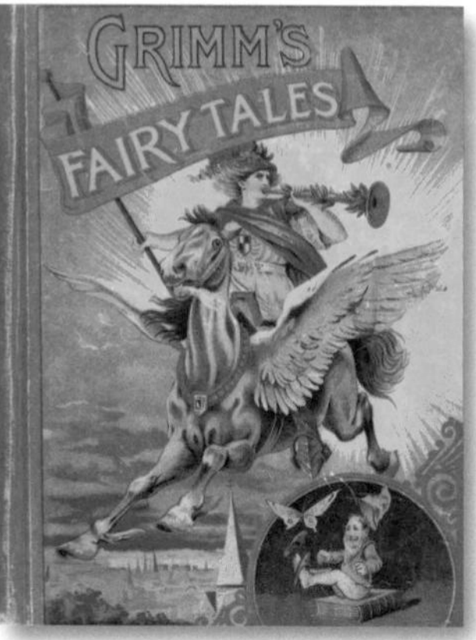

FAR LEFT *This German children's book from 1881, entitled* Märchenpracht und Fabelscherz *(*A Parade of Tales and Fun Fables*), embodies the Romantic trend in nineteenth-century German illustration and includes artwork by Fedor Flinzer (pages 41–46) and Heinrich Merté (pages 60–69).*

NEAR LEFT *In the 1820s, an English translation of the Grimms' tales featuring lively images by British artist George Cruikshank ushered in a new era of illustrated books. This 1899 book included special color versions of his images (page 161).*

OPPOSITE *The Grimms' tales continued to inspire artists into the 1910s and 1920s, the golden age of illustration. Kay Nielsen's watercolor of "The Goose Girl" appeared in his lavish 1925 book of the tales.*

tales with information about their age and place of origin, and the similarities and differences between their tales and versions from other countries. These annotations vaulted their collection well beyond other fairy-tale collections published up to that point, and laid the foundation for the study of folklore, becoming the DNA of all fairy-tale scholarship. Today, historians schooled in this two-hundred-year-old field love to remind us that the Grimms themselves did not strap on their chaps and ride horseback across the country knocking on doors and patronizing taverns on the hunt for fairy tales. In truth, they relied heavily on a few local sources for the oral tales, many of which have multicultural roots, and they also mined literary sources. Theirs was a quiet, scholarly pursuit, which they symbolized in their favorite local source, an innkeeper's daughter and their modern-day Minerva, Dorothea Viehmann, whose portrait they included as the frontispiece of their collection. It is this age-old image of a sage female storyteller that inspired twentieth-century British artist Arthur Rackham's silhouette of children listening attentively to a grandmotherly figure on page 18.

It is worth remembering that when the Grimms released their tales, Germany was not yet a unified country, but rather was composed of independent states loosely held together, sharing a common language but divided by hundreds of dialects, regional cultures, literatures, religions, fashions, and cooking traditions. Since the late 1700s, Europe had been rocked by the French Revolution in 1789, the ambitious wars of Napoleon Bonaparte, and the violent spasms of nation building as rapid industrialization swept the continent. In the face of this political turmoil and change, countries all across Europe turned inward and celebrated their vernacular treasures.

The rational thinking prized during the eighteenth-century Enlightenment attempted to cast strong, cleansing rays of empirical knowledge into the more mysterious corners of society to sweep away mysticism, the occult, and sentimentality, which were considered retrograde. Generations of scholars grappled with these issues, giving birth to legendary treatises on the power of the rational human mind. But in the decades leading up to the publication of the Grimms' tales, the pendulum had already started swinging back toward sentimentality and feeling, and this led to the blossoming of the Romantic movement, which prized authentic, unadulterated, direct communication with emotions and nature. Lurking beneath this discourse all the while was the oral tradition of everyday storytelling that the Grimms, as scholars of the German Romantic movement, would ultimately harness in their tales.

The Grimms' tales were published right at the cusp of a growing appreciation of the needs of children in learning and play. As public education and literacy grew, more reading material was needed, and fairy tales—particularly those with

moral lessons—filled the vacuum. In fact, the genre of fairy tales is one of the few literary genres to which both children and adults connect. Unlike nursery rhymes, which recede relatively quickly as childhood advances, fairy tales and the fantasy worlds they vividly evoke remain close at hand, inspiring literature for adults, memoirs, movies, animation, songs, opera, theater pieces, and video games. It was the narrative power of this primal, nonrational fantasy world that attracted the Grimms, the artists who responded to their tales, and adult and child readers alike.

The Era of Modern Book Illustration Begins

From 1823 to 1826 a two-volume illustrated translation of the Grimms' tales (the second ever up to that point) appeared that would have a profound impact on the way the tales were henceforth published, as well as on the Brothers Grimm themselves. This English translation was accompanied by the lively illustrations of the eminent British illustrator George Cruikshank, one of which can be seen in "The Shoemaker and the Elves" (page 161). As Cruikshank's work circulated in Germany, the Brothers Grimm realized they could enhance the reception of the tales if they too illustrated them, and they enlisted their younger brother, the artist Ludwig Emil Grimm. Although their brother's illustrations are not among the most critically acclaimed from the period and are not in this book, it was an important step by the Grimms. Over the course of their many subsequent editions, printing technology improved and the role of illustrations in books expanded, as can be seen in the selection of illustrations in this book. By the 1850s, for instance, German pioneer Gustav Süs (pages 268–274) had published his exquisite hand-colored lithographs of "The Hare and the Hedgehog," anticipating the playful, simple lines of Beatrix Potter's Peter Rabbit images. By the 1860s, serial illustrations and early protocartoons began to appear in popular broadsides of adapted versions of the tales. In the 1870s, England's book-designer extraordinaire, Walter Crane (pages 23–30), emerged as one of the most popular illustrators of his day, advancing the ideas of integrating text, image, and design inspired by the avant-garde Arts and Crafts movement and devoting much of his career to illustrating children's books, among them many of the Grimms' tales. Arthur Rackham (pages 172–174, 178, 181, 225, among others in this volume), one of England's most beloved and influential illustrators of the early twentieth century, created mysterious, riveting illustrations as well as silhouettes of the Grimms' tales and influenced generations of artists. Fantasy reigned supreme until World War I, exemplified by the work of the Danish illustrator Kay Nielsen, who also illustrated the Grimms' tales (for example, the single-page illustrations in this introduction, and

OPPOSITE, LEFT AND RIGHT *During the golden age of illustration, innovative artists such as Hanns Anker and Wanda Zeigner-Ebel, both from Germany, created colorful, uniquely designed children's books. Selections from Anker's 1910* Aschenbrödel *(*Cinderella*), left, are on pages 103–110, and Zeigner-Ebel's 1920* Sneewittchen *(*Snow White*) is on pages 184–199.*

RIGHT *The full-page images in this introduction are from Kay Nielsen's 1925 book* Hansel and Gretel and Other Stories by the Brothers Grimm. *Much admired for his original style, Nielsen was later hired by Disney to work on the animated movie* Fantasia *(1940).*

on pages 204, 210, 241, and 244) and who later was hired by Disney to work on *Fantasia* (1940). It was Disney who in 1937 released the first feature-length animated film, *Snow White and the Seven Dwarfs*, based on the Grimms' fairy tale and including art by Gustaf Tenggren, the best-selling Swedish-American artist and illustrator of two tales in this book (pages 146–157 and 253–265). This feature-length adaptation of a fairy tale would be the first of many made for the silver screen. While the boom in illustrated books began with Cruikshank's modest black-and-white images of the Grimms' tales in the 1820s, by the first decades of the twentieth century the golden age of book illustration, with lush, color editions printed with the latest four-color printing process, had fully arrived. During this period, the Grimms' tales were illustrated by many of Europe's most successful illustrators who dominated book publishing at that time.

Revival of an Appreciation for the Original Tales

In 2005, the Grimms' fairy tales were selected for inclusion in UNESCO's Memory of the World Register, an initiative to safeguard documents vital to world history. In light of this increased appreciation for the original stories, the time is right for a new illustrated approach to this time-less classic. To this end, I selected twenty-seven for the book, including all the famous tales, plus surprising gems that readers might otherwise not encounter and tales that have inspired generations of illustrators from many countries.

It has been nearly ten years since a major translation of the Grimms' fairy tales has been published in English, and in light of a resurgence in appreciation for the original stories, the time is right for new versions. The translator Matthew Price and I were surprised by what we found as we engaged with the text at the depth that translation requires: It is a text full of feeling, far more humorous and crackling with wit and spice than either of us remembered from the many adaptations we read growing up. We discovered the text anew and tried to bring the pleasure of its words to the forefront. For this reason, we tried to focus on vivid words to communicate the inner theater of the tales, for which Price's background in theater was essential, and to bring out the personalities of the characters, while keeping the English lively and engaging. We also tried hard to retain and capture as much of the oral quality of the tales as possible, by considering tonal range and color for every word, to make sure the text is as much fun to read aloud as it is to read alone.

Some of the tales in this book may differ from the versions readers recall from their childhood, or from similar tales by Charles Perrault. While most versions of the Grimms' tales are adapted, these translations are unabridged and follow the original tales closely. For this reason, we did not tamper

OPPOSITE *Due to the cost, Kay Nielsen created one image per tale for his 1925 Brothers Grimm book. His watercolor of "The Fisherman and His Wife" shows how artists often wove multiple scenes into a single image.*

NEAR RIGHT *Books of silhouettes, such as Käthe Reine's* Grimms Märchen *(*Grimms' Fairy Tales*) from 1925, are reminders of the simple but creative ways artists, especially many women, contributed to the Grimms' legacy.*

FAR RIGHT *Award-winning Swiss artist Herbert Leupin created cartoonlike images of "Puss 'n Boots" in 1946 (pages 279–287).*

with the occasional glimpses of violence that remain in these cleaned-up tales, for instance, at the ends of "Cinderella," "Snow White," "The Goose Girl," and "The Hare and the Hedgehog," which some adult readers may wish to adapt for young ears. Some of the tales are graceful and subtle, and others are dramatic and rough-hewn, but there is plenty of humor, spirit, and pitch-perfect narrative timing in the stories to offer a captivating spectrum of human emotion and to warrant rediscovery by readers of all ages. We, therefore, left all these elements in to allow readers to make up their own minds about the original tales.

Shadow Play and Shape-Shifting: The Heart of the Tales

The research for this project took me far and wide in my efforts to unearth the best vintage illustrations of the Grimms' tales that still exist. The famous tales were often interpreted by many artists, while the lesser-known tales were less frequently illustrated and required more sleuthing to uncover art that I could use. Also, wherever possible, I tried to find meaningful specimens that featured more than one image per story, which was challenging given the trend in many nineteenth- and twentieth-century books to feature one image per tale, or even every few tales, due to the printing expense. During my research visits to archives, however, I also came across beautifully made vintage albums of silhouettes of the Grimms' stories, and I decided to weave in these images, as well as newly commissioned silhouettes, to augment those tales with one illustration by artists whose inclusion was important to the book.

As a popular and democratic craft requiring only paper and a pair of scissors or perhaps a knife, fairy-tale silhouettes occupy an important place in the history of the visual arts and animation in the nineteenth and twentieth centuries, as can be seen, for instance, in the groundbreaking silhouette films of early animator Lotte Reiniger, whose oeuvre includes many short films of the Grimms' tales. The silhouettes in this book are a nod to this history and a reminder of the simple ways artists contributed to the visual landscape, even when prestigious art-school education (especially for many women) and more sophisticated technologies were not available to them. As cousins of shadow theater and magic-lantern slides, the silhouettes embody the essence of shadow play and shape-shifting, both of which are at the dramaturgical core of fairy tales. They are like shadowy Rorschach tests onto which we can project our fears, hopes, and dreams. Simple yet full of meaning, like fairy tales themselves, they resemble shadows at twilight—the moment of shifting from day to night and known to unknown. As darkness descends and reality fades, we enter a dream world onto which we project meaning, so aptly reflecting the journey into the words and images of fairy tales.

THE TALES

The Frog Prince

Although the story dates back to a medieval Latin manuscript from the thirteenth century, "The Frog Prince" is as fresh a tale as ever about the perils of breaking a promise and the pitfalls of judging a book by its cover. In modern versions, the frog's spell is broken not by throwing the frog against a wall, as in the Grimms' spirited tale, but by kissing him. As historian Maria Tatar has observed, this helped spawn the lively adage "You have to kiss a lot of frogs to find a prince" and made the enchanted frog one of the most parodied fairy-tale characters in the world. Both versions have at their heart the frog as a frisky, shape-shifting animal groom, which the artist Walter Crane has captured in an inventive protoanimation drawing on page 29. Shape-shifting, a favorite staple of love stories, has long been used in fairy tales, myths, and science fiction to reveal the hidden qualities of characters such as the gods and goddesses of ancient mythology, vampires, and the beastly paramour in "Beauty and the Beast." Stories of enchanted frogs have been found in Asia, and elements of the tale date back to the second-century "Cupid and Psyche."—ND

Color engravings by Walter Crane, British, 1874

"Stay calm, and dry your tears," the frog said. "But what will you give me if I bring your ball back?"

In the olden days, when children wished upon the stars, there lived a king whose daughters were all very beautiful. But the youngest was so radiant that the very sun, who had seen much indeed in her time, was filled with amazement every time she looked down upon the girl. Near the king's castle was a great dark forest, and in this forest, tucked away under a majestic linden tree, there bubbled a spring. Whenever the day became unbearably hot, the youngest princess would slip out into the woods and sit at the edge of its delightful coolness. And when she was bored, she would take out the little golden ball she always carried, toss it high over her head, and catch it as it came down. This was her favorite game.

One time it happened that she missed the golden ball as it whizzed past her outstretched hand, and it struck the ground and rolled straight into the water. She tried to see where it had gone, but the spring was deep, so deep that she could not see the bottom. She began to weep, and cried louder and louder until she truly could not console herself. But as she lamented, she heard a voice call out, "What has happened, Princess? Your wailing could make a stone beg for mercy." She looked around to see where the voice was coming from, but she saw only a frog stretching its fat, ugly head out of the ripples. "Oh, it's you, you old puddle jumper!" she said. "I'm crying for my little golden ball that's fallen down into the water." "Stay calm, and dry your tears," he responded. "I'm certain I can come up with an answer. But what will you give me if I bring your ball back?" "Whatever you desire, dear frog. My robes, my pearls and jewels, even the golden crown upon my head."

"I am not interested in your robes, pearls or jewels, or even your golden crown," answered the frog. "But if you would be fond of me, and cherish me, and if I were your friend and playmate, sitting next to you at your table, eating from your golden plate, drinking from your cup, and sleeping in your bed—if you will promise me these things then certainly I will slip down below and bring you back your golden ball." "Oh, yes!" she cried. "Whatever

OPPOSITE *"Youngest princess, let me in. Have you forgotten what you promised me by the spring? Let me in."*

PAGES 26–27 *"Push your plate over to me so we may eat together," said the frog. The princess did just that, but she did not do so gladly.*

you want, if you just bring me back my ball." But in her deepest thoughts she was wondering: What on Earth is this strange frog talking about? All it does is sit around in the spring, croaking with its own kind, and certainly it has no place among us humans. Still, the moment the frog heard her agree, he dipped his head down and plunged beneath the surface. Soon enough he paddled back up with the ball in his mouth and tossed it out onto the grass. The princess was overjoyed to see her shiny toy once more, and picked it up and skipped away. "Wait, wait!" called the frog. "Take me with you! I can't run like you can!" But what good did that do, even as he croaked after the girl with his loudest possible *ribbit, ribbit*? Deaf to all his cries, she ran straight back home. And soon enough she had forgotten about the frog, who was left to sink back down into the spring.

The next day, as she sat at the table with the king and all his court, eating from her golden plate, something could be heard flopping up the marble stairs—*squish, squash, squish, squash*—and then it reached the top and beat on the door, crying, "Youngest princess, let me in!" And so she ran over, anxious to see who might be outside, but when she opened the door all she saw was the frog. Hastily she slammed the door shut again and sat down at the table, trembling with fear. The king could tell that her heart was pounding, and asked, "My child, what troubles you so? Is there a giant at the door come to eat you?" "No, no giant," she replied, "but a horrible frog!" "What does this frog want from you?" "Oh, dear father, as I was playing by the spring yesterday, my golden ball fell in the water. And since I was crying so, the frog brought it back to me, and since the frog insisted on being my friend, I promised it could. But never did I think it could come out of the water and get all the way here. Now it's right outside and wants to come in and see me!" Just at that moment there came two more knocks on the door, and a voice rang out,

"Youngest princess, let me in.
Have you forgotten what you promised me
By the water of the cool, cool spring?
Youngest princess, let me in."

At that, the king said, "Whatever promise you have made, you must also keep. Go let him in."

She went and opened the door, and the frog hopped inside, following right at

She snatched him up and hurled him with all her strength against the wall. Yet as he landed, he ceased to be a frog.

her heels all the way to her chair, where he squatted, croaking, "Pick me up." Still she hesitated, until her father told her to. But as soon as the frog was in her seat, he wanted to climb onto the table; and once there he said, "Push your golden plate over to me, so that we may eat together." She did just that, although it was plain to see she did not do so gladly. For while the frog relished his meal, she could hardly swallow one bite. At last, licking his lips, he said, "I've had my fill and now I'm tired. Carry me to your chambers and turn down your silken bed. It is time for us to go to sleep." At this she burst straight into tears, since she was afraid of the cold and clammy frog, which she dreaded touching, but which was now set on sleeping in her sweet, clean bed. But the king became stern and said, "Whosoever has helped you in your time of need does not deserve your disrespect."

So she got up and gathered the frog, pinching him uncomfortably between her two fingers, then took him upstairs and dropped him down in the corner. No sooner was she snug in bed than he hopped over and said, "I am tired and I want to sleep just as nicely as you. Lift me into your bed or I will tell your father." But with this last demand she got mighty angry and snatched him up and hurled him with all her strength against the wall. "Now you can sleep as deeply as you like, you horrid frog!" Yet as he landed, he ceased to be a frog. Instead he became a prince with kind and winning eyes. He explained that he had been cursed by an evil witch, and that no one but the princess could dissolve this spell and free him from the spring, and that it was her father's wish that he become her true companion and husband. The next day, he told her, they would travel to his own father's kingdom.

And so they fell asleep, and as the sun rose the next morning, a carriage arrived, drawn by eight white horses adorned with ostrich feathers on their heads and harnessed in golden chains. At the back stood the young prince's attendant, Faithful Heinrich. Faithful Heinrich had been so downcast ever since his master was transformed into a frog that he had bent three iron bands around his chest, lest his sullen heart burst with grief.

"Heinrich, the carriage—is something wrong?"
"No, sir, the carriage rides on strong. That sound
is from the bonds loosed from my heart."

Now the carriage was there to bear the young royalties back to the prince's regained kingdom, and Faithful Heinrich helped them into the carriage and resumed his place at the rear, full of joy at his master's deliverance. After they had driven a ways, the prince heard a cracking noise behind him, like something breaking. Turning around, he called out:

> *"Heinrich, the carriage—is something wrong?"*
> *"No, sir, the carriage rides on strong.*
> *That sound is from the bonds loosed from my heart*
> *Meant to keep it from breaking apart*
> *While you were exiled to the spring,*
> *A mere frog, and not a king."*

Again and yet again it crackled along the way, and each time the prince thought it was the carriage breaking down. But in truth, it was one iron band after another bursting from Faithful Heinrich's heart, now that his master was restored and a happy man.

The Wolf and the Seven Little Goats

Immediately recognizable as the bad guy with his big teeth, gruff manner, and cunning, the wolf has been a symbol of danger for thousands of years. He has appeared to dramatic effect as the wily antagonist in ancient sayings such as "Beware a wolf in sheep's clothing" and in tales ranging from Aesop's fables and "Little Red Riding Hood" to "The Three Little Pigs" and Sergei Prokofiev's "Peter and the Wolf" (1936). The urbane cousin of the werewolf, the fairy-tale wolf roams enchanted forests threatening innocent creatures, but despite his rapacious appetite for lovable boys and girls and cuddly animals, he never wins. Instead, he is the agent for moral lessons that help his would-be victims come of age. In the Grimms' version from sources in Hesse, Germany, the winsome victims are hoodwinked by a wolf and swallowed whole, as in "Little Red Riding Hood," and are freed only when they are cut out of his belly and replaced with stones. This theme can be found in many ancient stories, including the story of Zeus, the father of the gods in Greek mythology, whose own father tried to prevent his usurpation of power by swallowing him, but unknowingly devoured a stone instead.—ND

Color lithograph by Heinrich Leutemann, German, 1893

"Dear children," the nanny goat said, "I am going out into the woods to forage. But be on your guard against the wolf!"

There once was an old nanny goat who had seven little baby goats, and she loved them just like a mother loves her children. One day she was about to leave for the woods to gather food, and she called all seven kids to her and said, "Dear children, I am going out into the woods to forage. But be on your guard against the wolf! If he gets inside, he will eat you up limb by limb. The villain can disguise himself well, but you'll always be able to recognize him by his husky voice and his black feet." The little goats replied, "Dear Mother, we will watch out for ourselves. You can go without worrying." The nanny goat gave out one loving bleat and went on her way, her mind at ease.

It was not long before someone knocked on the door and said, "Open up, you dear little children. Your mother's home and brought back something nice for each of you." But the little goats heard a husky voice and knew who it was. "We won't open up," they answered, "for you're not our mother. She has a fine and sweet voice, and yours is rough. You're the wolf!" The wolf backed off and went to the grocer, where he bought a big lump of chalk and ate it, which made his voice smoother. He went back to the goats' house, knocked on the door, and said, "Open up, you dear little children. Your mother's home and brought back something nice for each of you." But the wolf had put his black paw against the window, and, seeing it, the little goats cried, "We won't open up. Our mother does not have black feet like you. You're the wolf!" So the wolf went to the baker and told him, "I've hurt my foot. Spread some dough on it for me." Once the baker had covered his paw, the wolf ran over to the miller and told him, "Sprinkle my paw with your white flour." But the miller thought, "This wolf is trying to deceive someone," and he refused. Yet the wolf said, "If you don't do what I ask, I'll eat you up on the spot." The miller became afraid and turned the black beast's paw to white. Alas, that's mankind for you.

Now for the third time the villain sneaked to the goats' house, knocked on the door, and said, "Open the door for me, children. Your dear old mother has returned home and has a tasty little something from the woods for each of you." The younglings said, "Show us your paw

The wolf put his paw up to the window. And when they saw that it was white, they opened the door.

first, so we know you're our mother." He put his paw up to the window. And when they saw that it was white, they believed that everything he had said was true, and opened the door. Who came storming in but the wolf! They drew back in fear and ran to hide. One of them dove under the table; the second jumped into bed, and the third into the oven; the fourth hid in the kitchen, the fifth in the pantry, and the sixth under the washbowl; and the seventh hid inside the grandfather clock. But the wily wolf found them all, and without much ado, he gobbled them up one after the other in his maw. The youngest one, though, hiding inside the grandfather clock, that one he could not find. Once the wolf had satisfied his cravings, he toddled off and lay down outside in a green meadow under a tree, where he drifted off to sleep.

Not long thereafter, the nanny goat came home from the woods. Goodness, what did she find! The door was wide open; the table, chairs, and benches were all overturned; the washbowl lay in shards on the floor; and the pillows and covers were thrown from the bed. She searched for her children, but they were nowhere to be found. She called one after the other by name, but no one answered. At last, after she called out for her youngest, a little voice peeped, "Mother, I'm here inside the grandfather clock." She helped him out, and he told her how the wolf had gotten in the house and eaten all the others. You can imagine how bitterly she cried for her children.

Finally, in her misery, she went outside with her youngest at her side. As she reached the meadow, she saw the wolf lying asleep beneath the tree, rustling the branches with his snoring. As she looked him over, she noticed something moving inside his bloated belly. "Dear God," she thought. "Are my poor children, whom he

The seven little goats cried, "The wolf is dead! The wolf is dead!" And together with their mother, they danced for joy.

slurped down for his supper, still alive?" And immediately she sent her youngest running home to fetch scissors and a needle and thread. Then she slit the monster's belly open. And no sooner had she made the first snip than one little goat poked out his head, and with the next snips the others jumped out, one after the other. They were still alive and not even hurt, since the monstrous wolf had just swallowed them all whole in his blind greed. This was cause for great joy! They all hugged their mother and hopped about like a village tailor at his daughter's wedding. Then the nanny goat said, "Now go and find some rocks so we can fill up this godless brute's belly while he's still lying asleep." Her seven little ones hastily brought some stones over and filled his belly with as many as they could. Then their mother sewed it back up as quickly as possible so he wouldn't notice a thing, and indeed he did not move even one bit. When at last the wolf had finished sleeping, he got to his feet. The stones inside him were making him very thirsty, and so he made his way over to the spring to drink. But as he started off and moved back and forth with his steps, the stones began to knock into one another in his belly, and he cried out:

"What is it that bumps and clatters
In my stomach, now in tatters?
I thought six little goats would there moan,
But now I'd say I'm filled with stone."

As he reached the spring and bent over the water to drink, the heavy stones weighing him down pulled him in, and he drowned miserably. As the seven little goats saw this, they came running over and cried, "The wolf is dead! The wolf is dead!" And together with their mother, they danced for joy round and round the spring.

Little Brother and Little Sister

This endearing coming-of-age tale can be read as both a story about a girl who saves her brother and a psychological metaphor for the dualistic nature of man, composed of animal and rational impulses. To escape a cruel stepmother, the siblings seek refuge in a forest. Much like Hansel and Gretel, they comfort and look out for each other. But when the boy cannot control his urge to drink from an enchanted stream and is turned into a deer, his sister cares for him. Their opposing temperaments of impulsiveness and responsibility, described by critic Bruno Bettelheim, are drawn in sharp relief. Unable to control himself, the boy risks his life by repeatedly joining a nearby hunt; the girl is the voice of reason, and when she marries one of the hunters, a king, she secures her brother's freedom. Man as animal or half animal has had potent symbolic power in cultures around the world, and variations of this fairy tale have been documented in Europe, Africa, and Asia. The first known written tale of this type appeared in the *Pentamerone* (1634–1636), a collection of tales by Italian poet Giambattista Basile. The Grimms based their story on oral variations from Hesse, Germany.—ND

Details from a color lithograph by Fedor Flinzer, German, 1881

Little Brother bent over the spring to take a drink, and as the first drops touched his lips, he was turned into a fawn.

Little Brother took Little Sister by the hand and said, "Since our mother died, we haven't had one single happy moment. Our stepmother beats us every day, and when we try to go to her, she just pushes us away with her feet. Leftover hard crusts of bread are our only meal. The hound under the table has it better than we do; at least she throws him a hearty morsel of meat every now and then. God forbid if our poor mother knew. Come, it's time for us to go into the big wide world together." So they walked the whole day over meadows, fields, and rocks, and when it began to rain Little Sister said, "God and our hearts are crying together!" That night they came to a great forest, and were so exhausted from their sorrow, hunger, and long journey that they huddled together inside a hollowed-out tree and fell fast asleep.

When they awoke the next morning, the sun was already high in the sky. It beat down hot upon their tree. Little Brother said, "Little Sister, I'm thirsty. If I knew where a spring was, I'd go and drink from it. I think I heard one bubbling earlier." And he got up and took her by the hand, and they went to look for it. But their evil stepmother was a witch. She had seen the children leave and had secretly slunk after them, the way all witches slink, and had cast a spell on all the springs in the forest. When the children found one whose water glistened as it cascaded over the rocks, Little Brother wanted so badly to drink from it. But Little Sister heard it whispering among its bubbles: "Who drinks from me will a tiger be. Who drinks from me will a tiger be." And she cried out, "I'm begging you, Little Brother, please don't drink it. You'll turn into a wild beast and tear me apart." As aching as his thirst was, Little Brother did not drink, and said, "I'll wait until the next spring." But as they came upon a second spring, Little Sister could hear it speaking too: "Who drinks from me will a wolf be. Who drinks from me will a wolf be." And she cried out, "Little Brother, I'm begging you, don't drink it! You'll become a wolf and eat me if you do." Little Brother did not drink, and said, "I'll wait until we come to the next spring, but then I'll just have to drink from it, no matter what you say. My thirst is just too

strong." As they came upon that third spring, Little Sister could hear how it too spoke: "Who drinks from me will a deer be. Who drinks from me will a deer be." And she said, "Oh, Little Brother, I'm begging you, don't drink it. You'll turn into a deer and run away from me if you do." But Little Brother had already knelt down by the spring and bent over it to take a drink. And as the very first drops touched his lips, he was instantly turned into a fawn.

Now Little Sister began to weep for poor, bewitched Little Brother, and the fawn began to cry too, and lay so sadly next to her. At last the girl spoke, "Don't cry, little fawn. I will never leave you." Then she took off her golden garter and tied it around the fawn's neck, and gathered some reeds and braided them into a soft rope, which she tied to the animal. Then she led him on the rope and went deeper into the forest. After a long, long way, they came at last upon a little house. The girl looked inside, and, finding it empty, she thought, "We can settle here for a while." She gathered some leaves and moss to make the fawn a soft bed, and every morning she would go out to get roots, berries, and nuts for herself, and tender grass for the fawn, which he would eat out of her hand. That made him happy, and he jumped and played around her. In the evenings, when Little Sister grew tired, she would say her prayers and lie down, propping her head on the fawn's back. This was her pillow now, on which she would gently drift off to sleep. If only

The door opened, and the king stepped inside and saw a young woman more beautiful than any he had ever seen.

Little Brother had kept his human form, it would have been a wonderful life indeed.

And so it went on like this for some time, with the two living alone in the wilderness. But then it so happened that the king of the land held a great hunt in the forest, and soon their solitude was broken by the sounds of horns blowing, hounds barking, and the merry cry of the huntsmen, which rang through the trees. The fawn heard the noise, and longed to be a part of it all. "Oh, please, Little Sister," he said. "Let me go join the hunt. I can hardly contain myself." And he pleaded and pleaded until she gave in. "But come back in the evening," she told him. "I'll have the door locked to keep out the wild huntsmen. So that I know it's you, you must knock and say, 'My little sister, let me in,' and if you don't say just that, I won't open the door." With that, the fawn bounded out of the house, and he felt cheerful and happy to be in the open air. The king and his huntsmen saw the beautiful animal and went after him. But they could not keep up, and even when they thought they finally had him cornered, he jumped over the bushes and was gone. As darkness fell, he loped back to the little house, knocked on the door, and said, "My little Sister, let me in." She opened the little door for him, and he hopped inside and slept the whole night long on his soft bed.

The next morning the hunt began anew. And when the fawn heard the hunters' horns and the cries of "Heigh-ho!" he could not keep still. "Little Sister, open the door again. I must go out," he pleaded. She opened the door and told him, "But in the evening you must be back, and you must use your password." When the king and his hunters saw the fawn with the golden collar again, they gave chase, but again it was too quick and nimble for them. This went on the whole day long, until finally the hunters had the fawn surrounded. One of the hunters wounded him in the foot, and as he slowly limped away, the hunter was able to follow him back to the little house. He heard how the fawn called out, "Little Sister, let me in," and saw how the door was opened for him and just as quickly closed behind him. The hunter took note of this and went to the king and told him what he had seen and heard. The king declared, "Tomorrow we shall once again go hunting."

Little Sister had a horrible scare when she saw that her little fawn was

wounded. She washed the blood away and wrapped his foot with herbs, telling him, "Go lie in your bed, dear fawn, so you can rest and heal." The wound was so slight that he felt no pain from it the next morning. And when he heard the charge of the hunters outside again, he said, "I can't take it any longer, I must be out there with them! No one will catch me that easily." But Little Sister began to cry and said, "They'll kill you, and I'll be here in the woods all alone and abandoned. I won't let you out." "Then I'll die here of sorrow," he answered. "When I hear the hunting horns, I feel as if I might jump out of my skin with excitement!" There was nothing Little Sister could do, and with a heavy heart she opened the door. He bounded into the woods again, healthy and happy.

When the king spotted the fawn, he said to his hunters, "Go hunt him the whole day long and into the evening, but may no one harm him." As soon as the sun had set, the king said to the huntsman who had followed the fawn before, "Now come

"Will you come to my castle and be my wife?" the king asked. "Goodness, yes," she said. "But the fawn must come with us."

and show me where you found the little house in the woods." When at last the king came to the door, he knocked and spoke the words, "Little Sister, let me in." The door opened, and the king stepped inside and saw a young woman more beautiful than any he had ever seen. She was afraid when, instead of her little fawn, she saw a man wearing a golden crown. But the king looked at her kindly and offered her his hand with the words, "Will you come with me to my castle, and be my dear wife?" "Goodness, yes," answered the girl. "But the little fawn must come with us, for I will not leave him." The king replied, "He shall stay with you for as long as you live, and shall want for nothing." Just then, the fawn came bounding in, and Little Sister tied the soft rope to his collar again, and they left their place of solace in the woods.

The king took the beautiful girl on his horse, and together they rode to his castle, where they married in splendor and lived happily together for a long time. The fawn was devotedly looked after and cared for, and could prance about in the castle garden to his heart's content. Meanwhile, the evil stepmother from whom the children had fled into the forest was certain that Little Sister had been devoured by wild beasts, and that Little Brother, in his fawn form, had been killed by the hunters. But when she heard now of their happiness and good fortune, her heart was filled with envy and resentment, which gave her no peace. She became possessed by the sole thought of bringing misery to them. Her real daughter, who was as ugly as the night and missing an eye, would mope and whine, "I should have been so lucky to become queen myself." "Just be quiet," said the old woman, who then satisfied her with this thought: "When it's time, I will make it all right again."

And sure enough, the time came. The queen brought a handsome baby boy into the world. But the king was away hunting, so the old witch took the form of the royal chambermaid and walked right into the room where the queen was recovering, saying, "Come, your bath is ready. It will do your majesty good and give you renewed strength. Hurry now, before it gets cold." The witch's daughter was with her, and together they carried the queen into the bathroom and helped her into the tub. Then they closed the door behind them and ran away quickly. In the bathroom, they had conjured a sulfur hellfire, and

soon the beautiful young queen had suffocated on the fumes. Once this deed was done, the old woman took her daughter and put the queen's nightcap on her head, and tucked her into bed in the queen's place. Then the witch transformed her, giving her the queen's shape and likeness, except for her missing eye, which she could not replace. So that the king would not notice, she had the girl lie on her eyeless side.

When he returned that evening and learned that his son had been born, he was overjoyed and wanted to go to his dear wife's bed to see how she was faring. But the old woman interrupted: "Leave the bed curtains closed! Her majesty must not be exposed to the light yet. She needs peace and quiet." The king left, not knowing there was an impostor in his bed. But at midnight, when the rest of the house was asleep, only the nanny in the nursery was awake, sitting by the crib and watching over the baby. She saw the door open and the true queen come in. The queen took the baby from the crib, held him in her arms, and fed him. She then fluffed his pillow, laid him back down, and pulled the covers snugly over him. And, not forgetting the fawn, she went to the corner where he lay and stroked him along his back. Then, in complete silence, she went

The king rushed to her and said, "You can be none other than my dearly beloved wife." And she answered, "Yes, it is I."

to the door and left. The next morning the nanny asked the watchmen whether they had seen anyone enter the castle, and they answered, "No, we saw no one."

Night after night this went on, and never did the queen say a word. The nanny always saw her, but didn't dare speak about it to anyone. After some time, one night the queen at last spoke:

"How fares my child? How fares
my fawn?
Only twice more shall I come,
then forever I'll be gone."

The nanny did not reply, but as soon as the queen left, she went to the king and told him all that she had witnessed. The king exclaimed, "Dear God, how could this be? Tomorrow night I shall watch over the child myself." The next evening he went to the nursery, and at midnight the queen appeared again and said:

"How fares my child? How fares
my fawn?
Only once more shall I come,
then forever I'll be gone."

And before vanishing again, she cared for the child, as she had done for many nights. Not even the king could bring himself to speak to her, but he returned the next night, as did she. And once more she spoke:

"How fares my child? How fares
my fawn?
Only tonight can I come, then forever
I'll be gone."

Hearing this, the king could not hold back any longer, and he rushed to her and said, "You can be none other than my dearly beloved wife." And she answered, "Yes, it is I, your dearly beloved wife." At that very moment, through God's grace, she came back to life, glowing and healthy, with the color returned to her cheeks. She told the king of the cruel deceit committed by the evil witch and her daughter. He had them brought before the court, and a judgment was handed down. The daughter was taken to the woods, where the wild beasts devoured her, and the witch was thrown into a great fire, where she burned miserably to death. Just as she turned to ash, the fawn resumed his human form. And Little Sister and Little Brother lived together happily until the end of their days.

Rapunzel

Hair symbolizes power and attractiveness in many cultures, and "Rapunzel" features one of the most striking images of it ever conjured: A sorceress scales a tower using the locks of the maiden within. While the hair signifies the girl's emerging sexuality, it also defines her entrapment. Locked in a tower, Rapunzel and her tresses represent her captor's jealousy and ambivalence about her coming of age. Scholars have noted precursors to the story in the 1000 AD Persian tale of Rudaba in a tower, whose suitor climbs her hair, and in the early Christian story of Saint Barbara, whose father cloisters her in a tower. Readers and listeners have been captivated by the maiden's enigmatic name, Rapunzel, the German word for a salad plant known as rampion, which the girl's mother craves while pregnant. Although the tale had a lively oral tradition, the Grimms adapted their famous version from a 1790 book by Friedrich Schulz, who in turn counted as his source a 1698 French variant, an example of both the rapid multicultural migration of fairy tales and the Grimms' use of written sources. The earliest recorded version is in Giambattista Basile's *Pentamerone* (1634–1636), with the humorous title "Petrosinella" ("Little Parsley").—ND

Details from a hand-colored broadside by Otto Speckter, German, 1857

She knew she had no way of getting her hands on the delicious greens, and so she grew listless, pale, and miserable.

There once were a husband and wife who had long yearned for a child, but to no avail. At last the wife finally sensed that God would soon fulfill their wishes. From a small window at the back of their cottage they could see into a splendid garden, full of the loveliest flowers and herbs. But it was surrounded by a high wall that no one dared to cross, since it belonged to a sorceress of terrific powers feared by all the world.

One day the wife was standing at her window, looking into the garden, when she spied a particular bed thick with the most beautiful, buttery-looking rapunzel. This lettuce shone so fresh and green that she was overcome by a great craving, and soon felt a strong desire to eat some. And since she knew she had no way of getting her hands on the delicious greens, she grew listless, pale, and miserable. Seeing her so, the husband became alarmed and asked, "What's troubling you, dear wife?" "Oh," she sighed. "If I can't get just a little of that rapunzel from the walled garden, I will surely die." The husband cared for her greatly, and thought: "Before I let my wife die, I must go down and get her that lettuce, come what may!"

So that evening he scaled the wall into the magic garden by twilight, picked a handful of leaves in great haste, and brought it home to her. Immediately the good wife made herself a salad and devoured it with great delight. But because it was so good, so terribly delicious, the next day her craving was three times as great. And she would have no peace unless her husband ventured again into the forbidden garden. And so he went out once more under the cover of darkness.

But as he came down from the wall, he was stunned to see the sorceress standing before him. "How dare you!" she cried, rage growing in her eyes. "Like a thief, you climb down into my garden and steal my rapunzel! You will pay for this!" "Oh, please have mercy on me," he implored. "I came here only out of deepest desperation. My wife saw your lettuce from our window, and has been so overcome with the need for it that she will die if she cannot have more." The anger began to fade from the sorceress's face, and she replied: "If this is as you say, I shall let you take as much rapunzel as you like, but on one condition: You must

OPPOSITE *"How dare you!" the sorceress cried. "Like a thief, you climb down into my garden and steal my rapunzel! You will pay!"*

give me the child your wife will bear. The baby will be provided for indeed, since I shall care for her like a mother." Out of his dread the poor man agreed to all this, and as soon as nine months had passed, the sorceress immediately appeared again, named the child Rapunzel, and swept away with her.

Over time, Rapunzel grew into the most beautiful girl under the sun. But when she turned twelve, the sorceress took her deep into the woods and locked her high up in a tower with neither door nor stairs, but only a small window at the very top. Whenever the sorceress wished to visit her, she called up from below:

"Rapunzel, Rapunzel,
Let down your hair for me!"

For Rapunzel had the most magnificent long hair in the world, as fine as spun gold. And when she heard the woman's insistent voice from below, she would undo her braids, knot them around a hook at her window, and let them cascade their full length down the tower, to five stories below. There the sorceress took hold of them and climbed up to the window.

This went on for several years. But then it came about one day that the king's son was riding in the woods, and

BELOW *When Rapunzel heard the woman's voice, she would undo her braids, knot them around a hook at her window, and let them down.*

happened upon the tower. He could hear a voice so ravishing that he was brought to a halt and listened intently. It was Rapunzel, who in her loneliness spent her time singing, her sweet voice echoing through the woods. The prince wanted immediately to climb up to this wonderful being, but when he searched for an entrance, there was none for him to find. So he rode home, but her song had touched his heart so deeply that every day he went back to the woods to listen.

One morning as he eavesdropped from behind a tree, he saw the sorceress and heard her cry:

"Rapunzel, Rapunzel,
Let down your hair!"

Whereupon Rapunzel tossed down her long, shimmering golden hair, and the sorceress shimmied up, hand over hand. "Is that the ladder one needs to reach her? If so, I'll try my luck!" he thought. So the next day, as darkness was falling, he came to the foot of the tower and called up:

"Rapunzel, Rapunzel,
Let down your hair!"

Just then her tresses flowed down, and the prince made his way high up to the window.

At first Rapunzel was taken aback when she saw a man climb into her chamber, since in all her life she had never seen one like him before. But the prince addressed her with warmth and kindness, explaining how her song had moved him so deeply that he could not have rested until he saw her face-to-face. Rapunzel's initial fear melted away. And when the prince asked whether she would be with him always, seeing how young and handsome he was, she thought, "He will treat me more lovingly than the old sorceress!" and accepted straightaway, placing her hand in his with the words, "I will happily go with you, but I don't know how I can get down from here! Each time you come, bring a strand of silk, and I will weave a ladder. When it is finished, I will climb down and ride away with you." And they agreed that he would come each and every evening, since the old sorceress came only by the light of day.

The sorceress noticed nothing of this plan, until one day Rapunzel let slip, "Tell me, how is it that you are so heavy to hoist up here? It takes my young prince just a single instant!" "Oh, you godless child!" cried the sorceress. "What words do I hear coming from your mouth? I thought

The prince wanted immediately to climb up to her, but when he searched for an entrance, there was none to find.

I had sealed you off from the world forever, but you have betrayed me!" In her fury she grabbed Rapunzel's beautiful locks, wrapped them around her left hand, seized a pair of scissors with her right, and—*snip*, *snap*—the hair was gone! The lovely braids now lay lifeless on the floor. And so unforgiving was the sorceress that she took Rapunzel away at once, to live out

Rapunzel recognized him, and as she wept with joy, two of her tears flowed into his eyes, healing them and restoring his sight.

her meager days in hardship in a barren wilderness.

That same evening the sorceress tied the clipped braids to the hook by the window. And when the prince came to the tower and called up,

"Rapunzel, Rapunzel,
Let down your hair!"

she did so, as he expected. Up the prince climbed, but at the top he found not his beloved, but the sorceress, who stared him down with her vengeful, poisonous gaze. "Ha!" she sneered. "You have come for your little dearest. But the pretty little birdie is no longer in its cage. The cat came for her, and now it will scratch out your eyes! Rapunzel is forever lost to you. Never shall you set eyes on her again!" The prince was beside himself with heartbreak, and in his desperation he leapt from the window. His life was spared, but the thorny

bushes that broke his fall poked out his eyes. And so he passed his days wandering blindly through the woods, eating only roots and berries, and able to do nothing but cry for his lost love.

He spent year upon year in misery, until at last his wanderings brought him to the wilderness where Rapunzel was living hand to mouth with the twins she had borne, a boy and a girl. Suddenly he heard the voice he knew better than all others, and felt his way toward it. As he drew closer, Rapunzel recognized him and threw her arms around his neck. As she wept with joy, two of her tears flowed into his eyes, healing them and restoring his sight. And so together they went to his kingdom, where they were received with elation, and where they lived for many, many joyous years, happy and contented.

Hansel and Gretel

One of the most beloved stories of the Brothers Grimm, "Hansel and Gretel" tells of a brother and sister abandoned by their parents in a forest. In this tale, perhaps more than in any other in the Grimms' collection, we experience the world through the eyes of children. The forest, with its foreboding trees, wild animals, and witches, symbolizes a loss of innocence, while food represents the comfort and security at stake, whether as bread crumbs to follow home, or as the witch's edible cottage, the classic gingerbread house. While the names Hansel and Gretel may sound unconventional to non–German speakers, historian Christine Goldberg tells us that the Grimms carefully chose them as diminutives of Johannes (John) and Margarete (Margaret), meant to symbolize children everywhere. The tale fits within the folklore genre of children encountering ogres, and versions have been found in Italy, France, Sweden, Denmark, Hungary, Albania, Russia, and the Baltics. Scholars tell us that the Grimms got the story from several oral sources in their home state of Hesse, and that Wilhelm Grimm reworked it prodigiously, adding length and emotional color. By their fourth edition, the hard-hearted mother had been converted to a stepmother.—ND

Details from a color lithograph by Heinrich Merté, German, 1881

Once, at the edge of a large forest, there lived a poor woodsman with his new wife and his two children. The little boy was named Hansel, and the girl, Gretel. The father had very little food to give his family, and when scarcity gripped the land he could no longer afford to put bread on the table each day. One night in bed, as he worried and tossed and turned in despair, he sighed and said to his wife, "What will become of us? How can we feed our poor children when we have nothing for ourselves?" "You know what, husband?" his wife answered. "First thing in the morning let's take the children out to where the forest is thickest. We'll light a fire and give them each a piece of bread, then we'll go back to our work and leave them there alone. They won't know their way back home, and we'll be rid of them." "No, wife," said the man. "I can't do that. How could I possibly bring myself to leave my own children in the woods all alone? The wild beasts would soon come and tear them to pieces." "Oh, you fool," she said. "So all four of us will starve to death? Why don't you go start milling the wood for our coffins then?" And she would not leave him alone until he gave in. "How sorry I feel for the poor, poor children," he said.

The two children had been kept awake by hunger and overheard what their stepmother had said to their father. Gretel broke down in bitter tears and whispered

Hansel stopped and looked back, and each time, he took one of the white stones from his pocket and tossed it onto the path.

to Hansel, "That's it. We're done for."

"Shhh, Gretel, please don't worry," Hansel whispered back. "I'll find a way to help us." Once their parents had fallen asleep again, he got up, slipped on his coat, and sneaked outside. The moon was shining bright, and the white stones in front of the house glittered like shiny coins. Hansel bent down and put as many of them into his coat pockets as he could fit. Then he went back inside and said to Gretel, "Take heart, dear sister, and go to sleep without fear. God will not abandon us." And he lay down again in his bed.

As day was breaking, even before the sun was up, the woman came and woke

Gretel began to weep. "Let's wait until the moon comes up," Hansel said to comfort her. "Then we'll find our way out."

both the children: "Get up, you lazybones. We have to go into the forest and gather some wood." Then she gave them each a little piece of bread and said, "Here's something for lunch. But don't eat it up before. This is all you get." Gretel kept the bread in her skirt, since Hansel had his pockets full of stones. Then the whole family went into the forest together. After they'd walked a ways, Hansel stopped and looked back toward the house, and did this again and again. "Hansel, what are you looking at?" asked his father. "You're falling behind. Pay attention and keep your legs moving." "Oh, Father," he answered, "I'm just looking back at my little white kitten sitting on the roof. It wants to bid me farewell." The woman snapped, "You fool, that's not your cat. That's the morning sun shining off the chimney." But Hansel had not been looking at the kitten. Instead, each time, he had taken one of the white stones from his pocket and tossed it onto the path.

When they reached the depths of the forest, their father told them, "Now, go gather some wood, children. I'm going to light a fire so you won't catch cold." Hansel and Gretel brought back kindling and brushwood and piled them high. Once the fire was lit, and the flames climbed high enough, the woman said, "Now lie down by the fire and take a nap. We're going into the forest to chop wood.

When we're done, we'll come back to pick you up."

Hansel and Gretel sat by the fire, and as it turned midday they each ate their piece of bread. Because they heard what sounded like an axe striking wood, they thought their father was nearby. But it was not his axe making the noise. It was a loose branch he had tied to a withered tree, which made a striking sound while swinging back and forth in the wind. After sitting there for a long time, they got so drowsy they could no longer keep their eyes open and fell fast asleep. When at last they awoke, the night was pitch-black. Gretel began to weep and said, "How will we get out of the forest now?" "Let's wait a little while until the moon comes up," Hansel said to comfort her. "Then we'll find our way out." And once the full moon had risen, he took his sister by the hand and began to follow the white stones that were shimmering like newly minted coins, lighting their way home.

They walked the whole night through on foot and arrived at their father's house at daybreak. They knocked on the door, and as the woman opened it and saw that Hansel and Gretel were back, she snapped, "You naughty children! You slept so long in the woods, we thought you never wanted to come home." But their father rejoiced, since leaving the children behind had weighed heavily on his heart.

Still, after a short time the family's distress again worsened, and there was no relief anywhere in sight. One night the children heard their stepmother say to their father, "Everything we had to eat is gone again. We don't even have half a loaf of bread left, and after that the game is up. The children will have to go. We'll lead them deeper into the woods this time, so they really can't find their way out again. Otherwise we'll all be done for." His heart was pained, and he thought, "It would be better for me to share the last piece of bread with my children." But his wife wouldn't listen to any of his protests, and moaned and blamed him for their plight instead. Give someone an inch, and they'll take a mile: Since he had given in the first time, he had to knuckle under the second time as well. But the children were awake and overheard the whole grim conversation. When the grown-ups went back to sleep, Hansel got up and went to gather the white stones from outside as he'd done before. But the woman had locked the door, and he could not get outside. He tried to comfort Gretel just the same, saying, “Don’t cry, Gretel. Go to sleep. The good Lord will take care of us.”

Early in the morning the woman came and got the children out of bed. They were each given a little piece of bread, but this time smaller than the last. On the way to the forest Hansel began to crumble it in his pocket, and stopped often to toss the crumbs onto the ground. “Hansel, why are you stopping and looking back like that?” the father asked. “Keep moving.” “I’m just looking back at my little dove. It’s up on the roof and wants to bid me farewell,” Hansel answered. “You fool,” said the woman. “That’s not your little dove. That’s the morning sun shining off the chimney.” But Hansel kept at it, tossing crumbs along the way until the bread was gone.

The woman led the children even deeper into the woods, where they’d never been in all their lives. Again they built a big fire, and the stepmother said, “Just sit still, children. If you’re tired, you can sleep a little. We are going to chop some wood. In the evening, when we’re done, we will come back to pick you up.” At midday Gretel shared her bread with Hansel, who had strewn his piece on the forest floor. Then they fell asleep, and the evening came and went without anyone coming for the poor children. They did not wake again until the night was dark, and Hansel comforted his sister, saying, “Let’s wait, Gretel, until the moon comes up. Then we’ll see the crumbs I dropped along the way. They’ll show us the way home.” As the moon rose, they got up to start home, but couldn’t find any crumbs. The many thousands of birds flying around the forest and fields had come and eaten them all up. Hansel said, “We’ll still find the way.” But they did not. They walked all night long, and then the whole next day from morning till evening, but still they could not find their way out of the forest. They were so very hungry, for all they could find to eat were a few berries scattered on the ground. And because they were exhausted, and their legs could hardly carry them any farther, they lay down under a tree and went to sleep.

Now it was already the third morning since they’d left their father’s house. Wearily, they kept on walking, but they just kept wandering deeper and deeper into the woods. If help didn’t come soon they would surely perish. At midday they saw a little bird perched on a tree branch. It sang so beautifully that they stopped

They saw a little bird that sang so beautifully. They followed along behind it until they came to a little house.

to listen. When it was done, it spread its wings and flew off ahead of them. They followed along behind it until they came to a little house, where the bird landed on the roof.

As they drew closer, they saw that the house was made of bread and covered in cake, and that its windows were made of pure white sugar. "I say we dig in," Hansel said, "and enjoy this God-given meal. I'm going to munch on a piece of roof, Gretel, and you take some window. It'll taste so sweet." Hansel reached up and broke off a piece of the roof to give it a try and see how it tasted. Gretel went up to one of the windows and began to nibble at it. Just then a little voice rang out from inside:

"Nibble, nibble, little mouse,
Who's there nibbling on my house?"

And the children answered:

"Only the wind, the wind, says I,
That heavenly child from the sky."

And they kept right on eating without letting themselves be distracted. Hansel found the roof to be very tasty, and tore off a sizable chunk, while Gretel knocked out a whole piece of the windowpane and sat down to enjoy it.

All of a sudden the door opened, and a very old woman with a crutch came creeping out. Hansel and Gretel were so startled that they dropped what they'd been holding in their hands. The old woman shook her head and said, "Oh, you dear children. Who brought you here? Do come inside and stay with me. No one will harm you." And she took them both by the hand and led them inside the little house. She served up a nice meal of pancakes with sugar, apples, and nuts, along with milk, then made them two nice little beds with white sheets. Hansel and Gretel crawled in and thought they had just found heaven.

"Nibble, nibble, little mouse, who's there nibbling on my house?" All of a sudden the door opened, and an old woman came creeping out.

But the old woman had only pretended to be so friendly. She was actually an evil witch who lay in wait for little children and had built her gingerbread house just to draw them in. Whenever she managed to ensnare a child, she would kill it, boil it, and eat it. This was her very favorite way to feast. Witches have red eyes and cannot see very far, but they have a powerful sense of smell, just like an animal's, and they can tell from afar when humans are approaching. When Hansel and Gretel were getting close to her trap, she had cackled wickedly and sneered to herself, "I've got them! They can't get away from me now."

Early the next morning, before the children had awakened, she got up and gazed at them resting so sweetly, with their plump, rosy cheeks, and snickered to herself, "My my, won't they make tasty little morsels." And she grabbed Hansel with her scraggly hand and dragged him into a little pen, where she locked him up behind a barred door. He screamed all he could, but it did him no good at all. Then she went to Gretel, shook her awake, and said, "Get up, you little slowpoke! Carry water and make your brother something good to eat. He's sitting out in the pen and needs to be fattened up. And when he is, I will eat him!" Gretel began to weep bitterly, but it was no use. She had to do what the mean witch demanded.

Now Hansel was given the very best food, and Gretel got nothing but crab shells. Every morning the old lady crept to the pen and cried, "Hansel, stick your finger out so I can feel if you're fattening up!" But Hansel would instead stick out a little bone he'd found, and the old lady, thinking it was his finger, would wonder why he wasn't gaining weight. After four weeks of this, when Hansel still seemed skinny, impatience got the better of her and she could not wait any longer. "Hey there, Gretel!" she called. "Fetch some water, and be quick about it. Whether Hansel's chubby or thin as a rail, tomorrow I shall kill him and cook him." Oh, how his poor sister grieved for him as she carried the water, and how her tears spilled down her cheeks! "Dear God, please help us," she sobbed. "If only the wild animals had eaten us up in the woods. At least we'd have died together." "Spare me the bawling," the old lady hissed. "It won't help you at all."

Early the next morning, Gretel had to go out to hang up the big cauldron, fill it

Every morning the old lady crept to the pen and cried, "Hansel, stick your finger out so I can feel if you're fattening up!"

with water, and light the fire underneath. "But first let us do some baking," said the old lady. "I've already lit the oven and kneaded the dough." She pushed poor Gretel up to the oven, with flames licking its sides. "Crawl inside," said the witch, "and see if it's heating up properly before we put the bread in." Once Gretel was inside, the witch was going to slam the door on her and bake her, and then eat her up. But Gretel sensed what she had in mind, and said, "But I don't know how to

do that. How do I even get inside it?" "You silly goose," snarled the old lady. "The opening is big enough. Can't you see? Even I can fit through." She crept up to the oven and stuck her head in, and with that Gretel gave her a swift push, launching her into the oven. Then she slammed the iron door and jammed the bolt in place. Whew! And how the old woman began to wail and wail! But Gretel ran off, and the godless witch was burned miserably to death.

Gretel rushed to Hansel, opened up his little pen, and cried, "Hansel, we're free! The old witch is dead!" Hansel jumped out like a bird freed at last from its cage. Oh, how overjoyed they were! They fell into each other's arms, jumped up and down, and gave each other hugs and kisses. Now that they had nothing left to fear, they went inside the old witch's house and found chests of pearls and jewels in every corner. "These sure are better than our white stones," said Hansel, and stuffed his pockets full. And then Gretel said, "I want to bring something home too," and filled up her apron. "Now we must leave so we can get out of this godforsaken witch's forest," said Hansel.

But after they'd gone a few hours, they came upon a large body of water. "We

Gretel gave her a swift push into the oven. Then she slammed the iron door and jammed the bolt in place. Whew!

can't get across," said Hansel. "There's no path around it and no bridge across."

"There's no boat either," said Gretel. "But look! There's a white duck swimming over there! If I ask her, maybe she'll carry us over." And so she called out:

"Little duck, little duck,
We're Gretel and Hansel, nearly out of luck.
There is no bridge and we see no track,
Won't you please carry us on your back?"

And sure enough the duck swam over to them, and Hansel climbed onto her back, and told his little sister to come join him. "No," she replied. "That will be too heavy for the little duck. She should bring us over one after the other." And that is just what the good bird did.

Once they were happily across and had continued on their way a while, the forest became ever more familiar. At last they spotted their father's house in the distance and began to run. They burst inside and threw their arms around his neck. He had not had one single happy hour since he had left the children in the forest, and his wife had died of hunger. Gretel shook out her apron, and the pearls and jewels rained down and bounced and rolled around the room, and Hansel tossed out one handful after the other from his pockets. Now all their troubles had come to an end, and they lived on together in bliss. That's it for my story about this house, and, oh, there I see a little mouse! Whoever catches it could make a big, big fur hat out of it.

The Fisherman and His Wife

Marital friction has long been fertile ground for stories about ambition, betrayal, and the delicate dance of interdependence in human relationships. Here, the referee is a bewitched fish, who keeps his thoughts to himself as the wife demands ever more wealth and personal power, until the climactic moment when the expression "Be careful what you wish for" takes on a whole new meaning. The Grimms collected their tales at a time of great interest in folklore, spurred on by the Romantic appreciation of folk art. This story came to them in written rather than oral form from a friend, the Romantic poet Achim von Arnim, who edited an important collection of folk poems with fellow poet Clemens Brentano. They in turn had received the tale from the painter Philipp Otto Runge. The Grimms published the tale in its original Low German (Plattdeutsch) to retain its folk origins. They noted that parts of the story appear in *1,001 Nights*, and that the motif of a woman leading a man to dangerous heights recalls Eve in the Garden of Eden and Shakespeare's Lady Macbeth. Although the tale warns against overreaching, it also offers tantalizing details about the lifestyles of the rich and famous along the way.—ND

Drawings by Wanda Gág, American, 1936

"It's awful we have to live in this hovel," said his wife. "You could have wished for a cute cottage! Go call the fish."

nce upon a time there was a fisherman who lived with his wife in a filthy hovel near the sea, where the fisherman went every day to fish. And he fished and he fished. One day, as usual, he was sitting over his rod, staring into the shiny and calm water. And he sat and he sat. His lure sank deep down, right to the bottom, and as he pulled on it he brought up a big flounder. And the fish said to him, "Listen to me, fisherman, I ask you to spare me. I am not a real flounder, but a bewitched prince. What good would it do you to kill me? I wouldn't taste any good at all. Just put me back in the water and let me swim away." "Well," said the man. "Spare me your many words. A flounder that can speak is a flounder I should let live." With that he dropped the fish into the shiny water, and it swam back down to the bottom, leaving a long trail of blood behind it. Then the fisherman got up and went home to his wife in their hovel.

"Husband," said his wife, "you didn't catch anything today?" "No," he replied, "I caught a flounder, but he told me he was a prince under a spell, so I let him swim away again." "You mean you didn't wish for anything?" she asked. "No," he said. "What should I have wished for?" "Oh!" said the woman. "It's awful that we have to live here in this hovel. It's stinky and disgusting! For a start you could have wished for a cute little cottage! Go out and call him. Tell him we want a little cottage. He can surely do that for us." "How in the world am I supposed to do that?" "Man, oh man! You caught him and could have kept him, but you let him swim away. He'll do it for sure. Off with you right this minute!" He did not want to go back, but he wanted even less to go against his wife. So he

The fisherman went home and saw the little cottage. "Come have a look!" his wife said. "This is so much better now."

headed to the shore. As he approached, he saw the water was no longer shiny and calm, but had turned green and yellow. He stood at the water's edge and called out:

"Though a little man you claim to be,
Oh flounder, flounder, deep in the sea!
My dear wife, my Ilsebill,
What she wants is not my will."

Lo, the fish came swimming up and asked, "Well, what is it she wants?" "Well," answered the fisherman. "You know I caught you before. Now my wife tells me I should have made a wish. She can't stand our hovel any longer. She really wants a nice little cottage." "Go back home," said the fish. "She has it already."

So the fisherman went home, and found his wife was no longer cooped up inside the hovel. In its place was a little cottage, and she was sitting in front of it on a bench. She took him by the hand and said, "Come have a look! This is so much better now." They went inside, and in the cottage was a little entryway, and a wonderful little sitting room, and a bedroom with a bed for each of them. And there was a kitchen and pantry filled with everything needed for cooking: the best utensils and tools, made from the nicest tin and brass, all shiny and clean. Out back was a little courtyard alive with chickens and ducks, and a garden with fruits and vegetables. "See, isn't this nice?" asked the wife. "Yes," answered the fisherman, "and let's hope it stays this way. We can live happily like this." "We should think about that," said his wife. And with that they had a bite to eat and went to bed.

All the walls were bright and hung with splendid tapestries, and there were golden tables and chairs, and crystal chandeliers hanging from the ceiling.

It all went well for one or two weeks, until his wife said, "Listen, husband. This hut is really too cramped for us, and the courtyard and garden are much too small. That fish could have given us a bigger house. I'd really like to live in a big stone castle. Go down to the fish and tell him he should give us one." "Oh, woman," he said. "Our cottage is good enough. What on Earth do you want with a castle?" "Oh, come now," she said. "You go back down there. The fish can do this for us for sure." "No, dear. The flounder just gave us this cottage! I don't want to go back down there so soon and call him up to ask for more." "Just go!" she said. "He can easily do it, and he'll be glad to. Now go back down there." His heart felt heavy since he was against this idea, and he thought to himself, "This is just not right." But he went anyway. When he reached the sea, the water was no longer green and yellow, but was violet and dark blue, and gray and cloudy although mostly calm. He stood at the water's edge and called out:

"Though a little man you claim to be,
Oh flounder, flounder, deep in the sea!
My dear wife, my Ilsebill,
What she wants is not my will."

"Well, what is it she wants?" asked the fish. "Well," said the man, half in despair. "She wants to live in a big stone castle." "Go back home," said the fish. "She's standing in front of the door."

And so he left, set on returning to his comfortable cottage. But when he arrived, there was a large stone castle in its place, and his wife stood at the top of the steps waiting to go inside. She took him by the hand and said, "Come on in." So they went inside and found a large entrance hall with a seamless marble floor, and servants who threw open the great doors for them. All the walls were bright and hung with splendid tapestries, and inside the rooms were golden tables and chairs, and crystal chandeliers hanging from the ceiling. Carpets adorned the floors, and the tables sagged under the weight of ample food and the finest wines. And behind the castle was a large courtyard with horse stables, the very best carriages, and stalls for the cattle. There was also a magnificent garden with the most beautiful flowers and finely kept fruit trees, and a wooded park nearly a half mile long with bucks and their does, and rabbits and any other animals one might wish to find. "Oh!" exclaimed the wife,

“isn’t it just wonderful?” “Oh, yes,” replied the fisherman. “And may it remain so. It is time for us to live in our castle and be content with our good fortune.” “We shall see about that,” said the wife. “Let’s sleep on it.” And with that they went to bed.

The next morning, the wife awoke at daybreak, and looked out from her bed over the rich lands around the castle. The fisherman was just starting to stretch when she elbowed him, saying, “Get up and take a look out the window! Just think, we could reign over all the land we see. Go down to the fish. Let’s be kings!” “Wife, oh wife,” sighed the fisherman. “Why would we want to be kings? I certainly don’t want to be a king.” “Well, then,” she said. “You may not want to be king, but I do. Go to the fish and ask him. I want to be king!” “My dear, why would you want to be king? I don’t want to have to ask him this.” “Why not?” she asked. “Just go down there. I must be king!” And so off he went, feeling dismayed. “It’s not right. It’s just not right,” he thought. He did not want to go, but he did.

And as he reached the seashore, the water was black and gray and seething

His wife was seated high up on a throne inlaid with diamonds, wearing a mighty crown and wielding a scepter of pure gold.

from beneath, and it gave off a foul smell. He stood at the water's edge and called out:

"Though a little man you claim to be,
Oh flounder, flounder, deep in the sea!
My dear wife, my Ilsebill,
What she wants is not my will."

"Well," said the fish, "what is it she wants?" "Oh, dear," said the fisherman. "She wants to be king." "Go back home," said the fish, "she is already."

So the fisherman trudged off, and as he returned to the castle he found it transformed into a much larger palace, with a soaring tower and dazzling ornamentation. And the gates were adorned with a regal crest, and there were scores of soldiers sounding trumpets and kettledrums. As he entered the house, he saw that everything was made of pure marble and gold, and there were velvet carpets with long gold tassels. The doors opened onto a grand hall where the whole court was assembled, and his wife was seated high up on a gold throne inlaid with diamonds, wearing a mighty gold crown, and wielding a scepter of pure gold and precious gems in her hand. On each side stood six maidens in a row, each a head shorter than the last.

He went before his wife and said in awe, "Good heavens, wife! Are you king now?" "Yes," she said. "Now I am king." He stood there gazing at her, and after taking it all in for a moment he said, "That's wonderful—you as king! Now there is nothing left for us to wish for." "No, husband," she said, and suddenly became distraught. "It's so dull and boring, I can barely stand it any longer. Go back to the fish. I may be king, but I must also be emperor!" "Oh, dearest woman," he said.

"Why would you want to be emperor?" "Husband," she said, "go to your flounder. I want to be emperor." "My dear wife," he responded. "He cannot make you emperor. I can't possibly ask him. There is only one emperor in all the land. How could even this extraordinary fish possibly make anyone emperor? He cannot do it." "What?" she exclaimed. "I am king, and you are only my husband. Off with you, go ask him now! If he is a kingmaker, then he can make me an emperor just as well, and I want to be emperor. Go there now!"

And so he had to go. But on his way he grew even more troubled, and thought as he walked, "This is just not right and it will not turn out well. Emperor is just too outrageous. The fish will get tired of this." And with that he arrived at the sea, which was black all over now, and thick with inner ferment and foam. A wind came up and churned the water's surface, making the fisherman shudder. But he stayed put and cried out:

"Though a little man you claim to be,
Oh flounder, flounder, deep in the sea!
My dear wife, my Ilsebill,
What she wants is not my will."

"Well, what is it she wants?" asked the fish. "Oh, flounder!" he said. "My wife wants to be emperor." "Go back home," replied the fish. "She is already."

So the fisherman went back, and as he arrived he found the whole castle was now made of polished marble, with alabaster statues and gold adornments. Soldiers marched in front of the gate, blowing trumpets and striking kettledrums and snare drums. Inside, barons and counts and dukes kept busy in the great halls like servants. Now it was they who opened the doors for him, doors of solid gold. As he entered, he saw his wife seated on a towering throne, two miles high, made from a single piece of gold. She wore an imposing gold crown, three cubits tall, encrusted with brilliant-cut diamonds and rubies. In one hand she held a scepter and in the other the imperial orb. At her side stood her attendants in two ranks according to height, from the mightiest giant, standing two miles high, down to the tiniest dwarf, no bigger than my pinky finger. Assembled before her were also many princes and dukes.

The fisherman slipped through them and called up, "So, wife, are you now emperor?" "Yes," she said. "I am emperor." He drew closer and looked at her, and after a moment of taking in her splendor,

His wife was seated on a throne two miles high, and her attendants stood according to height, from the mightiest giant to the tiniest dwarf.

he said, "Well, what a great thing that you are emperor." "My dear," she interrupted. "Why are you standing there? I am emperor, and it is time for me to be pope, too. Off to the fish!" "Heavens, wife!" he stammered. "Is there nothing you don't want? You can't be pope. There is only one Holy Father in all of Christendom! That's not the fish's business." "Man, oh man," she steamed. "I want to be pope. Go there now! I must be pope before the day is out." "No, I just can't ask him," he said. "This will not end well, it's much too bold. Not even the fish can make someone pope." "What nonsense!" she said. "If he can make me emperor, he will make me pope. Go there instantly! I am the emperor and you are but my husband. Are you afraid of your little flounder now?"

With that he realized just how afraid he was, but still he went. He felt queasy. His limbs trembled and shook, and he was weak in the knees and wobbly in his calves. The wind ripped over the land, and the clouds rolled in, and the sky darkened as night fell. The leaves tore loose from the trees, and the ocean heaved and roared as if it were boiling, and pounded against the beach. On the horizon the fisherman saw ships firing their guns in distress as they danced and bounced up and down in the waves. A tiny spot of blue remained at the peak of the sky, threatened by the terrible storm around it. He stood at the shore, disheartened and afraid, and cried out:

"Though a little man you claim to be,
Oh flounder, flounder, deep in the sea!
My dear wife, my Ilsebill,
What she wants is not my will."

"Well, what is it she wants?" asked the fish. "Oh, my," the fisherman answered. "She wants to be pope." "Go back home. She already is."

He returned home, and by the time he arrived, their home was now a great cathedral surrounded by many palaces. He had to force his way through throngs of people to get nearer. Inside there were thousands upon thousands of candles, and his wife was clothed all in gold and sat upon a still-higher throne. She wore the triple crown of gold and was surrounded by statesmen of the church, and on both sides by rows of lights, the largest of which was as tall and wide as the biggest tower, on down to the smallest kitchen candles. And all the emperors and kings of the world were on their knees before her and kissed her

His wife sat upon a still-higher throne, and was surrounded by lights as tall as the biggest tower, down to the smallest kitchen candles.

feet. "Dear wife," the man said, staring at her in wonderment, "are you now pope?" "Yes," she answered. "I am pope." He stood before her and took a long look, and it was as if he were looking into the bright sun. After a moment he said, "Oh, my dear, it's magnificent that you are pope!" But she sat there as stiff as a board and did not move. "Be content, woman, now that you are pope. There is nothing more to wish for, nothing more to become." "I shall see about that," she said. With that, they both retired to bed.

But she was not content, and her greed kept her from sleeping as she thought of all that she still wanted to become. Her husband slept deeply and well since he had done much running back and forth that day, but she could not. She tossed and turned all night long, thinking all the while about what she wanted, and yet she had no clear idea what this might be. Soon the sunrise began, and as she saw the red of dawn through her window, she sat up in bed, staring out at the growing light. As she watched the sun break over the horizon, she thought, "Ha! Why couldn't I command the sun and the moon to rise?" She nudged her husband in the ribs and said, "Husband, wake up and go to the fish! I want to be just like God." The poor fisherman was still half asleep, but at that he was so startled that he fell straight out of bed. He thought he had misheard her, and rubbed his eyes. "What did you say, dear?" "Husband!" she said. "If I don't have the power to make the sun and moon rise, and have to sit and watch as they move each day, I simply won't be able to stand it. I'll never have a peaceful hour again if I cannot command them to rise myself." She gave him such a frightening look that he felt a chill down his spine. "Go back to the shore! I want to be just like God." "My wife," he pleaded, falling down on his knees, "the flounder cannot do this. Emperor or pope is another matter. I am begging you, look inside yourself and understand this, and just stay pope." With this she became enraged. Her hair flew wildly around her head, she tore at her nightgown and gave him a swift kick with her foot as she screamed, "I can't bear it! I can't bear it any longer! Go there immediately!"

He threw on his clothes and ran out as if his life depended on it. Outside, the storm was in its full fury, and roared with such menace that he could hardly

stay on his feet. The houses and trees were being whipped by the wind, and even the mountains shook, and the very cliffs tumbled into the sea. The sky was pitch-black, and thunder and lightning crackled around him. The black waves in the sea rose as tall as a church steeple and as high as mountaintops, and were capped with white sea foam. He screamed, scarcely able to hear himself:

"Though a little man you claim to be,
Oh flounder, flounder, deep in the sea!
My dear wife, my Ilsebill,
What she wants is not my will."

As the fisherman's wife (left) watched the sun break over the horizon, she thought, "Ha! Why couldn't I command the sun and the moon to rise?"

"Well, what is it she wants?" asked the fish. "Dear me," he faltered. "She wants to be just like God." "Well, then. Go home. She's sitting in your hovel again." And there, back in their filthy hovel, the fisherman and his wife are still sitting even to this day.

The Brave Little Tailor

"The Brave Little Tailor" is an adventure story about a spry tailor, the clown supreme of the Grimms' fairy tales, whose "little" name and stature contrast with his oversized bluster. Tickled with himself for killing seven flies at one blow, the tailor decides to pack in his trade and show the world his superhero talents, a theme that has enjoyed endless variation in popular culture. Using a sparkling blend of self-glorification, unrelenting swagger, and naive optimism, he outsmarts his foes in a series of slapstick scenarios, ultimately marrying a princess, inheriting a kingdom, and becoming king. Versions of the tale have been found all over Europe—for instance, in England, as "Jack and the Beanstalk," and in Scandinavia—and the Grimms cite as their source part of a 1557 story by the German writer Martin Montanus. Several of the Grimms' stories have a tailor as their main character, including "Tom Thumb's Travels" (pages 162–169). Folklorist D. L. Ashliman tells us that a tailor was often used in fairy tales to symbolize an everyday hero, and because tailors regularly traveled to ply their trade, they were often sources of news and intrigue, and ultimately earned a reputation for being good storytellers. —ND

Color halftone prints by Franz Wacik, Austrian, 1915

One summer morning a little tailor was seated at his sewing table by the window. He was in high spirits and stitched away with great zeal. A farmer's wife came along the road calling out, "Fine jams for sale! Fine jams for sale!" This rang sweetly in the little tailor's ears, and he stuck his delicate little head out the window and called down, "Up here, dear woman. Here you'll shed your load!" The woman climbed up the three flights of stairs with heavy basket in hand. At the tailor's request she unpacked all her jars for him to look over. He gazed at each one, held each one up to the light and to his nose for a sniff, and finally said, "This jam seems a rather good one to me. Weigh me out a few ounces, dear woman, and if it comes to a quarter pound, it doesn't matter to me." The good woman, who had thought she would sell him much more, did as he asked and then left, grumpy and upset. "Now, may God bless this jam for me, and may it give me vim and vigor!" he cried out. He took a loaf of bread down from the pantry, sliced it along its entire length, and spread it thickly with the jam. "This ought to be a sweet little nibble," he thought. "But I should first finish working on that jacket before I eat." He put the bread down next to him, and sewed away again happily, making bigger and bigger stitches.

In the meantime, the sweet smell of the jam made its way up the walls, where many flies were gathered. They were enticed by the bread and swarmed down on it in great droves. "Hey, who invited you?" cried the little tailor, and swatted them away with his hands. But the flies didn't understand his words, and, unimpressed, they came in ever greater numbers

He made himself a belt and embroidered on it: "Seven at one blow!" Swept away by it all, his heart beat with pride.

He set out on his way using nothing but his two legs, and since he was light and agile he could cover great distances.

until finally, as the saying goes, they were bugging him out of his mind. He reached for a rag and shouted out, "You just wait, I'll show you all!" and he snapped it down mercilessly upon them. Lifting it slowly, he counted no fewer than seven dead flies lying with their legs up in the air. "See, that's the kind of man you are," he said out loud, impressed by his own bravery. "The whole town shall hear about this!" And he quickly made himself a belt and embroidered on it the words: "Seven at one blow!" He went on musing, "You know what, little town? The whole world should know about this!" Swept away by it all, his heart beat with pride like a little lamb's tail.

He put his belt around his waist and was ready to set out into the world, since he felt his little workshop was now too small for so great a hero. Before he left, he looked around the house for a bite for the road, but all he could find was an old piece of cheese, which he nonetheless put in his satchel. Outside the town gate, he saw a bird stuck in the brambles, grabbed it, and put it in the bag with the cheese. He courageously set out on his way using nothing but his two legs, and since he was light and agile he could cover great distances without fatigue. The path led him over a mountain, and as he reached the peak he saw a mighty giant sitting there, gazing leisurely into the distance. The little tailor strode up to him and greeted him peppily, saying, "Good day, comrade. So, you're taking in the big wide world, are you? I'm on my way there, too, to try my luck. Want to come along?" The giant returned a glance of contempt and

BELOW *He took out the cheese and squeezed it until liquid came out. "There! Not so bad, am I?" The giant was speechless.*

OPPOSITE *The tailor said, "The way you do it, the rock will always fall back down. I'll show you a throw never to return."*

said, "You rascal! You miserable little half-pint!" "Oh, really?" replied the tailor, opening his coat and showing the giant his belt. "You can read right here what kind of man I am!" The giant read, "Seven at one blow!" and, thinking it referred to foes slain by the tailor, he began to change his attitude toward the little fellow.

Yet he wanted to test him first, and so he took a rock in his hand and squeezed it until water dripped out. "Now it's your turn," the giant spoke. "That is, if you have the strength." "That's all you ask?" replied the little tailor. "That's but child's play for the likes of me." He reached into his satchel and took out the soft cheese, and squeezed it until drops of liquid came out. "There! Not so bad now, am I?" The astounded giant was speechless. He found it hard to believe that the little man had managed the task. So he lifted another rock and threw it so high that it nearly flew out of sight. "Now you try that, you skinny little bird of a man." "That was decent enough," said the tailor. "But the way you do it the rock will always fall back down. I'll show you a throw that will never return." He reached into his satchel, took out the bird, and cast it straight into the air. It took flight, rejoicing in its newfound freedom, and soared skyward, never to return.

"What do you think of that little feat, comrade?" asked the tailor. "Well, you certainly can throw," admitted the giant. "But now let's see if you can carry a real load." He led the tailor over to a massive oak tree that lay felled on the ground, and said, "If you are strong enough, then help me carry this tree out of the forest." "Happy to!" replied the tailor. "You just take the trunk onto your shoulder, and I'll carry all the many branches, since they're the heaviest part." So the giant hoisted the

OPPOSITE *"Just take the trunk onto your shoulder," said the tailor, "and I'll carry all the branches, since they're the heaviest part."*

trunk onto his shoulder while the tailor scrambled up among the branches. Now, the giant could not see anything behind him and wound up carrying the whole tree, tailor and all. Much amused, the little man began whistling the tune "Three Tailors Went Riding Forth," as if hauling timber were just a game. After carrying the load a ways, the giant had to stop, and called out, "Listen, I have to drop the tree!" The tailor jumped spryly down to the ground, grabbed the tree with both arms, as if he had been carrying it the whole time, and said, "You're such a big fellow and can't even carry half a tree?"

They went farther along together until they came to a cherry tree. The giant seized its top, where the ripest fruit was hanging, bent the whole tree down, and handed it off to the tailor, telling him to eat the fruit. But the little tailor was far too weak to keep the tree bent, and when the giant let go, the trunk snapped straight and the tailor shot right into the air. As he hit the ground without a scratch, the giant chided him, "What happened? Aren't you strong enough to hold down that little twig of a tree?" "I have all the strength I need," replied the little tailor. "Do you think that would

BELOW *But the tailor was too weak to keep the tree bent. When the giant let go, the tailor shot right into the air.*

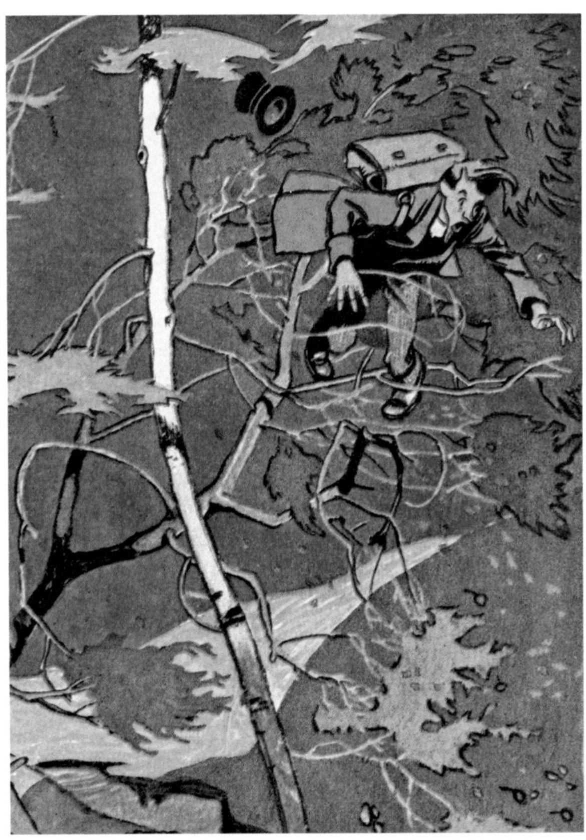

be difficult for someone who thrashed seven at one blow? I jumped over the tree because there are hunters shooting into the grove below. You should do the same—if, that is, you're able." The giant gave it his all, but could not clear the top of the tree. Instead, he got caught in the branches, leaving the tailor once again with the upper hand.

While he slumbered, courtiers looked him up and down, until they spotted "Seven at one blow!" on his belt. "Great heavens!" they exclaimed.

The giant grumbled, "If you are such a bold fellow, why don't you come to our cave and spend the night with us?" The little tailor was game and went along. As they arrived at the cave, the other giants were seated around a fire, each crunching away on a whole grilled sheep. "This place is much roomier than my little workshop!" thought the tailor as he looked around.

The giant showed him to a bed, and told him to lie down and sleep as long as he needed. But the bed was too vast, so instead he crawled into a comfy corner. At midnight, thinking that the tailor was fast asleep, the giant got up and took a heavy iron rod and smashed the bed with his full force, instantly splitting it in two. He was sure he'd pulverized the spindly little grasshopper of a man. At the first light of day he went out into the woods with the other giants and forgot all about the little tailor. But our little man, as high-spirited as always, soon caught up with the giants. They panicked, for they thought he had come to strike them down in revenge, and they tore away in haste.

So he continued on his way alone, ever guided by his sharp little nose. After wandering a long time he came upon the castle of a great king, and, exhausted, he lay down and fell asleep on the grass. While he slumbered, a crowd of courtiers gathered and looked him up and down from all sides, until at last they spotted the motto on his belt: "Seven at one blow!" "Great heavens!" they exclaimed. "What does this mighty warrior seek here in our peaceful kingdom? He must be a powerful lord indeed." They went and told the king

"I would be pleased to enter the king's service," declared the little tailor, and he was received with honors.

that if war were ever to break out, the man would be a powerful and useful ally, and at all costs should not be allowed to leave. The king thought this was wise counsel. He sent one of his courtiers to the little tailor to offer him the chance to serve in the royal army—that is, once he awoke. The messenger stood patiently by the sleeping guest, waiting until he had stretched his limbs from sleep and opened his eyes. Then he delivered the king's message. "That is exactly why I have come here," the tailor declared. "I would be pleased to enter the king's service." He was received with honors, and a special apartment was prepared for him.

But the other soldiers felt slighted by this generosity toward the newcomer, and wished he were a thousand miles away. "What will come of this?" they asked one another. "If there were ever any trouble with him and he lashed out, seven of us could go down all at once. We can't hold our own against that." And they decided as a company to go to the king to ask for leave. "We are not made for this," they said. "How can we stand fast against a man who can strike down seven at one blow?" The king was saddened to lose his most faithful servants for the sake of just one man. He wished that he had never laid eyes on him, and that he could be rid of him. But he thought it unwise to banish him, for he was afraid that the little tailor might take revenge by slaying him and all his people, and then seize the throne for himself. The king went back and forth in his mind until at last an idea came to him. He sent another messenger to the tailor to tell the little man that, because he was such a great warrior, he wished to make him an offer. In one of his kingdom's many forests, there were two giants wreaking havoc: thieving, murdering,

He slid down a branch so that he was seated right above the sleeping giants, and then he rained down one stone after another.

burning, and pillaging. Anyone who went near them put his life at risk. If the tailor overpowered and slew these monsters, the king would reward him with half the kingdom and his daughter's hand in marriage. He would also lend him a hundred knights in support. "This befits exactly the kind of man I am," thought the little tailor. "A beautiful princess and half the kingdom. This kind of offer doesn't come along every day!" "Oh, yes, your majesty," he answered, "consider those two monsters doomed already. But I won't be needing your hundred knights. Whoever can strike seven with one blow could never be frightened by two."

So the little tailor set out, and the hundred knights followed behind. As he came to the edge of the forest, he told them, "Stay here and wait. I shall deal with the giants alone." With that he started into the forest, looking left and right for the giants. After a while he spotted them lying asleep under a tree, snoring so powerfully that the branches swung up and down in rhythm. Hardly a lazy fellow, the little tailor packed his pockets full of stones and climbed into the tree. When he was halfway up, he slid down a branch so that he was seated right above the sleeping giants, and then he rained down one stone after another onto one giant's chest. It took some time before the giant felt anything, but finally he awoke and poked his fellow, saying, "What are you doing hitting me?" "You must be dreaming," answered the other giant. "I'm not hitting you." So they both lay back down and went to sleep.

But then the tailor pitched a stone down onto the second giant. "What was that?" he cried. "What are you doing chucking things at me?" The first giant growled back, "I'm not chucking anything at you." They bickered for a while, but since both were tired, they let it be and closed their eyes again. But the little tailor resumed his ruse, and took his heftiest rock and threw it down with all his might onto the first giant's chest. "Now that's going too far!" the giant screamed, leaping to his feet, and with blind rage he flung his partner in crime against the nearest tree, making it shake. The second giant gave him a taste of his own medicine, and soon they were in such a fury that they thrashed each other with trees ripped up from the ground, and did not stop until they both lay dead on the forest floor.

BELOW *He drew his sword and left deep marks in their chests, then went back to the knights to pronounce, "I've slain both giants."*

OPPOSITE *The unicorn rammed into the tree, spearing its horn into the trunk. "Now I've caught the little birdie!" the tailor cheered.*

The tailor jumped down and said, "What luck they didn't tear out the tree I was sitting in. I'd have had to leap into the next one like a squirrel. But we little fellows are a quick and agile lot!" And he drew his sword and left deep marks in the chests of both giants, then went back to the knights to pronounce, "The work is done. I've slain both the giants, but I must say it was tough. In their panic they tore up trees to beat me back with. But even that was no help against someone like me, who can strike down seven at one blow." "Are you not wounded at all?" the knights asked. "You are right to wonder," the tailor replied. "But they did not even touch a hair on my head." The knights could hardly believe him and rode into the woods, where they found the giants swimming in their own blood and, around them, the fallen trees.

So the little tailor returned to the king and demanded his reward. But the king regretted his promise and set his mind again on ridding himself of the hero. "Before you are entitled to my daughter and half my kingdom," he said to the tailor, "you must prove yourself with one more feat. A unicorn is running wild in our forest and doing great harm. You must first catch it and bring it to me." "I am less afraid of a unicorn than of two giants. Seven at one blow: That's my motto." So he took a rope and an axe and went out into the forest, and told his entourage again to wait. He did not need to search for long, for the unicorn soon came along and charged right at him, as if it wanted to gore the little man without any provocation. "Easy. Easy," he said. "Not so fast." He stood his ground and waited until the animal was dangerously close,

The boar entered the chapel, running at the tailor's heels. The tailor jumped out a window, ran around, and slammed the door.

then he leapt nimbly behind a nearby tree. The unicorn rammed into the tree at full speed, spearing its horn so deeply into the trunk that not even its mythical powers were enough to pull it out. And with that, the unicorn was captured. "Now I've caught the little birdie!" the tailor cheered. Coming out from behind the tree, he tied the rope around the unicorn's neck and used the axe to free the horn from the tree trunk. When he was finished, he led his prize out of the forest and brought it to the king.

Still, the king was reluctant to grant him the promised reward, and gave him a third challenge as a condition for earning it. Before the wedding could take place, the tailor was to capture a wild boar that was causing much damage to the royal forest. Again, a whole party of hunters would be there to help him. "Gladly," accepted the tailor. "That's mere child's play." He did not take the hunters with him into the woods, though, and they were relieved, for they had seen the frightful wild boar many times and were not inclined to go after it. As soon as the boar caught sight of the tailor, it ran at him head-on, foaming at the mouth and baring its spiked teeth, hoping to knock the man to the ground. But the nimble hero leapt into a little nearby chapel, and jumped right back out its window. The boar had entered, running at his heels, and the tailor ran around the outside and slammed the door. With that the animal was trapped inside, for it was too heavy and clumsy to escape out the window. The tailor called the hunters over to see the captive with their own eyes. The hero then made his way back to the king, who, like it or not, was now obliged to make good on his promise, and gave over his daughter and half the kingdom. Had he known that a little tailor, and not a famed warrior, stood before him, his heart would have weighed even heavier. And so the wedding was celebrated with great fanfare, if little joy, and out of a tailor was made a prince.

One night some time later, the young princess heard her husband talking in his sleep during one of his dreams: "Boy, make me that jacket and mend my breeches, or I will bash you over the head with my yardstick!" With that she realized what walk of life her mate had been born into. The next morning she confided her sorrow to her father, begging his help to get rid of this imposter, who was no more than a meager tailor. The king consoled her and said, "Leave the door to your bedchamber open tonight. My servants will be outside, and when he's fast asleep they will come in, tie him up, and put him on a ship bound for the lands beyond." The princess was relieved. But the keepers of the castle, who had heard all of this and were fond of the young new lord, warned him secretly of the ambush. "It will be easy enough to put a stop to this," the tailor said.

So that evening at the usual time, he went to bed with his wife. As soon as she thought that he was fast asleep, she got up, cracked the door, and lay back down again. But just then the little tailor, who was only pretending to be asleep, called out in his bright, full voice, "Boy, make me that jacket and mend my breeches, or I will bash you over the head with my yardstick! I have struck down seven with a single blow, killed two giants, caught a unicorn, and captured a wild boar, and you think I fear whoever stands at my door?" When the men posted outside heard him, they were overcome by wild terror, and took off running as if an entire army were after them. From that moment on, no one dared touch him. And so the little tailor became king, and remained so all the days of his life.

Cinderella

"Cinderella" is one of the most famous and ancient fairy tales in existence. Over its thousand-year history, seven hundred versions have flourished worldwide, including in ancient Egypt, Africa, Japan, Brazil, and Asia. The earliest version, from China circa 850–860 AD, is about a girl named Yè-Xiàn who is helped by a magic fish, and parts of "Cinderella" date back even further. In 1697 Frenchman Charles Perrault published a new version featuring a pumpkin, glass slipper, and fairy godmother upon which Disney based its 1950 animation. Critic Bruno Bettelheim notes that most of the world's Cinderella stories do not descend from this version but, like the Grimms', are based on older strains where our heroine relies on her wits to outsmart her oppressors. Along with themes of self-reliance, the Grimms' version contains an impassioned ending where, as Bettelheim puts it, Cinderella's stepsisters "stop at nothing." Indeed, they cut off parts of their feet to fit the shoe and win the prince, a deception they pay for with the loss of their eyesight. In this ancient morality tale, good dramatically prevails over evil, and the stepsisters' blindness represents their inability to perceive the goodness of Cinderella and the wickedness of their ways.—ND

Color lithographs by Hanns Anker, Austrian, circa 1910

There once was a rich man whose wife became very ill. As she felt her end drawing near, she summoned her little daughter, her only child, to her deathbed. She told her, "My sweet child, if you remain faithful and good, the dear Lord will always be with you, and I will be watching over you from Heaven and will always be with you." With that she closed her eyes and passed away. Every day the girl went to her mother's grave and wept, and remained faithful and good. As winter came, snow buried the grave beneath a white blanket, and by the time the spring sun had melted it, her father had chosen another woman as his wife.

This woman brought into the household two daughters of her own, pretty and fair in appearance, but evil and dark in their hearts. This was the beginning of hard times for the new stepchild. "Is this silly goose supposed to sit in the parlor with us?" they would ask. Or, "Whoever wants to eat bread has to earn it. Put the little kitchen maid back to work!" They took her nice clothes away and gave her an old smock instead, along with wooden shoes. "Look at the proud princess; how nicely done up she looks!" they said, mocking her and pushing her back into the kitchen. She toiled away there from morning till night, waking before sunrise, drawing and hauling the water, lighting the fire, cooking and cleaning. And on top of all this, the sisters taunted her and trampled on her feelings, playing such cruel tricks as shaking all the peas and lentils into the ashes, where she would have to crouch and sort out every last one of them again. At nighttime, after she'd been worked to the bone, she had no bed to go to, but instead had to huddle by the hearth near the cinders. From all this she was forever dusty and dirty, and so they took to calling her Cinderella.

One day her

The stepsisters would say, "Put the kitchen maid back to work!" They took her nice clothes away and gave her an old smock instead.

father decided to go to the great fair, and he asked his stepdaughters what he might bring them. "Beautiful clothes," said the first. "Pearls and precious gemstones," said the second. "And you, Cinderella," he asked, "what would you like?" "Oh, Father, the first branch to brush your cap on the way home, please snap it off and bring it to me." He bought beautiful clothing, pearls, and precious gemstones for his two stepdaughters. And on his way home, he rode through a green thicket, and a branch from a hazel tree knocked his hat off. He snapped the branch off and took it home. When he arrived he gave his stepdaughters what

"You sweet little doves," Cinderella said, "and all you birds in the sky, come help me sort the good lentils into the pot."

they had wished for, and gave Cinderella the hazel branch. She thanked him and went out to her mother's grave, where she planted it. She cried so hard that her streaming tears fell upon it and watered it, and it grew steadily into a lovely tree. After it had matured enough, Cinderella would go sit beneath it every day three times to cry and pray. And each time, a little white bird came and perched in the tree. Whenever Cinderella made a wish, this little bird would toss down to her what she had wished for.

Now it so happened that the king was preparing a three-day festival, and invited all the young beauties in the land so that

Just as before, all the birds of the sky came chirping and flocking into the kitchen and began to peck, peck, peck, peck.

his son might choose a bride. When the two stepdaughters learned they had been invited, they were overjoyed and called to Cinderella, "Brush our hair, clean our shoes, and snap our clasps. We are going to the festival at the king's palace!" Cinderella obeyed, but she wept silently, since she too would have so gladly gone to the dance; and she asked her stepmother whether she might go. "You, Cinderella," she said, "all covered in dust and dirt? You want to go to his majesty's festival? You have no proper clothes or shoes, and you want to dance?" But Cinderella kept asking, and finally the stepmother said, "I have poured a bowl of lentils into the ashes. If you pick them out within two hours, then you may go."

The girl went out the back door into the garden, and called out:

"*You sweet little doves, you little turtledoves,*
And all you birds in the sky,
Come help me sort the good ones into the pot,
And the bad ones into your crop."

Two little white doves flew in through the kitchen window, and then a flock of turtledoves, and finally all the birds of the sky came flapping into the kitchen, settling down by the cinders to help. The doves nodded their heads and began to *peck, peck, peck, peck.* Then the others joined them and began to *peck, peck, peck, peck*, and the birds sorted all the good lentils into a bowl. Hardly an hour had passed when they were finished, and they flew back out the window. Cinderella carried the bowl to the stepmother, and was so happy, for she thought she could now go to the ball. But all the woman said was, "No, Cinderella. You have no clothes and you cannot dance. You will just be laughed at." As Cinderella began to cry, her stepmother offered, "If you can sort two bowls of lentils out of the ashes in one hour, then you may go." Yet she thought to herself, "There is no possible way she can."

With that, she emptied the two bowls of lentils into the ashes. The girl then went out into the garden again and called out:

"Dear little tree," said Cinderella, "shake your branches and flutter your leaves, and let gold and silver fall down over me!"

"You sweet little doves, you little turtledoves,
And all you birds in the sky,
Come help me sort the good ones into the pot,
And the bad ones into your crop."

Just as before, the two white doves flew in through the kitchen window, and then the flock of turtledoves, and finally all the birds of the sky came chirping and flocking into the kitchen, settling down by the ashes. And the doves nodded and began to *peck, peck, peck, peck*. Then the others joined them and began to *peck, peck, peck, peck*, flicking the good seeds into the bowls. And after a mere half hour they were all done, and flew off again. Cinderella took the bowls to her stepmother, again so happy, thinking she could surely go to the ball now. But the woman said, "This won't help you. You are not coming with us. You have no clothes, nor can you dance. You would do nothing but disgrace us." With that, she turned her back on the girl and rode off with her two proud daughters.

Now the house was empty, and Cinderella went to her mother's grave under the hazel tree, where she called out:

Cinderella returned to the hazel tree, and the bird tossed down an even more magnificent gown than the previous night's.

> *"Dear little tree,*
> *Shake your branches and flutter your leaves,*
> *And let gold and silver fall down over me!"*

Then the bird dropped down a gold and silver evening gown, and slippers embroidered in silk and silver. In great haste, Cinderella put on the dress and dashed off to the ball. Her sisters and her stepmother did not recognize her, and thought she must be a princess from a far-off land, so beautiful was she in her golden gown. That it might be Cinderella never occurred to them. They assumed she was sitting at home in her filthy clothes, picking lentils from the ashes. But the prince came straight up to Cinderella and took her by the hand and danced with her. The whole night he danced with her and no one else, not letting go of her hand. If another suitor tried to cut in, he refused, saying, "She is my partner."

They danced well into the evening, until Cinderella felt she must go home. But the prince protested, "I will come along and accompany you home." He was eager to see what family the lovely girl belonged to. But she slipped away toward home and disappeared into her father's pigeon coop. The prince waited until her father arrived, and told him that he thought the mysterious girl had escaped into his dovecote. The old man thought, "Could it be Cinderella?" And he was brought an axe and a pick so he could break it open. But there was no one inside. As he went back into the house, he saw Cinderella lying in her dirty clothes among the cinders, with a dim oil lamp burning in the chimney nearby. She had sneaked out the back of the dovecote and

She astonished each and every guest at the ball with her beauty. The prince took her by the hand and danced only with her.

run to the hazel tree, and left her evening clothes at her mother's grave, where the bird had taken them back. And then she had dashed back to the kitchen and the cinders, once again wearing her old smock.

The next day the festivities began anew, and after her father, stepmother, and stepsisters had left the house, Cinderella returned to the hazel tree and said:

"Dear little tree,
Shake your branches and flutter your leaves,
And let gold and silver fall down over me!"

The bird tossed down an even more

The prince had ordered the entire staircase covered in pitch, and as Cinderella ran off, one of her slippers got stuck in it.

magnificent gown than the previous night's. When Cinderella appeared wearing it at the ball, she astonished each and every guest with her beauty. The prince had been waiting for the unknown girl to arrive, and took her right away by the hand and danced only with her. When other hopefuls came and asked to cut in, he again refused, saying, "She is my partner."

As evening fell, she wished to return home. The prince followed her, since he still wanted to see where she lived. But she slipped away into the garden behind their house, where there was a beautiful, big tree with the most wonderful pears.

She climbed up among the tree limbs as nimbly as a squirrel, and the prince could not see where she had gone. He waited until her father came out, telling him, "The mysterious girl has escaped me, and I think she climbed into this pear tree." The father thought, "Could it be Cinderella?" He called for an axe, and felled the tree. But no one was in it. And as he went into the kitchen, there was Cinderella lying among the cinders as usual. For she had crawled down the other side of the tree, brought her lovely gown back to the hazel-tree bird, and put on her dirty smock.

On the third day, once her father, stepmother, and stepsisters had ridden away, she returned to her mother's grave and called up to the tree:

"Dear little tree,
Shake your branches and flutter your leaves,
And let gold and silver fall down over me!"

The bird unfurled a gown so splendid and dazzling that the likes of it had never been seen before, and her slippers were woven of pure gold. As she arrived at the wedding celebration, the guests were struck speechless with amazement. Once more, the prince danced only with her, and when someone else asked for a dance, he again refused, saying, "She is my partner." As darkness fell, Cinderella felt she must leave, and the prince again wanted to go with her. Yet once again she slipped away so quickly that he could not follow. But the determined prince had used a little cunning: He had ordered the entire staircase covered in pitch, and as Cinderella ran off, one of her slippers got stuck in it. The prince picked it up, and it was tiny and precious and all gold.

The next morning he rode to the father to tell him, "None other shall be my wife than the one who fits this gold shoe." The two stepsisters were delighted, for their feet were quite beautiful. The elder sister took the shoe into her room, and tried it on with her mother by her side. But she could not fit even her big toe into it. The shoe was simply too small for her. Her mother handed her a knife and told her, "Cut off your toe. Once you are queen, you'll no longer need to walk anywhere." With that, the girl cut off her toe, forced her foot into the shoe, swallowed the pain, and went out to the prince. He then asked her to be his wife and rode away with her on his horse. But they had to pass by the

The prince handed her the golden shoe. She removed her clog and slid on the slipper, which fit as if made just for her.

mother's grave. There the two doves were perched in the hazel tree, and called out:

"Roocki dee goo, Roocki dee goo
There is blood in that shoe
The shoe's too small, and not enough wide
By your side sits not the right bride."

The prince looked down at the stepsister's foot, and saw the oozing blood. He swung his horse around and brought the false bride home.

He announced that she was not the right one, and that the other sister should try on the shoe. So she went into the bedroom, and put her toes gleefully into the shoe. But her heel was far too big. So her mother handed her a knife, and said, "Hack off a piece of your heel. Once you are queen you'll no longer need to walk anywhere." So the girl sliced off part of her heel, forced her foot into the shoe, swallowed the pain, and went back out to the prince. He swept her up onto his horse, and they rode away. But as they passed by the little hazel tree, the two doves called out:

"Roocki dee goo, Roocki dee goo
There is blood in that shoe
For it presses on her bone
While your true bride still sits alone at home."

He looked down at her foot, and saw blood leaking from the shoe, staining its way up her white stockings and turning them bright red. Once again he turned his horse around and took the false bride back to the house.

"This one is not the right one either," he said. "Do you not have another daughter?" "No," answered the father, "only the grimy little Cinderella from my wife who died. It is simply not possible that she's the chosen bride." Nevertheless, the prince asked for her to be sent out. The stepmother protested, "Oh, no, she is much too dirty to be seen." But he stood his ground: Cinderella must come out. First she washed her hands and face, and then she came out and bowed before the prince, who handed her the golden shoe. She sat on a footstool, removed her heavy wooden clog, and slid on the slipper, which fit as if made just for her. As she stood up again and turned her face toward the prince, he recognized the lovely girl he had danced with, and exclaimed, "This is my true bride!" The stepmother and her daughters reeled in shock and turned pale with anger. But he lifted Cinderella onto his horse and they rode away together. As they passed by the hazel tree, the two white doves sang out:

"Roocki dee goo, Roocki dee goo
There's no blood in that shoe
That shoe fits to save her life
For this one's your only true wife."

And after they had said this, they flew down and landed on Cinderella, one on each of her shoulders, where they perched.

And on the day of the royal wedding, the two deceitful sisters came, hoping to grovel their way into good favor and share in the couple's fortune. As the bride and groom went into the church, the elder daughter pushed alongside to the right, and the younger to the left, and the two doves swooped down on either side and each pecked out one of the sisters' eyes. After the service, the elder sister hobbled out on the left and the younger sister on the right, and the doves pecked out the eyes they had left. And so, blind for the rest of their days, the stepsisters paid dearly for their wicked and treacherous ways.

Mother Holle

This morality tale features a fairy godmother in the mold of an ancient European mythological figure, Mother Holle. In this story made famous by the Grimms, a kind and hardworking girl pricks her finger while spinning and falls through a magical well to Mother Holle's underground world. When she returns with gold, her cruel stepmother sends her own selfish daughter for more. The girls' separate journeys are tests of their characters, and they find the underworld much like Earth: Bread needs to be baked, apples picked, and beds made. When Mother Holle's feather comforter is shaken, it snows on Earth, a reference to her power over the weather and her roots in old Germanic mythology as a primeval Earth goddess, noted by the elder brother Jacob Grimm in his book *German Mythology*. The ancient meanings associated with Mother Holle are also evident in her affiliation with spinning, which, according to historian Bernhard Lauer, reflects her influence over the girls' fates. The Grimms based their version on an oral tale from Hesse, Germany, told to them by Henriette Dorothea Wild, whom Wilhelm Grimm married in 1825. The first written variation of this type of tale appeared in Giambattista Basile's fairy-tale collection *Pentamerone* (1634–1636).—ND

Color lithographs by Herbert Leupin, Swiss, 1949

The poor girl had to go out each day and sit near a well by the roadside, and spin until her fingers bled.

There was once a widow with two daughters. One of them was a hard worker and very pretty, while the other one was ugly and lazy. But the widow loved the ugly, lazy one much more, since she was her real daughter. The other one was left to do all the chores, just like Cinderella. The poor girl had to go out each day and sit near a well by the roadside, and spin until her fingers bled.

Now it once so happened that the bobbin got bloodied, so she bent down over the well to wash it off. But it slipped out of her hands and fell in. She began to cry, ran to her stepmother, and told her of the mishap. But all she got was a merciless scolding: “If you let the bobbin fall in, then you’d better go get it out.” So the girl went back to the well, not knowing how on Earth she’d get the bobbin out. In her heartfelt fear, she leapt into the water after it and lost her senses.

When she came to, she was in a beautiful meadow where the sun was shining and thousands of wildflowers were in bloom. Strolling through the meadow, she came upon a baker’s oven full of bread, and the bread called out to her, “Oh! Take me out, take me out! Otherwise I’ll burn. I’ve been done for a while already!” So she stepped forward and got all the loaves of bread out with a spatula, one after the other. Then she went on her way again,

She came upon a baker's oven, and the bread called out to her, "Oh! Take me out, take me out! Otherwise I'll burn."

and soon came to a tree that was weighed down heavily with a great crop of apples. It called out to her, "Oh! Shake me, shake me! We apples are ripe already!" And so she shook the tree until the apples rained down, and kept shaking until not one was left on the branches. Once she'd piled them high, she again went on her way. At last she came to a little house. An old woman was looking out the window. She

OPPOSITE *At last she came to a little house. An old woman with awfully big teeth was looking out the window.*

PAGES 120–121 *Mother Holle said, "Be sure to shake out the pillows and feather bed so the feathers fly. Then it will snow in the world above."*

had such awfully big teeth that the girl was afraid and wanted to run away. But the woman called after her, "What are you afraid of, dear child? Stay here with me. If you do all the housework, you'll be taken care of. You just have to be sure to make my bed well, and to shake out the pillows and feather bed hard enough that the feathers fly. Then it will snow in the world above. For Mother Holle am I."

Because the old woman spoke so kindly to her, the girl took heart and agreed to work for her. She took care of everything according to her mistress's wishes, and shook out the pillows and feather bed thoroughly each and every day so that the feathers flew around like snowflakes. For all her hard work, she had a good life in the old woman's house, with plenty of sweet hot drinks and well-grilled meats, and never a harsh word spoken.

But after some time at Mother Holle's, the girl became sad. At first she didn't know what was wrong, but then she realized she was homesick. Even though she was treated a thousand times better here, she still felt a longing for home. So finally she went to the old woman and said, "I'm aching to go home. And even though I'm so much better off down here, I just can't stay any longer. I need to go back up to my people." Mother Holle answered, "I'm pleased that you feel a longing for home. And since you've served me so very well, I shall take you back up there myself." So she took the girl by the hand and led her to a great gate, which opened for them. And just when the girl passed through it, a veritable cloudburst of gold came pouring down over her, and she was completely covered in gold. "This is all for you, since you've been such a dedicated girl," said Mother Holle, and gave her back the bobbin she had lost. And then the gate closed, and the girl found herself back up in the world she knew, not far from her stepmother's house. As she came into the yard, the rooster that was perched on the edge of the well crowed, "Cock-a-doodle-do! Our golden girl is here anew!" The girl went inside, and since she was still covered in gold, she was warmly received by her stepmother and stepsister.

She then told them everything that had happened, and when the stepmother heard how this sudden wealth had come to her, she wanted to get the same good fortune for her other daughter—the ugly, lazy one. So now she was made to go sit

When the lazy girl walked under the great gate, instead of gold a great cauldron full of black pitch emptied over her.

by the well and spin. And to bloody her bobbin, she pricked her finger and dragged her hand through the thorny hedges. Then she threw the bobbin into the well and jumped in after it. She came to the meadow just as her stepsister had, and walked along the same path. When she reached the baker's oven, the bread cried out again, "Oh! Take me out, take me out! Otherwise I'll burn. I've been done for a while already!" But the lazy girl replied, "I would if I felt like getting dirty," and walked on. Soon she came to the apple tree, which cried, "Oh! Shake me, shake me! We apples are ripe already!" But she answered, "Well, just my luck. One of you might fall on my head," and with that she walked on. When she reached Mother Holle's little house she was not afraid, since she had already heard about her monstrous teeth, and right away she agreed to work for her.

On that first day she worked with all her might. She was hardworking and followed each and every one of Mother Holle's instructions, thinking of all the gold she would give her. But on the second day she began to drag her feet, and by the third day she was even worse. That morning she did not even feel like getting out of bed. She did not make Mother Holle's bed as she should have, nor did she shake out the pillows or the feather bed, nor did the feathers fly.

In no time, Mother Holle had had enough of this, and let the girl go. The lazy girl was perfectly happy with this, for she still thought the gold would soon be showering down upon her. But when Mother Holle led her to the great gate and she walked under it, instead of gold a great cauldron full of black pitch emptied over her. "That is the reward you get for your service," said Mother Holle. And with that, she shut the gate. The lazy girl made it home, but covered in pitch from head to toe. And the rooster that was perched on the edge of the well crowed, "Cock-a-doodle-do! Our dirty girl is here anew!" But the pitch would not come off, and for the rest of her life, try as she might, it was stuck to her for good.

Little Red Riding Hood

No other fairy tale is as inextricably linked to a piece of clothing as is "Little Red Riding Hood." Wearing a red bonnet like a beacon of innocence, Little Red Riding Hood ventures into the forest with much to learn about talking to strangers before she arrives at her grandmother's house. This cautionary coming-of-age tale about an innocent girl and a scheming wolf has had a long, colorful, and varied oral tradition. Versions have been found from Italy to Japan, and scholars have noted that a story about a girl wearing red who encounters wolves existed as far back as the eleventh century in what is now Belgium. The tale was first written down in France in 1697 by Charles Perrault, who, according to historians, added the iconic cap. The Grimms based their tale on a version they heard from a woman of French Huguenot heritage in Hesse, Germany, and added the lifesaving hunter. They continually revised the story through the seventh and final edition of their collection in 1857, and this last version has become the most widely known. Historians identify the story as an example of the widespread genre of folk and fairy tales about children and fearsome ogres.—ND

Color images by Divica Landrová, Czech, 1959

Her grandmother gave her a little red-velvet bonnet, which suited the girl so well that she never wanted to wear anything else.

There once was a sweet young maiden who was adored by everyone who laid eyes on her. Most of all, though, her grandmother loved her, and didn't know what she might possibly give to the child next. One time she gave her a little red-velvet bonnet as a gift, which suited the girl so well that she never wanted to wear anything else. So everyone took to calling her Little Red Riding Hood. One day her mother told her, "Now, Little Red Riding Hood, take this slice of cake and this bottle of wine to Grandmother. Ill and weak as she is, she'll be delighted to take strength from them. Hurry along now before it gets hot, and as you go, tread very carefully and keep to the path. For if you wander off, you could trip and break the bottle, and then Grandmother will have to go without. When you reach her place, don't forget to wish her good morning, and don't go poking around in everything." "I'll do everything just as you say," said Little Red Riding Hood to her mother, and squeezed her hand as a promise.

But her grandmother lived deep in the woods, a good half hour from the village. And just as the girl entered the woods, a wolf approached her. Little Red Riding Hood had no idea how treacherous an animal this was, and was not in the least afraid. "Good day, Little Red Riding Hood," he said. "Oh, thank you kindly, Mr. Wolf." "Where are you off to so early this morning?" "To my grandmother's house." "And what do you have there beneath your apron?" "Cake and wine. We baked yesterday for my poor, sick grandmother, who needs something to enjoy and make herself strong again." "And where does your grandmother live, Little Red Riding Hood?" "She's about a quarter hour from here in the woods, under the three

BELOW *"Good day, Little Red Riding Hood," said the wolf. "Where are you off to so early this morning?"*

PAGES 128–129 *She stepped off the path into the woods to pick some flowers, venturing deeper and deeper into the woods.*

oak trees. That's where her house stands. Just below are the nut bushes, which I'm sure you must know," Little Red Riding Hood answered.

All along the wolf was thinking, "This tiny young thing will make a juicy mouthful. She'll go down much better than the old woman. I've got to be very cunning to get them both!" And so after he had padded alongside Little Red Riding Hood for a while, he said, "My dear, take a good look at these lovely flowers all around us. Why not look around a little? I don't think you're hearing the sweet birdsong either. You're just walking along as if you had to go to school. But out here in the woods it's so magical!" So Little Red Riding Hood widened her eyes, and as she saw the sunlight streaming and dancing through the trees, and how thick the ground was with flowers, she thought, "I bet a fresh bouquet would make Grandmother happy too. It's still early enough that I'm sure to arrive on time."

And so she stepped off the path into the woods to pick some flowers. Whenever

The wolf turned the handle and the door sprung open. Without another word he went straight to the grandmother's bed and gobbled her up.

she plucked one, though, she thought she spotted another much more beautiful one up ahead, and went after it, venturing deeper and deeper into the woods. But the wolf went straight to her grandmother's and knocked on the door. "Who is there?" "It's your Little Red Riding Hood, with cake and wine. Open on up!" "I feel too weak to get up," she called. "Just turn the handle." The wolf turned the handle and the door sprung open, and without another word he went straight to the grandmother's bed and gobbled her up. Then he wriggled into her clothes and her nightcap, climbed into her bed, and pulled the bed curtains shut.

Meanwhile, Little Red Riding Hood had been running around after flowers, and only when she had gathered so many that she couldn't carry any more did she remember her grandmother, and set out anew for her house. She was surprised to find the door open, and as she entered, the house felt very strange to her. She thought, "Good heavens, how frightened I feel today. And I usually enjoy being at

BELOW RIGHT *The wolf wriggled into her grandmother's clothes and nightcap, and climbed into her bed.*

PAGES 132–133 *"But, Grandmother, what an awfully large mouth you have!" said Little Red Riding Hood. "All the better to eat you with!"*

Grandmother's so much." "Good morning!" she called out, but got no answer. She went over to the bed and opened the curtains. Her grandmother was lying there with her nightcap pulled down low over her face, and looked very strange. "Oh, Grandmother dear, what large ears you have!" "All the better to hear you with." "Oh, Grandmother, what big eyes you have!" "All the better to see you with." "Oh, Grandmother, what large hands you have!" "All the better to hold you with." "But, Grandmother, what an awfully large mouth you have!" "All the better to eat you with!" Hardly had these words escaped the wolf's mouth when he dashed from the bed and gobbled up poor Little Red Riding Hood.

Now that the wolf had satisfied his cravings, he lay back down in the bed and fell into a glutton's slumber, and began to snore noisily. It just so happened that a huntsman was passing by the house, and he thought, "Goodness, how the old lady's snoring. I should check to make sure she is all right." He entered the house and went over to the bed, and he saw the wolf lying in it. "So here you are, you old scoundrel!" he said. "I've been looking for you a long time." He was just bringing up his rifle when he realized the wolf might have the grandmother inside, and he might still be able to save her. Instead of firing, he grabbed a pair of shears and began cutting the sleeping wolf's belly open.

After just a couple of snips he saw a red bonnet within. Another couple slices and Little Red Riding Hood jumped out and cried, "Oh, I was so frightened. It was so dark inside the wolf!" And then her grandmother came out, too, still alive though barely able to breathe. Little Red Riding Hood quickly gathered some large stones, and they filled the wolf's stomach with them. When he awoke, he tried to jump up and escape, but the stones were so heavy that he sank back down and keeled over dead. So all three were elated. The hunter skinned the wolf and took its pelt home. The grandmother relished the cake and drank the wine her granddaughter had brought, and felt so

The huntsman entered the house and saw the wolf lying in the bed. "So here you are, you old scoundrel!" he said.

much better. And Little Red Riding Hood vowed to herself, "My whole life long I will never again go off the path into the woods when Mother has told me otherwise!"

It's also been said that another time when Little Red Riding Hood was bringing her grandmother some more baked goods, another wolf tried to charm her from the path. But this time, Little Red Riding Hood knew to beware and kept on going. She told her grandmother that a wolf had come up to her and said hello, but that there was a devilish glint in his eyes. "If we hadn't been on the open road, I'm sure he would have eaten me." "Come now," said her grandmother. "Let us lock the door so he can't get in." Only a short while later, there was a knock at the door, and a growly voice called out, "Open up, Grandmother! It's your Little Red Riding Hood with bundles of baked goods for you!" They kept quiet inside and did not go near the door. The old Grayhead sneaked around the house several times, then

With a stomach full of stones, the wolf keeled over dead. The hunter skinned the wolf and took its pelt home.

jumped onto the roof. He planned to wait there until Little Red Riding Hood left for home, so he could follow her silently and eat her up as night fell.

But the grandmother could tell what he had in mind. In front of her house there was a big, heavy stone trough. So she said, "Now take this bucket, Little Red Riding Hood, and carry the water I boiled yesterday's sausages with to the trough." The girl did as she was told until the whole long trough was full. The sausage scent began to rise up to the wolf's nose. He sniffed and he sniffed and he bent down to see what smelled so good, stretching his neck so long that he lost his balance and began to slide. Finally he fell straight off the roof and down into the trough, where he drowned. Little Red Riding Hood went happily home, and no one did her any harm along the way.

The Bremen Town Musicians

This tale is a heartwarming comedy of errors starring a lovable motley crew of farm animals. Maltreated by their owners and considered too old to be useful, a donkey, dog, cat, and rooster hatch a plan to strike out on their own and become musicians in the nearby town of Bremen, Germany. They are drawn by the lure of the big city and are eager to regain their self-respect, but on their way they come upon a band of robbers in a den with pilfered loot. With the help of their earsplitting cacophony, the four animals disband the thieves and win their stash of riches; and when one of the robbers comes back for it, the animals scare them off for good. The ragtag band of animals—more humane and good than any of the humans—triumph over the robbers, the real beasts in the story, with their teamwork. The Grimms reportedly heard the tale from Dorothea Viehmann in their hometown of Kassel. An innkeeper's daughter, Viehmann was a key oral source of a number of their tales, and the Grimms featured her portrait at the beginning of their collection to promote its folk origins.—ND

Details from a hand-colored broadside by Rudolf Geißler, German, 1892

The donkey said to the dog, "I'm on my way to Bremen to become a town musician. Come make music with me."

nce there was a donkey who for many years had faithfully carried his master's sacks of grain to the mill. But now his strength was fading, and he was less and less fit for work, so his master began to think about getting him out of the way. But the donkey got wind of the trouble ahead, and took off for the town of Bremen. There, he thought, he'd have a chance at becoming a town musician. After he had been on his way for a while, he came across a hunting dog who was worn out in the middle of the road and panting as if he'd run a mile too many. "Hey, why are you panting so hard, Old Wheezer?" the donkey asked. "Oh, me," said the dog. "It's because I'm old and getting weaker by the day. And since I can no longer hunt, my master was planning to do me in. So I skedaddled! But how on Earth can I earn my daily bread now?" "You know what?" said the donkey. "I'm on my way to Bremen to become a town musician. Come along and make some music with me. I'll play the lute, and you can beat the drums." The dog liked the idea, and they walked on together.

It wasn't long before they saw a cat sitting by the side of the road. She had a look on her face like a month of rainy Sundays. "Hey, what's rubbed you the wrong way, Whisker Washer?" asked the donkey. "How could I be amused when I've had it up to here?" replied the cat, rubbing her neck with her paw. "Now that I'm getting old, my teeth aren't sharp anymore, and I prefer sitting behind the warm stove and dreaming up schemes to actually chasing mice. And guess what? My mistress even tried to drown me! Thankfully I managed to run away. Advice doesn't come cheap, but still I ask: Where on Earth do I go now?" "Come with us to Bremen!" said the donkey. "You can make

BELOW LEFT *It wasn't long before they saw a cat sitting by the road. She had a look on her face like a month of rainy Sundays.*

a little night music, can't you? You could become a town musician with us." The cat thought this sounded like a good idea, and went along.

Soon enough, the three refugees came upon a farm, where a rooster was sitting on the gate crowing his lungs out. "Your scream is getting under my skin, right into my bones!" the donkey exclaimed. "What in the world are you up to?" "All I was doing was predicting good weather," said the rooster, "since it's the day our Good Lady washes the baby Jesus's swaddling clothes and hangs them out to dry. But tomorrow guests are coming for Sunday lunch, and the mistress has no mercy. She's told the cook she wants me

BELOW RIGHT *They came upon a rooster crowing his lungs out. "Why don't you come with us?" they said. "We're off to Bremen!"*

in the soup, and that she should chop off my head tonight! So now I'm screaming for all it's worth for as long as I still can!" "Know what, Red Head?" said the donkey. "Why don't you come with us? We're off to Bremen! You're sure to find something better than death no matter where you go. But you have a good voice, and I bet if we make music together, it will be very memorable!" The rooster liked the suggestion, and the wayfarers, now four, went on together.

But they couldn't reach Bremen in just one day, and so when evening came they slipped into the woods, where they planned on spending the night. The donkey and the dog stretched out under

Once they built their pyramid, they began their music: The donkey hee-hawed, the dog bellowed, the cat meowed, and the rooster crowed.

a big tree, while the cat and the rooster scrambled up into the branches, and the rooster flew up to the very top, the safest spot for him. Before the rooster fell asleep, he looked out in all four directions one last time. He thought he saw a little sparkle of light in the distance and he called down to the others to tell them there must be a house not far off where a light was burning. "Let's get up and go there, since our lodgings here are pretty poor," the donkey suggested. The dog said he could imagine he'd be better off, too, finding some bones and a little gristle.

And so they set out again toward the light, which shined bigger and brighter as they drew nearer, until at last they stood in front of a brightly lit robbers' den.

Since the donkey was the tallest, he went up to the window and looked inside. "What do you see, Flea-bitten Gray?" asked the rooster. "What do I see?" replied the donkey. "A table decked out with food and drink, and hairy bandits seated around it having a grand old time." "Ooh, that'd be something for us," mused the rooster. "Oh, yes. Ohh, yes," added the donkey. "If only we were inside."

So the animals debated how they might drive the robbers out, and at last settled on an idea. The donkey propped his forelegs on the windowsill; the dog leapt up onto the donkey's back; the cat clawed her way up onto the dog; and finally the rooster flew up to the tippy-top and sat on the cat's head. Once they had built their pyramid, they gave a signal and began their music: The donkey hee-hawed, the dog bellowed, the cat meowed, and the rooster crowed. Then, all at once, they crashed through the windows into the robbers' den, shattering the windowpanes. The robbers jumped up in wild alarm at this cacophony, convinced that a ghost was upon them, and in their terror they fled headlong into the woods.

The four friends sat down at the table and helped themselves eagerly to the remains of the meal, eating as if four weeks of starvation lay ahead of them. Once our troubadours were full, they blew out the candles and found themselves

All at once, they crashed into the robbers' den. The robbers jumped up in alarm at this cacophony and fled into the woods.

comfortable places to sleep, each according to his or her needs. The donkey lay down outside in the straw; the dog went behind the door; the cat sought the stove and snuggled herself up near the warm ashes; and the rooster took to the beams above. And since they were tired from their long journey, they all soon fell asleep.

After midnight, the robbers could see from afar that no lights were burning

BELOW LEFT AND RIGHT *The cat leapt at the robber's face, spitting, hissing, and scratching. The dog sunk his teeth into the man's leg.*

in the house. Their leader growled, "We shouldn't have been browbeaten so easily," and sent one of his men back to the house to inspect it. The robber found everything silent and still, and went into the kitchen to light a candle. But he mistook the cat's fiery eyes for glowing coals and held his match up to them to light it. This did not amuse the cat in the least, who leapt at the man's face, spitting and hissing and scratching at him. The man reeled back in shock and tried to escape through the back door. But instead, he ran into the dog lying there, who leapt up and sunk his teeth into the man's leg. And as the robber fled through the courtyard past the straw, the donkey gave him a nasty kick with his hind legs, while the rooster, who had also been awakened by the noise, let out an earsplitting shriek from the rafters: "Cock-a-doodle-doo!"

BELOW LEFT AND RIGHT *As the robber fled, the donkey gave him a nasty kick, and the rooster let out an earsplitting "Cock-a-doodle-doo!"*

The robber hobbled as best he could back to his leader, and said, "Oh! There is a terrible witch in that house who spewed her poison over me and scratched my face with her long fingernails. And there was a man in front of the door who stabbed me in the leg with his knife. And in the courtyard there was a black monster who clubbed me with his wooden cudgel. And up on the roof there sat a judge who shouted, 'Bring me that rascal!' I got out of there as fast as I possibly could!" From then on, the robbers dared not go near the house. The four Bremen town musicians, however, had such a marvelous old time that they decided never to leave. And somewhere out there without fail, there's another tongue still warm from telling this same tale.

The Devil with the Three Golden Hairs

In this tale, a baby boy is born with an auspicious membrane called a caul over his head, and the townspeople interpret it as a sign that he will marry the king's daughter. The belief that a caul foreshadows greatness dates back to medieval Europe. Given its protective second-skin quality, it was also sometimes believed to offer lifelong protection against drowning. In the story, the king thinks he has drowned the baby boy in a box, only to discover that, like Moses, the child was saved. Years later, the king challenges him to bring back three hairs from the Devil before he can marry his daughter. With the limitless optimism common to the everyday heroes in the Grimms' tales, the boy succeeds with the help of the Devil's kindly grandmother. The Grimms noted that similar stories appeared in Scandinavia and in Britain—for instance, in "Jack and the Beanstalk," where Jack is helped by a giant's compassionate wife. Folklorists have also noted the resemblance to the myth of Prometheus, who stole fire from the gods. Here, however, no harm comes to the boy from the tractable Devil, who lives with his grandmother and snoozes in her lap while she lovingly picks his lice.—ND

Tempera drawings by Gustaf Tenggren, Swedish-American, 1955

The king rode away with the baby in a box until they came to a river, where he threw the box right in.

Once there was a poor woman who gave birth to a little boy. Since he was born with a caul, considered a sign of good luck, it was foretold that in his fourteenth year he would marry the king's daughter. Shortly after his birth, it so happened that the king came to the village, but no one knew he was really the king. When he asked the villagers what the latest news was, they answered, "Just a few days ago, a child was born with a caul. Whatever this child does in life, it's bound to turn out well. It's even said that he will marry the king's daughter in his fourteenth year." But the king had a mean heart and was upset by this prophecy. He went to the boy's parents, pretended to be friendly to them, and said, "You poor people, why don't you let me take care of your child?" At first they refused, but once the stranger offered heaps of gold, they thought twice about it: "He's a lucky child, after all. This will surely turn out to be for the best." And at last they consented and handed over the boy to him.

The king placed the baby boy in a box and rode away with him until they came to a deep river. There the king stopped and threw the box right in. "Now once and for all I'll keep this unintended suitor away from my daughter," he thought. But instead of sinking, the box floated like a little raft, and not a drop of water leaked in. It drifted along until it was two miles from the king's castle, where it got hung up in a milldam. The miller's apprentice standing nearby happened to see the box, and pulled it out with a crook. He thought he might find treasure, but when he opened it, there inside was a handsome little boy, rosy-cheeked and cheery. He brought the baby to the miller

There inside was a handsome little boy, rosy-cheeked and cheery. The miller and his wife, who had no children, were over the moon.

and his wife, and since they had no children, they were over the moon, and said, "This is a gift from God." They took good care of the foundling, and he grew into a loving, kind, and generous young man.

One day the king ducked inside the mill seeking shelter from a storm. He asked the miller and his wife whether the tall lad was their son. "No," they replied. "We found him. Fourteen years ago he floated into the dam in a box, and our apprentice pulled him out of the water." At that moment, the king realized it was none other than the lucky lad he himself had thrown in the river, and he said, "Good people, could that boy take a letter to my wife, the queen? I'll give him two gold coins as a reward." "As your majesty wishes," they answered, and told the lad to get ready. Then the king wrote a letter to the queen that said, "As soon as the young man carrying this letter arrives, he is to be put to death and then buried. And this should be done before I return."

The lad took the letter and set out on his way, but he took a wrong turn and at nightfall ended up in a big forest. Through the darkness he spotted a flickering light. He went toward it, and came to a little cottage. When he went inside, he saw a little old lady sitting alone by the fire. She was startled to see the young man, and asked, "Where are you coming from, and where are you going?" "I'm from the mill," he answered. "And I'm on my way to deliver a letter to the queen. But I've lost my way in this forest, and I was hoping to spend the night here." "Oh, you poor boy," the old woman said. "You've ended up in a robbers' den, and when they get home, they'll kill you." "Let come what may," replied the boy. "I'm not afraid. But I'm so tired that I can't go on." And with that he stretched out on a bench and fell fast asleep.

PAGES 148–149 *The hard-hearted criminals were moved with sympathy for the boy, tore up the letter, and wrote a new one in its place.*

OPPOSITE *The ferryman said, "Tell me why I have to row with no one to relieve me." "I'll find out for you," the boy replied.*

Soon afterward the robbers came and asked angrily who the boy on the bench was. "Oh," said the old woman, "he's just an innocent boy lost in the woods, and I've let him stay here out of the goodness of my heart. He's taking a letter to the queen." The robbers opened the letter and read it, and it said that the boy was to be killed the minute he handed it over. The hard-hearted criminals were moved with sympathy for him, and their leader tore up the letter and wrote a new one in its place. This letter said that the boy was to marry the king's daughter as soon as he handed it over. They let him sleep in peace and quiet on the bench until morning, and when he awoke they gave him the letter and sent him off in the right direction. When the queen received the letter and read its instructions, she did just as it said: She called for a magnificent wedding celebration, and her daughter was married to the lucky lad on the spot. And since he was handsome and kind, she lived happily and joyfully together with him.

After a time, the king returned to the castle and saw that the prophecy had been fulfilled, and that the lucky lad had married his daughter. "How could this possibly have happened?" he asked. "I gave completely different orders in my letter." But the queen showed him the letter, and told him to see for himself what it said. He read it, and sure enough, the letter had been switched. He asked the young man what had become of the letter he'd been given, and why he'd brought another. "I have no idea," he answered. "It must have been swapped while I spent the night in the forest." The king became enraged and said, "It will not be that easy for you. If you want to marry my daughter, first you must bring me from Hell three of the Devil's golden hairs. Only if you bring me what I ask may you keep my daughter." Of course the king was really hoping to be rid of the boy forever. But the lucky lad answered, "I'll get you the golden hairs. I'm not afraid of the Devil." And with that he took his leave and started on his journey.

The way led him to a large city, where the watchman at the city gate asked him what his trade was, and what he knew. "I know everything," answered the lucky lad. "Then you can do us a favor," said the watchman, "and tell us why the fountain at the market that has always flowed with wine is all of a sudden dry. It won't even give out water." "I'll find out for you," the

boy replied. “Just wait until I get back.” He went on until he came to another city, and again the watchman at the gate asked him what his trade was, and what he knew. “I know everything,” he answered. “Then you can do us a favor and tell us why a tree in our town that has always grown golden apples no longer even grows leaves.” “I’ll find out for you,” the boy replied. “Just wait until I get back.” Then he walked on farther until he came to a big river, which he had to get across. The ferryman asked him what his trade was, and what he knew. “I know everything,” he answered. “Then you can do me a favor,” said the ferryman, “and tell me why I always have to row back and forth, with no one to relieve me.” “I’ll find out for you,” the boy replied. “Just wait until I get back.”

Once he had crossed the river, he came upon the entrance to Hell. It was black and sooty inside, and the Devil was not at home. But his grandmother was there,

The Devil returned home, and hardly was he inside when he sensed something in the air. "I smell…I smell human flesh!" he said.

sitting in a great big armchair. "What do you want?" she asked him, and didn't look so mean at all. "I'd like three golden hairs from the Devil's head," he answered. "Otherwise I won't be able to keep my wife." "That's asking a lot," she said. "If the Devil comes home and finds you here, it's going to get very hot under your collar. But I feel sorry for you, and I'll see if I can help." She then turned him into an ant, and said, "Crawl into the folds of my skirt. You'll be safe there." "Yes," he answered, "that should work well, but there are three things I'd also like to know: why a fountain that has always flowed with wine has now dried up, and won't even give out water; why a tree that has always grown golden apples now doesn't even grow leaves; and why a ferryman has to row back and forth without relief." "These are difficult questions," she answered. "But keep quiet and listen carefully to what the Devil says when I pluck the three hairs from his head."

As evening fell, the Devil returned home. Hardly was he inside when he sensed something in the air. "I smell…I smell human flesh!" he said. "Something's not right here." He searched high and low, but found nothing. The grandmother gave him a scolding. "I just swept up in here and put everything in order, and now you've come and made a mess," she said. "You always have the smell of human flesh in your nose! Just sit down and eat your supper." Once he finished eating and drinking he grew tired. He lay his head down in his grandmother's lap, and asked her to pick some lice from his head. Before long he fell asleep, snoring and whistling gently through his lips. Then the grandmother took hold of a golden hair, plucked it out, and put it down next to her. "Ouchie!" the Devil cried. "Why did you do that?" "I just had a very deep dream," said the grandmother. "And I must have grabbed your hair." "What were you dreaming?" asked the Devil. "I dreamt there was a fountain at a market that usually flowed with wine, but it had dried up and wouldn't even give out water. What could be the matter with it?" "Ha! If they only knew!" the Devil said. "There's a toad underneath one of the fountain's stones. If they kill it, the wine will flow again."

The grandmother went back to picking his lice until he fell asleep again, and he snored so loudly that he made the window-panes rattle. Then she tore out a second

The grandmother spoke soothingly, and he fell asleep again. She then ripped a third golden hair out, and up the Devil leapt, screaming.

hair. "Ow! Ah! What are you doing?" the Devil cried angrily. "Please don't be upset," she answered. "I must have been dreaming." "What were you dreaming?" he asked. "I dreamt there was a kingdom with an apple tree. It had always grown golden apples, but now it wouldn't even grow leaves. What could be the reason?" "Ha! If they only knew!" the Devil said. "There's a mouse gnawing at its roots. If they kill it, the tree will bear golden apples again. If it keeps gnawing at it, though, the tree will wither and die. But stop bothering me with these dreams of yours. If you disturb me once more while I'm sleeping, you'll get a nice slap!"

The grandmother spoke soothingly to him as she picked his lice, and he fell asleep again and began to snore. She then took hold of a third golden hair and ripped it out. Up the Devil leapt, screaming and ready to visit the same pain on her. But she calmed him again, and said, "It was just a bad dream again! Who can help it?" "What were you dreaming this time?" he asked, curious again, despite himself. "I dreamt there was a ferryman who was complaining that he had to row back and forth, and no one ever came to relieve him. Why is this happening to him?" "Ha! What a nincompoop!" the Devil said. "If someone comes and wants to cross over, he simply has to give that person his oars, and make him do the rowing. Then he's free!" Now that the grandmother had plucked the three golden hairs, and the three questions were answered, she let the old dragon sleep in peace until morning.

Once the Devil had gone out again, the old woman lifted the ant out from the folds of her skirt and restored the lucky lad to his human form. "Here are the three golden hairs," she said. "I assume you heard what the Devil said about your three questions?" "Yes," he replied. "I heard it and I'll remember it well." "So now I've helped you, and you're free to go on your way," she said. He thanked the old woman for helping him in his distress, and put Hell behind him, happy that

everything had gone so well. When he reached the ferryman, the man asked him for the promised answer to his question. "First take me over to the other side," said the lucky lad. "Then I'll tell you how you can set yourself free." Once they had landed on the other side, the lad gave him the Devil's advice: "The next time

someone comes and wants to cross over, simply give him your oars." He kept walking and came to the town in which the barren tree stood, and the watchman demanded an answer from the lad, so he gave him the Devil's advice: "Kill the mouse gnawing on the tree's roots, and the tree will bear golden apples again." The watchman thanked him, and gave him two donkeys laden with gold as a reward. Finally he came to the city with the dried-up fountain. And there he gave the watchman the Devil's advice: "There's a toad sitting under one of the fountain's stones. You must find it and kill it. Then the fountain will flow with abundant wine again." The watchman thanked him, and also gave him two donkeys laden with gold.

At long last the lucky lad returned home to his wife. Her heart was filled with joy when she saw him again and heard all about his successful adventures. He presented the Devil's three golden hairs to the king as requested, and when the king saw the four donkeys and the gold, he was mighty pleased and said, "Now you've satisfied all the conditions,

OPPOSITE *At long last the lucky lad returned home to his wife, and her heart was filled with joy when she saw him again.*

BELOW *From then on, the king had to ferry people from shore to shore as punishment for his sins.*

and you may keep my daughter. But, dear son-in-law, please tell me, where did you get all this gold? It's a sizable fortune indeed." "I was ferried across a river," he answered, "and that's where I found it. There, the riverbank is gold instead of sand." "Can I get some for myself?" the king asked, growing greedy. "As much as your heart desires," he answered. "There's a ferryman at the river. Have him take you across, so you can stuff your bags full." At once the greedy king hurried on his way. When he reached the river, he motioned to the ferryman to take him across. The ferryman came and told the king to get on board. As soon as they reached the other shore, he pushed the oars into the king's hands and jumped out. From then on, the king had to ferry people from shore to shore as punishment for his sins. "Is he still rowing?" you might ask. What do you mean? Of course he is! There's no one who will come and take those oars.

The Shoemaker and the Elves

Although brief, this tale is the most popular of the Grimms' stories about *Wichtelmänner,* gnomelike creatures commonly called elves in English. The story hinges on surprising circumstances that a shoemaker and his wife cannot understand: Each morning they awake to find beautiful shoes made of leather they left out the night before. Although the mischievous elves don't reveal themselves until the end, their anonymous actions reflect their puckish identity, which has delighted listeners and readers since the little creatures emerged in medieval European folklore. This story of a hardworking shoemaker currying favor with two elves is the quintessential portrait of a folkloric world where humans and otherworldly creatures intermingle along the fissures of unexplained events. Other magical characters who exist on this plane are dwarfs, goblins, trolls, and fairies. In contrast to tales that occur in hypothetical kingdoms and forests, this one takes place in a humble workshop—a down-to-earth setting where not a prince, princess, or witch is to be found, suggesting that no matter what one's status is in life, elevation of one's circumstances is always possible. Though it originally bore the simple title "The Elves," the tale is popularly known today as "The Shoemaker and the Elves."—ND

Color lithograph of an 1823 black-and-white illustration by George Cruikshank, British, 1899

nce upon a time there was a shoemaker who one day, through no fault of his own, found himself so poor that all he had left in the world was enough leather for one last pair of shoes. That evening he cut the leather to size, since he wanted to take up work on the shoes the next morning. Then with a good conscience he got into bed, prayed for the dear Lord's grace, and fell asleep. In the morning he said his prayers and was about to sit down to work when he saw the shoes lying finished on his workbench. He was amazed, and did not know what to say. He picked up the shoes to take a closer look: So finely were they crafted, without a single stitch out of place, that they looked just like a masterpiece. A moment later a customer walked in who loved the shoes so much that he paid more than the usual price for them.

With this money the shoemaker was able to buy enough leather for two pairs of shoes. He cut the patterns for them that evening, and planned to get to work on them the next morning. But there was no need, for when he got up the shoes were already finished. Soon customers came and paid him so much money that he could now buy enough leather for four pairs of shoes. First thing the next morning, he found these four pairs finished, and so this went on: Whatever he sized up in the evening was finished by morning. Soon enough he was making a good living again, and in time became a prosperous man.

One such evening, not long before Christmas, when he'd finished cutting the leather just before bed, he said to his wife, "How about we stay up tonight to see who on Earth has been lending us such a helping hand?" His wife liked the idea and lit a lamp. Then they hid in the corner behind the clothes hanging there, and kept watch. At the stroke of midnight, two little bare men came and sat down at the shoemaker's bench. They took the cut leather and began to work. Their tiny fingers were so deft and fast at punching the holes, stitching, and hammering that the astonished shoemaker could not take his eyes off them. They did not let up until everything was done, and the shoes lay finished on the workbench. Then they hurried off.

They hopped and danced, leaping over the chairs and the bench, until at last they danced their way merrily out the door.

The next morning the shoemaker's wife said, "These little elves have made us rich, and we should show our gratitude. They're running around here with nothing to wear, and must be freezing cold. You know what? I'll knit some little shirts, coats, vests, and pants for them, and for each a pair of stockings too. Why don't you make them some tiny shoes?"

"That's a great idea," her husband said. And in the evening when they'd finished everything, instead of the next day's leather they laid their gifts out on the workbench. Then they hid once again, hoping to see what the little elves would do. At midnight they came bounding in, ready to get down to work. But instead of leather for their shoemaking, they found darling little clothes laid out for them. At first they were puzzled, but then they jumped for joy. As fast as they could, they got dressed and straightened their new garments out with their hands, singing:

"Aren't we fellows so neat and smooth? Let's quit shoemaking and make a new move."

Then they hopped and danced around the room, leaping over the chairs and the bench, until at last they danced their way merrily out the door. From then on, they never returned. But the shoemaker continued to prosper, succeeding at everything he put his hands to.

Tom Thumb's Travels

This story tells the adventures of Tom Thumb, a boy no bigger than a thumb who has appeared for centuries under many names in fairy tales and nursery rhymes of various cultures. In the Grimms' collection, the character—originally called Thumbling—appears in two tales that playfully invert the classical epic of the globe-trotting hero in the mold of Homer's *Ulysses*. Tiny, clever, and cheeky, Tom Thumb sets out to experience life on his own. The fast-paced tale entertains with episode after episode of folly and farce in his supersized world, where danger lurks around every corner, as do plenty of opportunities to outwit the lumbering humans overhead. In Tom Thumb's world, his petite size is not a disadvantage but an impetus to ingenuity, exemplified in his repurposing a coin into a glider and similar creative maneuvers. As a popular character in folklore for hundreds of years, Tom Thumb has endeared audiences with his tenacious spirit and unlikely heroism. The Grimms noted that versions of his character date back to ancient Greece, and folklorists Iona and Peter Opie have confirmed that tales of being swallowed, a fate that befalls Tom Thumb, can be found in Europe, India, and Japan.—ND

Details of a hand-colored broadside by Oswald Sickert, German-British, 1852

Though he was small, he was a gutsy fellow, and said to his father, "I feel I have to go out into the world."

Once there was a tailor who had a son who was very much on the short side. In fact, he was no bigger than a thumb, and so was called Tom Thumb. Even though he was so small, he was a gutsy fellow, and said to his father, "Father, I feel I have to go out into the world." "You're right, my son," said the old man, who took a sewing needle and made a little handle on the end of it with melted sealing wax. "And here you have a sword to take with you on your way." Our little tailor wanted to have one last home-cooked meal, and skittered into the kitchen to see what his mother was cooking. The meal was ready, and his bowl was keeping warm on the hearth. "Mother, what are we having to eat today?" he asked. "Take a look for yourself," she said. So Tom Thumb leapt onto the hearth and peered into the bowl. But he had stretched his neck out a bit too far, and the steam rising from the food lifted him up into the chimney, and he rode the hot air for some time before he finally sank back to Earth.

Now the little fellow was out in the big, wide world. He wandered around, and eventually became an apprentice with a master tailor. But there the food was not good enough for him. "Mrs. Tailor, if you don't give us better vittles," said Tom Thumb one day, "I will leave, and tomorrow morning I'll be back to write on your door in white chalk: 'Too many potatoes and too little meat. Auf Wiedersehen, Potato Queen!'" "You've got some nerve, you little grasshopper," she said, getting mad, and she grabbed a rag and tried to swat him with it. But our little tailor slipped nimbly under her thimble. Then he looked out from underneath and stuck out his tongue. The master's wife picked up the thimble and

"You've got some nerve, you little grasshopper," she said, getting mad, and she grabbed a rag and tried to swat him.

tried to snatch him, but little Tom Thumb hopped into the rag first. As she unfolded it to try to find him, he jumped into a crack in the table. "Yoo-hoo! Mrs. Tailor!" he called out, poking his head out, and when she tried to squash him, he dove into the drawer. But finally she cornered him and chased him out of the house.

So he roamed around once more until he came to a great forest. There he ran into a band of robbers who were planning to steal the king's treasure. When they saw Tom Thumb, they thought, "Such a tiny little thing can crawl right through the keyhole and be our picklock." "Hey, you giant Goliath," one of them called out. "How'd you like to come with us to the king's treasure room? You can crawl inside and hand the money to us." Tom Thumb thought for a moment, finally agreed, and went with them to the treasury.

There he searched the door up and down for a crack, and before long he found one wide enough to crawl through. He was just about to wriggle through the crack when one of the watchmen at the door noticed him, and said to the other, "What kind of awful spider is that crawling over there? I'm going to squash it." "Let the poor little thing be," said the other. "It hasn't done you any harm." Just then Tom Thumb slipped safely through the crack into the treasury, opened the window, and began tossing one silver coin after another to the robbers below. He had just begun to work at a solid clip when he heard the king coming to check on his treasure, and so he dashed into hiding. The king noticed instantly that some of his silver currency was missing, but he could not fathom how that could be. The door had been tightly bolted, and as usual everything was kept under lock and key. The king left the room and said to the two watchmen, "Be on your guard. There is someone after my money."

Once Tom Thumb resumed his work, the watchmen could hear the sound of

the money moving and clinking inside—*cling, clang, cling, clang.* They burst in, thinking they would catch the thief red-handed. But our little tailor had heard them coming, and was too quick for them. He scampered into a corner and took cover under a coin, and he began to tease the watchmen, calling out, "Here I am!" They ran toward the voice, but by the time they got there, he was already hiding under a coin in another corner. He called out, "Yoo-hoo! Here I am!" The watchmen hurried over, but Tom Thumb was long gone, and from a third corner he teased, "Yoo-hoo! Here I am!" Again and again he made fools of them, and had them running in circles around the treasury until they were worn out and finally left.

He was then able to get back to work, tossing the coins one after the other out the window. He heaved the very last one with all his might, then leapt onto it, and flew out the window on its face. How the robbers sang his praises! "You're a real hero!" they exclaimed. "Do you want to be our leader?" Tom Thumb thanked them kindly, but said his plan was to see the

OPPOSITE *One of the robbers said, "How'd you like to come with us to the king's treasure room? You can crawl inside and hand us the money."*

BELOW *One of the maids saw Tom Thumb, mowed him right up with the grass, and then secretly fed him to the cattle.*

world first. They divvied up their loot, and Tom Thumb asked for only one small coin, since that was all he could carry.

He strapped on his sword again, bade the robbers farewell, and set off on his own two little legs. He worked as an apprentice to several different masters, but had little appetite for the work. Finally he was hired as a servant boy at an inn. But the maids could not stand him, since he always saw the mischief they were up to without their knowing he was even there, and he would tell the owners what they stole from the guests' plates and took for themselves from the cellar. "Just you wait. We'll teach you a lesson," they snapped, for they planned to play a prank on him.

A short while later, when one of the maids was mowing the garden and saw Tom Thumb jumping up and down in the weeds, she mowed him right up with the grass, bundled up the cuttings in a towel, and secretly fed it all to the cattle. There was a big black cow among them, and she swallowed Tom Thumb along with the grass without hurting him. But he did not like it down inside her at all, since it was terribly dark and there was not a single candle burning anywhere. While the cow was being milked, Tom Thumb called out, "Strip, strap, stroll. Isn't the bucket already full?" But the sound of milking was so loud that no one could hear him. Soon the innkeeper came into the stall and said, "Tomorrow that cow is to be slaughtered." Understandably, this made Tom Thumb quite afraid, and he cried out in a shrill voice, "Let me out! I'm stuck inside!" The man heard this, but did not know where the voice was coming from. "Where are you?" he asked. "In the black one," Tom Thumb answered. But the man did not understand what that could possibly mean, and he walked away.

BELOW LEFT *Our little man screamed at the top of his lungs, "Don't hack so deep, don't hack so deep! I'm right down here within the meat!"*

BELOW RIGHT *But he could not escape and got stuffed into a sausage with the last pieces of meat. These new quarters were really very tight.*

Indeed, the next morning the cow went to the slaughterhouse. Fortunately Tom Thumb did not suffer during the chopping and hacking that followed. Instead, he ended up among the sausage meat. As the butcher came over to begin his work, our little man screamed at the top of his lungs, "Don't hack so deep, don't hack so deep! I'm right down here within the meat!" But not a soul could hear his cries over the noisy chopping. Now he was in dire straits, but his panic gave him strength, and our fellow ran and hopped right through the army of chopping knives, and got through without a nick.

But even so he could not escape entirely, since he couldn't see a clear way out, and so he got stuffed into a blood sausage with the last pieces of meat. These new quarters were really very tight, and to add to his predicament, he was hung out in the smokehouse, where time seemed to stand still. He wasn't taken down until winter, when his sausage was to be served to a guest. The minute the innkeeper's wife began to slice it, Tom Thumb had to take great care not to stretch his neck out too far, lest he lose his head. Finally, seeing the light of day, he seized his moment and burst right out of the sausage.

He had no desire to stay in the house where he had been treated so poorly, and so he struck out again on his journey. But

The fox carried him home, and when the father saw his little boy again, he gladly gave the fox all the chickens he owned.

his newfound freedom was not to last very long. Out in the open fields he crossed paths with a fox, who snapped [illegible] without a second thought. "Hey, Mr. Fox," cried the little tailor. "It's me who's stuck in your throat. Let me out!" "You're right," answered the fox. "You're hardly the meal I was looking for. Promise me the chickens in your father's yard, and I'll let you out." "I'd be more than happy to!" said Tom Thumb. "I promise you every chicken in the coop." So the fox let him out, and even carried him home. When the father saw his little boy again, he gladly gave the fox all the chickens he owned. "It's not all a loss, Father," said Tom Thumb. "In return here's a nice piece of silver I brought you." And he handed his father the small coin he had earned along the way.

"Why, oh why, did that fox get to eat those poor chirping chickens?" you might ask. Aha, you silly! Your father, too, would be much happier to have his child home than to have all the chickens in the yard.

Sleeping Beauty

The Brothers Grimm sometimes lengthened the tales they collected, but they trimmed "Sleeping Beauty" to its essence, creating the world's most memorable version of this classic tale. The story is brisk and full of unforgettable images—a castle covered in thorns, a princess asleep, and a prince's kiss—that have captured the imaginations of writers and artists for more than six hundred years. Although Sleeping Beauty is asleep for most of the story, her plight mesmerizes the people of the countryside for generations and unleashes a swirl of activity as prince after prince tries unsuccessfully to reach her. Historians have interpreted the tale as a story about self-knowledge and love, and the initiation of a girl and boy into adulthood. Interestingly, the tale has a limited oral history; it appeared first in writing in the French prose romance *Perceforest* circa 1330. Parts of the tale also rec[illegible] sleeping, fire-ensconced heroine Brunhilde in an old Norse saga, and seventeenth-century fairy-tale collectors Giambattista Basile of Italy and Charles Perrault of France both published more adult versions. Drawing from sources in Hesse, Germany, the Grimms called their tale "Brier Rose" for the flowers that bloom from the thorns as the princess's curse is broken.—ND

Color lithographs by Herbert Leupin, Swiss, 1948

ong, long ago, there lived a king and queen, who each and every day cried to one another, "Oh, if only we had a child!" And yet none ever came. But one day, as the queen was sitting in her bath, a frog crawled out of the nearby pond and spoke to her: "Your wish will be fulfilled—before a year has passed, you shall bear a daughter." The frog's prophecy came true, and the queen bore a little girl so beautiful that the king could hardly contain himself, and he called for a great celebration. He invited not only the royal family, his friends, and many townspeople, but also the Wise Women, whom he wanted to take kindly to the newborn child. But there were thirteen of these women in the kingdom, and since the king had just twelve gold plates for such important guests to eat from, one of the powerful women had to remain uninvited.

The festivities were celebrated with great splendor, and at the end each Wise Woman stepped forward to bless the child with a marvelous gift: the first with virtue, the next with beauty, the third with riches, and so on, until they had given her everything that one could possibly wish for on Earth. But after eleven of them had spoken, the thirteenth Wise Woman suddenly appeared. She was set on revenge for not having been invited, and neither offered words of greeting nor met anyone's eye. In a booming voice she then pronounced: "On her fifteenth

OPPPOSITE *The queen bore a little girl so beautiful that the king could hardly contain himself, and he called for a great celebration.*

BELOW *The thirteenth Wise Woman suddenly appeared and pronounced: "On her fifteenth birthday the princess will prick her finger and fall down dead."*

birthday the princess will prick her finger on a spindle and fall down dead." And without another word, she spun around and fled from the hall. As the guests stood dumbstruck, the twelfth Wise Woman stepped forward to resume her turn. Although she was powerless to undo the evil curse, at least she could recast it, and so she proclaimed, "It shall not be death into which the fair girl will fall, but a deep sleep to last one hundred years."

The king, who wanted desperately to spare his child from even this harsh destiny, decreed that every single spindle in the entire kingdom should be burned. As the girl grew, the gifts of the other Wise Women ripened, and she blossomed into such a beautiful, well-mannered, loving, and understanding child that everyone who saw her fell under her sweet spell. On the day she was to turn fifteen, the king and queen happened to be away from court. Left at home by herself, the girl wandered through the castle, exploring its endless rooms and chambers, until at last she came to an old tower. She climbed up its winding staircase and arrived at a door. In its lock was a rusty old key. She turned it and the door sprang open. There, in a tiny room, she saw an old woman busily spinning flax at her spinning wheel.

"Good day, dear old lady," the princess said. "What are you doing there?" "I'm spinning," replied the old woman, nodding her head. "What is that funny thing bobbing up and down?" the princess asked, reaching for the spindle, wanting to spin too. But scarcely had she touched it when the prophecy came true, and she pricked

OPPOSITE *She saw an old woman at her spinning wheel. "What is that funny thing bobbing up and down?" the princess asked.*

herself in the finger. In the very moment she felt the tiny stab, she collapsed onto the bed next to her and sank into a deep sleep, which spilled out over the whole great castle. The king and queen, who had just returned home and entered the great hall, began to drowse, and all their court with them. The horses fell asleep in their stalls, as did the dogs in the courtyard, the doves on the roof, and the flies on the wall; even the flames flickering in the hearth dimmed into embers, and the roast above ceased its sizzling. The cook, who was just about to grab his apprentice by the hair for making a mistake, stopped short and began to snore. The winds themselves died away, and in the castle woodlands not a leaf rustled anymore.

All around the castle wild rosebushes began to grow, and every year the thicket grew taller and thornier, until finally it enveloped the castle so that not a single turret could be seen, nor even the flag atop the highest tower. All over the kingdom people began to whisper of Sleeping Beauty, as the princess was now called, and also of the many high and noble princes who came from time to time, hoping to force their way through the thorny hedge to her. But this they failed to do, for the thorns held together as tightly as clasped hands, and each prince inevitably met a miserable end trapped in the briar.

RIGHT *The girl wandered through the castle, exploring its endless rooms and chambers, until at last she came to an old tower.*

PAGES 176–177 *All around the castle wild rosebushes began to grow, and every year the thicket grew taller and thornier.*

OPPOSITE *All over the kingdom people began to whisper of Sleeping Beauty, and of the many princes who tried to get to her.*

After many, many years there came yet another prince into the land. He heard from an old man the tale of the brambles surrounding a hidden castle, and of the beautiful princess known as Sleeping Beauty, who was said to have been sleeping there for nearly one hundred years along with the king and queen and their entire court. The old man knew from his grandfather that many princes had come with high hopes and sharp swords, intending to cut through the thorny rosebushes, but had gotten caught among the pitiless thorns and died woeful deaths. But still the young man said, "I am not afraid. I shall go and find Sleeping Beauty." The good old man tried to dissuade the prince, but his words went unheard.

What no one knew was that the hundred years were nearly at an end, and that the day had come when Sleeping Beauty was to shake off her spell. As the prince approached the wall of thorns, it burst into beautiful flowers, parted before him to let him pass through unharmed, and then gently closed behind his heels into a hedgerow. Once inside the castle's outer walls, he found the horses and speckled hunting dogs still under the spell's power. On the roof he saw the doves standing with their heads tucked beneath their wings. And as he entered the castle, the flies slept on the walls; the cook in the kitchen still held up his hand, frozen in midair over his apprentice; and a maiden sat with a black hen, as if ready to pluck its feathers. He went farther on and found all the courtiers asleep in the hall, and the king and queen lying at the foot of the

LEFT *The prince said, "I am not afraid. I shall find Sleeping Beauty." The old man tried to dissuade him, but his words went unheard.*

OPPOSITE *As the prince approached the wall of thorns, it burst into beautiful flowers, and parted to let him pass through unharmed.*

BELOW *The prince bent to kiss Sleeping Beauty. Just as his lips touched hers, she opened her eyes and awoke.*

throne. And on he went, and the place was so hushed that he could hear his every breath. Finally he reached the staircase to the old tower, climbed up, and opened the door to the little room where Sleeping Beauty lay. She slept so peacefully, and was so lovely, that he could not take his eyes off her. He bent to kiss her. Just as his lips touched hers, she opened her eyes and awoke, and gazed at him tenderly.

Down they went together, and the king and queen roused, as did their court, and they all looked at one another in wide-eyed astonishment. The horses in the courtyard stood and shook themselves; the hunting dogs leapt and barked and wagged their tails; the rooftop doves looked up from beneath their feathers and took flight into the fields; the flies on the wall began their buzzing anew; the hearth's fire flamed up again and cooked the food, the roast sizzling away once more; the apprentice squealed as the cook finally boxed him on the ears; and the maiden began to pluck the black hen. And the prince and Sleeping Beauty were married in a dazzling celebration, and they lived in contentment all the days of their lives.

Snow White

Known for its unique iconography—white as snow, red as blood, black as ebony—"Snow White" is one of the most famous fairy tales of all time. Even though it appeared only three hundred years ago, which is recent by fairy-tale standards, it has had a vivid, multicultural oral legacy, with four hundred variations found across Europe, the Americas, Asia Minor, Africa, and the Caribbean. Some historians speculate that the story was inspired by real-life people and places in premodern Europe. This version here has deep roots in Hesse, the birthplace of the Brothers Grimm as well as the first variations of the tale to feature dwarfs. Like Sleeping Beauty, Snow White succumbs to a deep sleep. Snow White's sleep is brought on when she is poisoned by her conniving stepmother, whose narcissism and mastery of witchcraft have been colorfully rendered by many artists and filmmakers, as in Walt Disney's 1937 *Snow White and the Seven Dwarfs*. In the end, her stepmother is forced to dance herself to extinction in hot iron shoes, an act that also appeared in an early Danish saga, an example of the tale's more violent variations that have existed around the globe.—ND

Color lithographs by Wanda Zeigner-Ebel, German, 1920

OPPOSITE *The stepmother had a magic mirror and would often ask: "Mirror, mirror on the wall, who is the fairest of them all?"*

Once upon a time, deep in the middle of winter, as snowflakes were floating out of the sky like feathers, a queen sat and sewed by her open window, whose frame was of dark ebony. And as she sewed and looked out at the snow, she accidentally pricked herself in the finger. Three drops of blood fell into the snow, and the redness on the white drifts struck her as so beautiful that she thought to herself, "If only I had a child as white as snow, as red as blood, and as dark as the wood of the window frame." A short time later, she gave birth to a little baby girl who was as white as snow, as red as blood, and with hair as black as ebony, and she was called Snow White. But sadly, just as the child was born, the queen died.

A year passed, and the king married another woman. She was beautiful, but arrogant and proud, and she simply could not tolerate the possibility that anyone else might surpass her in beauty. She had a magic mirror, and would often stand in front of it admiring herself, and ask:

"Mirror, mirror on the wall,
Who is the fairest of them all?"

And the mirror would reply:

"Your majesty is the most beautiful far and wide."

And so she was content, since she knew the mirror spoke the truth.

But Snow White grew and grew and became more and more radiant. By the

The hunter took the child away into the woods. She began to weep and plead, "Oh, dear hunter, please spare my life."

time she was seven years old she was as beautiful as the brightest day, and more so than the queen herself. This time, when the queen challenged the mirror,

"Mirror, mirror on the wall,
Who is the fairest of them all?"

it had to answer:

"Your majesty is the fairest one here,
But Snow White's beauty shines
a thousand times more clear."

This dealt the queen a cruel blow, and her face turned yellow and green with envy. From that hour on, whenever she saw Snow White her heart turned inside out, she hated the girl so. Her envy and vanity grew in her like weeds, higher and higher, until she had no peace day or night. She summoned a hunter and told him, "Take that child out into the woods. I don't want her ever to offend my eyes again. You are to kill her and bring me her lungs and liver to show you have." And so he obeyed, and took the child away. But as he drew his bow to shoot straight through Snow White's innocent heart, she began to weep and plead, "Oh, dear hunter, please spare my life. I promise to run deep into the woods and never, ever return again." He took pity on her and said, "So run away, you poor little thing!"

"The wild beasts will eat you up in no time," he thought. Yet it was as if a weight had been lifted from his shoulders, since now he would not be forced to kill her himself. Just then a young buck bounded by, and he turned his arrow on it instead, offering its lungs and liver to the queen. The cook boiled the organs in salt water and the evil woman ate them, thinking they were Snow White's.

Now the helpless child was deep in the woods, completely alone. She was so afraid that she stared at every leaf on every tree, trying hard to calm herself through their peaceful green. Yet she could not fathom how to escape her predicament. So she fled, leaping over sharp stones and through thorns, and the wild beasts bounded past her, doing her no harm at all. She ran as far as her feet could carry her, until dusk, when she saw a little cottage and stumbled into it to rest.

Inside the cottage everything was tiny and delicate, and neat beyond description. There was a tiny little table, covered with a white tablecloth and set with seven tiny plates, each one with a tiny spoon, and just as tiny a knife, fork, and cup. Up against the wall stood seven little beds lined up neatly in a row, each covered with a snow-white sheet. Snow White was so hungry and thirsty, but since she did not want to reveal her presence by finishing any one plate, she took a little bite of bread and vegetables from each of the plates, and sipped a drop of wine from each of the cups. At last exhaustion overcame her, and she lay down on one of the beds, but she didn't fit. Some were too long, and the others too short, until at last the seventh bed felt just right. She stayed in that bed, asked for God's grace, and fell fast asleep.

The Dwarfs came running over with their tiny lamps, holding them up to examine their visitor more closely. "Oh, my goodness!" they exclaimed.

Darkness arrived, and with it the owners of the hut. These were the Seven Dwarfs, who worked in the mountains each day digging and mining for mineral ore. They lit their seven tiny lamps, and as it became lighter inside the hut, they saw that someone had been there, since it was clear that their things were not as neat as they had left them. The first one said, "Who sat in my chair?" The second one fussed, "Who ate from my plate?" The third one cried, "Who nibbled my bread?" The fourth one snapped, "Who ate of my vegetables?" The fifth one hooted, "Who used my fork?" The sixth one rumbled, "Who cut with my knife?" And the seventh one grumped, "Who drank from my cup?"

Then the first one gazed around and spotted a small rumple on his bed. "Who has been lying in my bed?" he wondered. The others came running, and one called out: "Someone's been lying in mine, too." "And in mine!" "And mine!" "And mine!" "And in mine, too!" But as the seventh went to his bed, he found Snow White lying there, fast asleep. He called to the others, who cried with astonishment and came running over with their tiny lamps,

PAGES 190–191 *As morning came, Snow White awakened, and when she saw the Seven Dwarfs she was taken aback. But they were friendly.*

holding them up to examine their visitor more closely. "Oh, my goodness! Oh, my heavens!" they exclaimed in muted tones. "What a beautiful child!" They took such joy at seeing her that they let her sleep on. The seventh dwarf bunked with his fellows, with each for one hour, until the night was up.

As morning came, Snow White awakened, and when she saw the burly Seven Dwarfs she was taken aback. But they were friendly, and asked her name. "I am Snow White," she answered. "How did you come to be in our house?" they inquired further. She told them about how her stepmother had tried to have her killed, and how the hunter had let her live, and how she had then run the whole day until she eventually came upon their cottage. The Dwarfs said to her, "If you would like to take care of our house—do the cooking, make the beds, handle the sewing and knitting—and if you can do all this in a clean and neat fashion, then you may live with us and you will lack for nothing." "Oh, yes," said Snow White. "I would love to!" And so she stayed on with them and kept their home in order. In the mornings they left for the mountains in search of ore and gold, and when they returned in the evenings their supper had to be ready. Since Snow White was alone during the days, the good little Dwarfs warned her, saying, "You must beware of your stepmother. Soon she will know that you are here. Let no one inside!"

But the queen—thinking she had supped on her stepdaughter's lungs and liver—was certain she was again the single most beautiful woman. So she went to her mirror and tested it:

"Mirror, mirror on the wall,
Who is the fairest of them all?"

But the mirror had to answer:

"Your majesty is the fairest one here.
But over the mountains with the Seven Dwarfs lives Snow White,
Whose beauty shines a thousand times more clear."

She drew back in shock, because she knew the mirror could not lie. She realized that the hunter had deceived her, and that Snow White must still be alive. And so she pondered and schemed about how to be rid of the girl for good. For as long as the queen was not the most beautiful woman in the whole land, her envy would know no bounds. Once she had pieced together her plan, the queen painted her face and disguised herself as an old

woman from the market, becoming totally unrecognizable. In this costume she went out through the seven mountains to the home of the Seven Dwarfs. She knocked on the door, calling out, "Fine goods for sale, fine goods! Get your fine goods!"

Curious, Snow White peeped out of the window and said, "Good day, ma'am. What do you have for sale?" "Nice goods, very fine goods," she answered. "Laces in every color." She held out some finely woven laces made of colorful silk. "I can let this honest woman in," thought Snow White. She unlocked the door and bought herself the cute laces. "Child," the old lady said, "you should see yourself! Come here! I'll lace up your bodice properly for you." Snow White saw no harm in this, and stood in front of the lady to let herself be laced up with the new laces. But the old lady's hands worked so quickly and laced her so tightly, that soon Snow White could no longer breathe, and she fell down as if dead. "Well, then. You *were* the most beautiful one of all," pronounced the evil queen, and hurried away.

Soon after, around dusk, the Seven Dwarfs returned home and were horrified to find Snow White lying on the ground, not stirring or moving. They lifted her, and having noticed how tightly laced up she was, they quickly cut the laces in two. At last she began to breathe a little, and slowly revived. When the Dwarfs heard what had happened, they said, "That old junk peddler was nothing but the godless queen herself. You must guard against her! You cannot let anyone inside when we are not here with you."

Once at home, the wicked woman went to her mirror and asked:

"Mirror, mirror on the wall,
Who is the fairest of them all?"

And the mirror answered, as before:

"Your majesty is the fairest one here.
But over the mountains with the Seven Dwarfs lives Snow White,
Whose beauty shines a thousand times more clear."

As the queen heard this, the blood drained from her face, since it was clear that Snow White was still alive. "Well, then," she seethed, "I will find some other way to destroy you!" She set about using the dark arts of witches to create a poisonous comb. She then disguised herself, this time as a different old woman, and went out through the seven mountains to the home of the Seven Dwarfs. She knocked on the door and called out, "Precious

The Dwarfs said to Snow White, "You must guard against the queen! You cannot let anyone inside when we are not here with you."

goods for sale, precious goods! For sale, for sale!" Snow White looked out and said: "Please go away. I am not allowed to let anyone in." "But surely you're allowed to look," the old woman said, and pulled out the poisonous comb, tempting her. The child liked it so much that she was transfixed, and she opened the door. As soon as the girl had bought the comb, the old woman said, "And now I will give you a good combing." Poor Snow White thought nothing of it, and she let the old woman do as she pleased. But hardly had the comb touched her hair when the poison began to take effect. She fell to the floor, unconscious. The evil woman cursed her on her way out the door: "Our little paragon of beauty: Now you are finished for good!" Luckily it was nearly evening, and the Seven Dwarfs soon returned home. When they saw Snow White lying on the floor again as if dead, they immediately suspected her stepmother. They searched and found the poisonous comb, and as soon as they removed it, Snow White woke up and told them what had happened. They warned her a third time to watch out for herself, and not to open the door for anyone.

When the queen was home again, she went before her mirror and asked:

"Mirror, mirror on the wall,
Who is the fairest of them all?"

And the mirror answered, just as before:

OPPOSITE *Snow White craved the perfect-looking apple and could no longer resist. She held out her hand and took the poisoned half.*

PAGES 196–197 *They placed her inside a glass coffin and took her high up into the mountains, where they took turns keeping watch.*

"Your majesty is the fairest one here.
But over the mountains with the Seven Dwarfs lives Snow White,
Whose beauty shines a thousand times more clear."

As she heard the mirror's answer, she shook and trembled with rage. "Snow White must die!" she howled. "Even if it costs me my own life!" She withdrew and shut herself inside a secret, hidden room, where she made a very, very poisonous apple. It looked so delicious, bright white with red cheeks, that whoever saw it would crave it. Yet anyone who ate even the smallest piece would perish.

When the apple was ready, she again painted her face and disguised herself, this time as a farmer's wife. She went through the seven mountains to the home of the Seven Dwarfs, and knocked. Snow White poked her head out the window and said, "I am not allowed to let anyone in. The Seven Dwarfs forbid it." "That is fine by me," answered the farmer's wife. "I only want to get rid of my apples. Here, I will give you one as a gift." "No," said Snow White. "I cannot accept anything." "Why? Afraid of being poisoned?" said the old woman. "Look: I'll cut this apple into two pieces. You can eat the red part, and I will eat the white." She had crafted the apple such that only the red part was poisonous.

Snow White craved the perfect-looking apple, and as she watched the farmer's wife taste it, she could no longer resist. She held out her hand and took the poisoned half. Hardly had she taken a bite into her mouth when she fell to the floor, dead. The queen stared at her with a dreadful gaze, and cackled loudly, "White as snow, red as blood, and black as ebony! This time the Dwarfs will not be able to wake you—ever again!" Once she got home again, she challenged her mirror:

"Mirror, mirror on the wall,
Who is the fairest of them all?"

Finally, it answered:

"Your majesty is the fairest in all the land."

Her jealous heart now had peace, to the extent a jealous heart can.

As the Dwarfs returned home in the evening, they found Snow White lying on the floor. They could hear no breath passing from her lips. She was dead. They lifted her up, and searched for anything poisonous. They untied her laces, they combed her hair, they washed her with water and with wine, yet none of it did any good. The dear little child was dead,

and remained so. They laid her on a bier, and all seven of them sat with her and cried, mourning her for three whole days. They had planned to bury her, but she looked just as fresh as if alive, with her pretty cheeks still flushed red. They said, "We cannot put her down into the black earth looking like this." So they had a transparent glass coffin made for her, which showed her from every side. They placed her inside and wrote her name in gold lettering on it, making special note that she had been a royal: a princess. Then they took the coffin high up into the mountains, where they took turns keeping watch over it at all times. And the animals came too and cried for her—first an owl, then a raven, and then finally a dove. Snow White lay in the coffin a long, long time, but she never showed any sign of decay. In fact, she looked just as if she were asleep, since she was still as white as snow, as red as blood, and with hair as black as ebony.

One day a prince rode into the forest and came upon the Dwarfs' cottage, where he stayed for the night. He found the coffin upon the mountainside, saw Snow White lying within, and read what was written in gold lettering. He then went to speak with the Dwarfs: "Let me have the coffin. I will give you whatever you want for it." But the Dwarfs answered, "For all the gold in the world, we would not give it up." So he said, "Then give it to me as a present, for I cannot live without seeing Snow White, whom I will honor and respect as the love of my life." Hearing him moved in this way, the kindly little Dwarfs felt sympathy for him and gave him the coffin. The prince had his servants carry it away on their shoulders, but on their way, one of them tripped over a shrub. The jolt jostled the piece of poisoned apple loose from Snow White's throat. Not long after, she opened her eyes, lifted the coffin lid, and sat up, alive again. "Dear God, where am I?" she cried. The prince sighed with joy, "You are with me," and told her what had happened. "I love you more than anything in the world," he confessed. "Come with me to my father's castle and be my wife." Snow White accepted. She went with him, and their wedding was prepared with great finery and splendor.

Yet Snow White's godless stepmother was also invited to the celebration. After she had readied herself in her extravagant clothing, she went to her mirror and asked:

"I love you more than anything in the world," the prince confessed, and their wedding was prepared with great finery and splendor.

"Mirror, mirror on the wall,
Who is the fairest of them all?"

The mirror answered:

"Your majesty is the most beautiful here,
But the young queen's beauty shines a thousand times more clear."

The evil witch cursed out loud. She was struck with such horror, such horror, that she could not contain herself. At first she refused to attend the wedding. But even so she found no peace, and was driven by envy to go and see the young queen. And as she arrived, she recognized Snow White, and in her fear and shock she stood frozen, unable to move a limb. Meanwhile, nearby, slippers made of iron were heated over coals. They were carried over to the wicked queen with tongs, and placed at her feet. Then she was made to walk in those red-hot shoes, and to dance in them. And she did so until she fell to the ground, dead.

Rumpelstiltskin

In this tale, an odd little man helps a maiden spin straw into gold. In return, she must give him her firstborn child, whom she can only win back by guessing the man's name. The power of a name is an important theme in mythology, folklore, and fantasy tales: As long as Rumpelstiltskin's identity is concealed, he has the upper hand, reflecting an age-old belief that to know an evil spirit by name is to defeat it. Many versions of the tale exist worldwide. Some, like the English, use variations of the German name Rumpelstilzchen, which historians believe dates to a 1575 children's book. Although the name's meaning is debated, some speculate it relates to the bumping (*rumpeln*) and clacking of "stilts" (furniture posts) by otherworldly creatures in the home. Other versions of the name include Ricdin-Ricdon in France, Tremotino in Italy, Tom Tit Tot in England, and Whuppity Stoorie in Scotland. Historian Maria Tatar notes that the tale is known in nearly every culture where clothes are made from spinning, which highlights the special relationship between spinning and the use of storytelling to pass the time. The Grimms adapted their famous version from four tales they heard in Hesse, Germany.—ND

Watercolor by Kay Nielsen, Danish, 1925

here once was a miller who was poor, but he had a beautiful daughter. It so happened that he crossed paths with the king, and, trying to impress him, the miller claimed, "I have a daughter who can spin straw into gold." The king said to the miller, "Such an art would please me well. If your daughter is as gifted as you claim, bring her to the castle tomorrow. I will put her to the test." When the girl was brought before the king, he led her to a chamber filled with straw, gave her a spinning wheel and a bobbin, and said, "Now set to work. If you have not spun this straw into gold by dawn, then you must die." He made sure the room was locked, and left the poor girl alone inside.

She sat there fearing for her life, having no idea what to do. She knew nothing about how to spin straw into gold, and her worry grew with each passing moment until she finally broke down in tears. Suddenly the door opened, and a little man stepped in, saying, "Good evening, Miss Miller. Why are you crying so?" "Oh, dear me. I've been told I have to spin all this straw into gold, and I have no idea how." The little man said, "What will you give me if I spin it for you?" "My necklace," she answered. So the little man took the necklace, sat down at the wheel, and—*whirr, whirr, whirr*—with three spins the spool was full. He loaded another spool, and—*whirr, whirr, whirr*—with three more spins the second spool was just as full. And so it went on till morning, when all the straw had been spun, and all the spools were laden with gold.

At sunrise the king appeared, and when he saw the mass of gold he was altogether astounded and mighty pleased. But his heart grew greedy for more. So he had the girl brought to another chamber full of straw, even bigger than the last one, and ordered her to spin all of it during the coming night, if she valued her life. Again she didn't know what to do and began to weep, and again the door swung open and the little man appeared, asking, "What will you give me if I spin all this straw into gold for you?" "The ring on my finger," she replied. The little man took the ring and let the spinning wheel fly again, and by morning he had spun all the straw into shining gold. The king was thrilled at the sight of the yellow metal, but his hunger

The little man said, "Promise you will give me your first-born child." She gave in, and once more he spun the straw into gold.

for gold had not been satisfied, and he had the girl taken to a still-bigger chamber and said, "Another night's work for you. But this time if you succeed, you shall be my wife." He thought to himself, "Even if she is just a miller's daughter, I won't find a richer woman in all the world."

She was hardly alone again when the little man came back a third time, asking, "What will you give me now, if I spin this straw for you once more?" "I have nothing left to give," she answered. "Then promise me that when you become queen, you will give me your first-born child." "Who knows how all this will end?" thought the girl. In her distress she could think of no other way out, and she gave in to the little man's demand, and once more he began to spin the straw into gold. The next morning the king came and found what he had hoped for, and, as promised, he married her. And so the beautiful miller's daughter became a queen.

A year later she brought a precious baby into the world, and thought nothing more of the little man. But suddenly he strode into her chambers, and said, "Now give me what you promised." The queen was terrified, and offered the little man all the riches of the kingdom, if only he would leave the newborn child alone. But he insisted, "No, a living being is worth far more to me than all the treasures of the world." The queen began to grieve and cry so terribly that the little man finally felt sympathy for her. "I will give you three days' time," he said. "And if you know my name by then, you may keep your child."

All night long the queen struggled to think of every last name she'd ever heard, and sent a messenger out across

"The Devil told you that!" he screamed. And he stamped his right foot so hard that he drove his leg down through the floor.

the kingdom, scouring far and wide for any other names. When the little man returned the next day, she began with names such as Caspar, Melchior, and Balthazar, and tried all the names she knew, one after the other. But with each one the little man said, "That is not my name." On the second day she had all the families surrounding the castle questioned, and she offered the little man their rarest and strangest nicknames: "Could your name be Ribsfiend? Or Muttonchops? Or Lacelegs?" Each time, he answered, "No! That is not my name either."

On the third day the messenger returned and reported, "I could not find one single new name. But as I was pressing on through the hinterlands, by a high mountain along the forest's edge, I passed a little house. And in front of the house there was a fire burning, and around the fire was a ridiculous-looking little man hopping around on one leg, singing:

"Today I bake, and tomorrow I brew
The next day I steal the queen's baby-boo.
Oh, it's so good, and surely no shame
That not a soul knows
Rumpelstiltskin's my name!"

Now you can imagine how delighted the queen was, hearing the name. Not long after, the little man came in and asked, "Now, dear queen, what is my name?" At first she asked, "Can it be Tom?" "No." "Or Dick?" "No." "What about Harry?" "No!" "Oh dear. Then could it possibly be… Rumpelstiltskin?!"

"The Devil told you that! The Devil told you that!" screamed the little man. And he stamped his right foot so hard that he drove his leg down through the floor, all the way to his waist. Then, in a fit of rage, he pulled at his left foot with both hands and tore himself right in two.

The Three Feathers

In several of the Grimms' fairy tales, the main characters are endearing simpletons. Ridiculed by others, these characters always win the day, proving that the weak and downtrodden are as heroic as the strong and powerful. In addition, they also function as foils against which the others reveal their worst sides. This storytelling device is a humorous way to show the full spectrum of human nature, both the good and the bad, and to impart moral lessons on behavior. The question of inheritance appears regularly in the Grimms' fairy tales—for instance, in "Puss 'n Boots"—and provides a backdrop against which the characters must prove themselves. Contrary to the old-fashioned custom of the firstborn's inheriting the family fortune, the king in this tale uses three feathers in a game of chance to decide whom to leave his kingdom to, which allows all three sons to compete. The simpleton shows courage in enlisting the help of an underground toad, who like a genie in a magic lantern grants his wishes. Versions of this tale have appeared in Scandinavia, Greece, and India. The Grimms adapted this tale from one of their favorite sources in Hesse, Germany, the innkeeper's daughter Dorothea Viehmann.—ND

Watercolor by Kay Nielsen, Danish, 1925

nce there was a king who had three sons, two of whom were clever and sensible. But the third did not speak very much and was simpleminded, and the others hard-heartedly called him Dimwit. As the king grew old and weak, and began to contemplate the end of his life, he was not sure which of his three sons should inherit the kingdom. He said to them, “Go out into the world, and whoever brings me back the finest carpet shall be king after my death.” So that there would be no dispute among them, he took them out in front of the castle and blew three feathers into the air. “As the feathers fly, so must you follow,” he said. One of the feathers floated toward the east, the second toward the west, and the third flew straight ahead, but not very far, then sank right to the ground. The first brother went left, the other went right, and they laughed in chorus at Dimwit, who went to the spot where the third feather had landed and just stayed put.

Dimwit sat there and was sad, but then all at once he noticed a trapdoor right next to the feather. He pulled it open to find a staircase, and started down. Soon he came to another door and knocked on it, and heard a voice call from inside:

“Dear little maiden, green and merry,
Limpy Leg says to her little frog fairy:
Limp on over. Don’t wait at all.
Let’s see right now who’s come to call.”

The door opened slowly, and he saw a big fat toad squatting on the ground, surrounded by other, smaller toads. The big fat one asked him what he wanted, and he answered, “I’m looking for the most beautiful and wonderful carpet there is.” She called over to one of the little ones, saying:

The door opened slowly, and he saw a big fat toad squatting on the ground, surrounded by other, smaller toads.

The frog had her bag brought over and gave him a ring so spectacular that no goldsmith on Earth could possibly have made it.

"Dear little maiden, green and merry,
Limpy Leg says to her little frog fairy:
Limp on over. Don't wait at all.
Bring the big bag and its contents all."

The young toad brought the bag, and the fat one opened it and handed Dimwit a carpet from inside. It was so beautiful and so fine that no one up above on Earth could ever have woven the likes of it. He thanked her and climbed back up the stairs.

Meanwhile the two other brothers were convinced silly Dimwit would never find anything to bring back. They said, "Why should we bother to search far and wide?" So they took a coarse tunic worn by the very first shepherd's wife they encountered along the way, and brought it back to the king. Dimwit returned at the same time, carrying his sumptuous carpet. When the king saw it, he was astonished and said, "If the law will allow it, this means my youngest shall inherit the kingdom." But his other two sons would hear nothing of it, and said it was impossible that Dimwit, dim and witless as he was, could become king. They asked the king to set another condition, and so their father said, "Whoever brings me back the most beautiful ring shall inherit the kingdom." He then took his sons outside, and again blew three feathers into the air for them to follow.

The two elder sons went toward the east and the west again, while Dimwit's feather flew a short distance straight ahead and landed by the trapdoor. And so he went down the stairs to the big fat toad, and told her he needed the most beautiful ring. She had her big bag brought over, and from inside it she gave him a ring so spectacular, shimmering all over with precious stones, that no goldsmith on Earth could possibly have made it. Meanwhile the two elder brothers were laughing about Dimwit, off looking for a golden ring, and they put no effort at all into the task at hand. Instead they took the nails out of the iron rim of a wagon wheel and brought this as their ring back to the king. When Dimwit presented his golden ring, their father once again proclaimed, "His is the kingdom." But the two elder sons would not let up, and tormented the king with protests until he came up with a third condition: that the kingdom would pass to the one who

The instant the toad was inside, she turned into a beautiful woman, while the turnip turned into a carriage and the mice into horses.

brought the most beautiful girl to the castle. Again he blew three feathers into the air, and again they flew as before.

Without hesitation, Dimwit went straight down to the big fat toad and said, "I must bring home the most beautiful girl." "Aha," answered the toad. "The most beautiful girl! She is not exactly here right now, but you'll have her." She handed him a hollowed-out yellow turnip that had six tiny mice tied to it with string. Dimwit said, very sad, "What should I do with this?" The toad answered, "All you need to do is put one of my little toads inside." He grabbed for the first one he could reach from the circle of toads, and placed her inside the odd yellow contraption. The instant the toad was inside, she turned into a beautiful young woman, while the turnip turned into a carriage and the six mice into six horses. Then he kissed her, just like that, and off they raced in their horse-drawn carriage back to the king.

His brothers returned too, but they had not put any effort into finding a beautiful girl. Instead, they brought along the first farmers' daughters they could find. As soon as the king saw them, he said, "The kingdom shall belong to my youngest son after my death." But the elder brothers numbed the king's ears with their howling protest: "We won't allow Dimwit to be king!" They demanded a new condition: that only the brother whose wife could jump through a hoop hanging in the middle of the hall could win. They thought to themselves, "The farmers' daughters can do that, since they are strong enough, but his dainty little girl will fall over dead trying."

The old king gave in to this one last condition. The two farm girls jumped and made it through the hoop, but they were so plump that they fell down hard, and their stout arms and legs broke in two. Then the beautiful young woman brought by Dimwit jumped through the hoop as easily as a doe, putting an end to the complaining once and for all. And so the youngest brother received the crown, and he ruled wisely for a long, long time.

The Golden Goose

As in "The Three Feathers," the main character in this tale is a simpleton, translated here as Peabrain, who has two clever older brothers. Unlike his selfish brothers, the simpleton compassionately shares his meager rations with a little old man in the woods. The man then gives the boy a golden goose, which sparks a chain of events leading to his good fortune. The tale, adapted from stories from Hesse and nearby Paderborn, Germany, unfolds like a farce, with people accidentally hurting themselves, getting stuck to the golden goose, and creating a spectacle so hilarious it tickles the funny bone of a princess previously unable to laugh. Heightening the tale's subversiveness, along the way Peabrain and the band of fools stuck to him meet a sexton and a pastor, figures of moral authority who are pulled into the fun. On the surface the story is a morality tale about being nice to others no matter what the consequences. But on a deeper level, it is about the wisdom derived from comedy and the role of clowning in satirizing social hierarchies. Although portrayed as the dummy, Peabrain becomes the story's straight man in comedic terms, while everyone around him is made a fool.—ND

Watercolors and drawings by L. Leslie Brooke, British, 1905

The eldest son hit himself in the arm with the axe and staggered home. All this befell him because of the little old man.

Once upon a time there was a man who had three sons. The youngest was called Peabrain, and everyone mocked and ridiculed him, and put him down at every turn. One day the eldest son was headed to the forest to cut wood, and before he left, his mother gave him a delicious freshly made pancake and a bottle of wine to take along so that he would go neither hungry nor thirsty. As he entered the forest, he met a little old gray-haired man who wished him a good day and said, "Oh, would you give me a piece of the pancake in your pocket, and let me have a sip of your wine? I'm so hungry and thirsty." But the clever son answered, "If I gave you my pancake and my wine, I'd have nothing left for myself. Now mind your own business." And he walked off, leaving the little man standing there. He began to chop down a tree, but it wasn't long before he swung and missed his mark: He hit himself in the arm with the axe, and staggered home to get it bandaged. And all this befell him because of the little old gray-haired man.

Soon afterward, the middle son set off for the forest, and his mother gave him a pancake and a bottle of wine, just as she had given his brother. Again the little old gray-haired man appeared and stopped to ask the brother for a little piece of pancake and a drink of wine. But the middle son merely gave the same matter-

Peabrain went to take out his ash cake and found it had turned into a tasty pancake, and his sour beer had become wine.

of-fact answer: "Whatever I give you is my loss. Now mind your own business." And he walked off, leaving the little man standing there. But he couldn't outrun his punishment: After striking the tree just a couple of times, he gouged himself in the leg with the axe, and needed to be carried home. Then Peabrain said, "Father, for once let me go out and chop wood." But his father answered, "Your clever brothers hurt themselves doing that. Just forget about it. You don't know the first thing about chopping wood." But Peabrain kept asking until his father finally gave in: "Alright, go ahead. If you get hurt, at least you'll learn from your mistake." His mother gave him a pancake that was made with water, not milk, and baked in the hearth's ashes, and with it a bottle of sour beer.

As he entered the forest, he too met the little old gray-haired man, who said, "Give me a piece of your pancake and a drink from your bottle. I'm so hungry and thirsty." Peabrain answered, "All I have is this pancake baked in ashes, and some sour beer. If that's all right with you, then we can sit together and eat." So they took a seat, and as Peabrain went to take out his ash cake, he found it had turned into a nice, tasty pancake, and his sour beer had become fine wine. They ate and drank, and afterward the little man said, "Because you have a good heart and can share what's yours with others, I want to bestow some good luck upon you. See that old tree over there? If you cut it down, you'll find something special among its roots." And with that, the little man took his leave.

BELOW *Peabrain went over and cut down the tree, and sure enough, nestled among the roots was a goose with feathers of pure gold.*

OPPOSITE *The next morning he took the goose and left, untroubled by the three girls hanging on, who had to run along behind him.*

Peabrain went over and cut down the tree. As it toppled, sure enough, nestled among the roots there was a goose with feathers of pure gold. He picked it up, took it with him, and went to an inn, where he planned to spend the night. The innkeeper had three daughters who saw the goose and became curious. They wanted to know what kind of wondrous bird it was, and above all they wanted to have one of its golden feathers. The eldest thought, "I'm bound to find the right moment to pluck one of those feathers and keep it for my very own."

Sure enough, when Peabrain had gone outside, she reached out and grabbed the goose by its wing. But her fingers and hand became stuck to it. A moment later the second sister came, and could think of nothing but getting her hands on one of the feathers. Hardly had she brushed up against her sister when she got stuck. Finally, the third sister came, set on the same idea. The others screamed, "Stay away! For heaven's sake, stay away!" But she didn't understand why she should stay away, and thought, "If they're doing it, so can I." She ran toward them, but just as she grabbed her sister, she got stuck to her, and so they had to spend the whole night with the goose, in very close quarters.

The next morning Peabrain took the goose under his arm and left, untroubled by the three girls hanging on. They had to run along behind him, wherever his legs took him. Out in the fields they came upon the pastor, and as he caught sight of their unusual caravan, he said, "Naughty girls! You should be ashamed of yourselves,

YE
BOKE
OF
JOKE

OPPOSITE *When the princess saw the chain of seven followers stumbling and bumping into one another, she burst into laughter.*

BELOW *Peabrain led the man down to the king's wine cellar, where he drank and drank until his sides hurt.*

following a young man through the fields like that. Is that how good girls behave?" With that he took hold of the youngest girl's hand, intending to pull her away. As soon as he touched her he got stuck too, and had to walk in tow like the others. A short while later, the church sexton came along and saw the pastor following close behind the girls. He found this quite odd, and said, "Hello there, Reverend, where are you off to in such a hurry? Don't forget the baptism later today." He ran up and tugged the pastor's sleeve, but stuck fast too. As the five followers trotted along in their funny human chain, two farmers came in from the fields, carrying their hatchets and hoes. The pastor called out to them and asked them for help getting him and the sexton loose. Hardly had they touched the sexton when they too were suddenly stuck to the group, now seven in number, running along behind Peabrain with his goose.

Afterward, Peabrain came to a town ruled by a king whose daughter was so serious that no one had ever been able to make her laugh. For this reason the king had decreed that whoever could make her laugh could marry her. Upon hearing this, Peabrain went before the king's daughter with his goose and their entourage. When she saw the chain of seven followers stumbling and bumping into one another, she burst into peals of laughter, and enjoyed it so much she just did not want to stop. And so Peabrain claimed her as his bride, but the king was not at all pleased with him as a candidate and raised all kinds of objections. Finally, he said Peabrain would first have to bring him a man who could drink an entire wine

The man from the woods dove right in and began eating, and within a day the whole mountain of bread was gone.

cellar dry. Peabrain remembered the little old gray-haired man—maybe he could help!

He went back to the spot in the forest where he had chopped down the tree, and saw a man sitting there with a very sad face. He asked him what was troubling him so, and the man answered, "I have such a terrible thirst that I can't quench. I tried this cold water and couldn't stomach it, and though I just emptied a cask of wine, it felt like a mere drop of water on a hot stone." "I can help you," Peabrain said. "Just come with me. You'll have your fill." And so he led the man down to the king's wine cellar, where he took on the great barrels, and drank and drank until his sides hurt. Before a day had passed, he had emptied the entire cellar of wine, and Peabrain went once again to claim his bride. But the king was upset that such an unfitting man was to take away his daughter, let alone someone known as Peabrain. And so he came up with a new stipulation: First the young man would have to find someone who could eat an entire mountain of bread.

Peabrain needed only a brief moment's thought before he decided to return to the forest again. There at the same spot sat a man who was tightening his belt around his waist. He made a pained face and said, "I just ate an entire oven's worth of bread, but what good does that do for someone with such an epic hunger? My stomach is still empty, and I've got to tighten my belt so that I don't die of hunger." Peabrain was delighted to hear this, and said, "Get up and come with me. You'll have your fill." He took the man to the castle courtyard, where

The king sought to slip out of his bargain, and insisted Peabrain bring him a ship that could sail on both land and sea.

the king had all the flour from his entire kingdom baked into a huge mountain of bread. The man from the woods dove right in and began eating, and within a day the whole mountain was gone.

Now, for the third time, Peabrain demanded his bride. But again the king sought to slip out of his own bargain, and insisted that Peabrain bring him a ship that could sail over both land and sea. "As soon as you sail up in it," he said, "you shall have my daughter as your bride." Peabrain went straight to the forest, and there sat the little old gray-haired man, the same one he had given his pancake to. The man said, "It was I who drank and ate for you, and I will give you the ship too. All of this I do because you showed me kindness." And so he gave him the ship, and indeed it could sail on both land and sea, and when the king saw it, he could no longer deny Peabrain his daughter. Their wedding was celebrated, and upon the king's death, Peabrain inherited the kingdom, and he lived for many years in happiness with his wife.

Jorinda and Joringel

This story tells of two young lovers so devoted to one another that even their names are nearly identical. Like Romeo and Juliet, they cannot bear to be apart, which sets the stage for the separation they will face and hints at the obsessive nature of their love. Historians have interpreted the tale as an allegory for the individuation that is necessary to experience true love: The young lovers must find themselves before they can find each other. When a sorceress gleefully turns Jorinda into a bird and hides her in a cage in her castle with seven thousand other unlucky maidens, the lovers' trial begins. With its dark forest, shape-shifting sorceress, foreboding castle, and magical blood-red flower, the tale is laden with supernatural and symbolic details. Its gothic tone is markedly different from other tales by the Grimms, and this may be accounted for by the fact that they sourced the story from the 1777 autobiography *The Life of Heinrich Stillings*, written by a friend of German writer Johann Wolfgang von Goethe. The book is emblematic of the German Romantic literary tradition and is the only known source for this tale, which folklorists identify as unique to Germany.—ND

Watercolor by Arthur Rackham, British, 1909

nce upon a time there was an old castle nestled within a thick forest. An old woman lived inside all by herself, and she was a great sorceress with mastery of the dark arts. During the day, she took the shape of either a cat or a night owl, but in the evening she returned to her human form. She had the power to entice game and birds to draw close to her, whereupon she would catch and cook them, roasting their meat. Whoever came within a hundred paces of her castle would be frozen in place, unable to move until she chose to dissolve the spell. Whenever an innocent young maiden crossed into this circle, the sorceress would turn her into a bird, lock her up in an old wicker cage, and carry it off to a special chamber in her castle. There, she had as many as seven thousand such cages, each with a rare bird inside.

Now, there was a young maiden called Jorinde, and she was more beautiful than any other. She and a very handsome young man named Joringel had promised themselves to one another. They were in the middle of their engagement and took the greatest pleasure in being with one another. One day, so that they could speak in private, they went for a walk in the forest. "Just be careful," said Joringel, "that you don't get too close to the castle." It was a beautiful evening, with the long rays of the low-lying sun shining through the trees into the deep woodland green. And a turtledove was singing mournfully from atop an old beech tree.

Suddenly Jorinde began to cry, and sat down weeping in the sunshine. Joringel began to weep too. They were so distraught that they felt as if they might die, for when they looked around they realized they were lost, and had no idea which way was home, and the sun had already sunk halfway behind the mountains. As Joringel looked through the bushes, he saw the old castle wall not far away, and was gripped by fear. Then Jorinde began to sing:

> *"My little bird with the little red ring,*
> *Sadly, sadly, sadly sings.*
> *It mourns the dove who now is dead*
> *Sings sadly, sad—wee-cleck-cleck-cleck."*

Joringel turned to look for Jorinde, but she had been turned into a nightingale, and sang, "*Wee-cleck, wee-cleck, wee-cleck-*

A great sorceress lived in a castle all by herself, and during the day she took the shape of a cat or a night owl.

As Joringel looked around, he saw the old woman sneakily grab a basket with one bird in it and head toward the door.

cleck-cleck." A night owl with glowing eyes flew around her three times, each time crying, "*Shoo-hoo, shoo-hoo, shoo-hoo.*" Joringel could not budge, and stood there like a stone, unable to cry, speak, or move his hands or feet.

The sun had now set, and the owl flew into the bushes. Within an instant a buckled-over old woman emerged. She looked jaundiced and thin, and had great big red eyes and a crooked nose that almost reached her chin. She was whispering something, and scooped up the nightingale in her hand and carried it off. Helpless, Joringel could not say anything, nor move from the spot, and the nightingale was gone. Eventually the woman returned, and said in a muffled voice, "Greetings, Zachiel. When the moon shines on the cage, Zachiel, set him free. When the time is right." With that, Joringel was set free.

He fell on his knees before the woman and begged her to give him back his Jorinde. But she said he would never see her, ever again, and then she left. He cried and he wept and he moaned, but all in vain: "Oh! What ever will become of me?" Joringel made his way to an unfamiliar village. For many years he kept the sheep there, and he would often walk around the castle, keeping a safe distance. Then one night he dreamt that he'd found a blood-red flower with a beautiful large pearl in the heart of its petals. He plucked the flower and went with it to the castle, where everything he touched with this flower was released from its spell. And he also dreamt that in this way he regained his Jorinde. After he awoke the next morning, he went searching high and low, through mountains and valleys, for such a flower. On the ninth day of searching, early in the morning, he found the blood-red flower. In the heart of its petals was a dewdrop as big as the most beautiful pearl. With flower in hand, he walked day and night until he finally reached the castle. As he walked within the fateful hundred paces, he did not freeze, but kept moving toward the gate. Now his spirits were high, and as he touched the gate with the flower, it sprang open.

He entered through the courtyard, listening for the sound of the many birds, and finally he heard it. He kept going until he found the chamber where the sorceress was feeding the birds in their seven thousand cages. When she spotted Joringel, she was angry, very angry. She cursed him, and spat poison and gall at him. But she could not get within two steps of him. He did not take her on, though, and turned instead to search through the birdcages. But lo, there were several hundred nightingales. How should he find his Jorinde again? As he looked around, out of the corner of his eye he saw the old woman sneakily grab a basket with one bird in it and head toward the door. Straightaway, he ran after her and touched the cage, and then the sorceress, with the flower.

From that moment on the sorceress could no longer cast a spell on anything, and suddenly Jorinde appeared before Joringel as beautiful as before, and wrapped her arms around his neck. Then he turned all the other birds back into maidens, and went home with his Jorinde. And they lived for many years happily together.

The Goose Girl

This tale features some of the most memorable and moving motifs in all of fairy tales: A princess is dethroned by her sly waiting maid and reduced to a lowly goose girl; tragically, her beloved talking horse is then killed, and his head is hung at the village gates; when her fellow goose herder pesters her in the meadow, she magically summons the wind to whisk away his cap so she can comb her hair in peace. This chorus of plaintive, poetic imagery expresses the princess's physical and emotional isolation and exemplifies the depth of feeling that fairy tales can communicate. In their annotations the Grimms remark on the beauty of the tale, which they adapted from Dorothea Viehmann of Hesse, Germany. They also observe that many of the motifs are ancient, including the talking horse and speaking drops of blood on the princess's handkerchief. At the close of the story, the deceitful maid meets a morbid end that she herself unwittingly decrees and that stands in stark contrast to the tale's incandescent lyricism. Variations of this type of tale have been found in oral traditions worldwide; the first published versions appeared in seventeenth-century France and Italy.—ND

Oil and charcoal painting by Jessie Willcox Smith, American, 1911

here once lived an old queen whose husband had died many years before, and she had a beautiful daughter. When the child came of age, she was betrothed to a prince who lived far away across the land. When the time came for them to be married, the princess was to travel a long way to his kingdom. Her mother packed up a great many useful and precious things: jewelry, gold and silver, goblets, and other little treasures—in short, everything a royal dowry should include, for she loved her child from the bottom of her heart. She also sent a waiting maid to ride with the girl and safely deliver her to the groom. Each young woman had her own horse, but the princess's horse, named Falada, could talk. When it was time to say goodbye, the aging queen went to her bedchamber, took a small knife, and cut her finger until it bled. She held a white handkerchief underneath and let three drops of blood fall onto it; then she gave it to her daughter, and said, "My sweet child, take good care of this, for it will help you on your journey in times of need."

With that, the two said their sad farewells, and the princess tucked the handkerchief into her bodice, then mounted her horse and rode off to her prince. When they had ridden an hour, she became parched and said to her waiting maid, "Get down and fill up the cup you brought for me with water from that brook. I would really like a drink." "If you're thirsty," replied the chambermaid, "then get down and go to the brook yourself, and get your own drink. I have no desire to wait on you." The princess was so thirsty that she dismounted, but without her golden cup, she had to kneel down beside the brook to drink. She whispered, "Oh, dear God!" And the three drops of blood said back to her, "If your mother only knew, her poor heart would burst in two." But the princess was humble, and so she got back on her horse without saying a word.

They rode for several more miles, but the day grew even hotter and the sun beat down on them, and soon the princess was thirsty again. As they came upon a stream, having forgotten the way she'd been treated before, the princess called out once more to the waiting maid, "Get down and get me a drink in

"If you want a drink," said the maid, "get it yourself." While the princess was leaning over the water, the handkerchief fell out and floated away.

my golden cup." But the waiting maid replied even more haughtily, "If you want a drink, get it yourself. I will not wait on you." Since she was so thirsty, the princess dismounted again, and bent down over the flowing water, cried, and said, "Oh, dear God!" And the drops of blood answered again, "If your mother only knew, her poor heart would burst in two." And while she was leaning over the water drinking, the bloodstained handkerchief fell out of her bodice and floated away. But she was so distressed that she did not even notice.

The waiting maid had been watching all this, and relished the thought that she was now gaining sway over the princess. Without the three drops of blood the princess had become weak and powerless. As the princess went to mount Falada again, the waiting maid said, "I belong on Falada, and you belong on this nag," and the princess had no choice but to yield. Then the waiting maid brazenly told her to remove her royal finery and to put on her own poor clothes. Finally, she made her swear to the heavens that she would not tell anyone at the royal court about this, and told her that if she didn't swear to this oath, she would be killed on

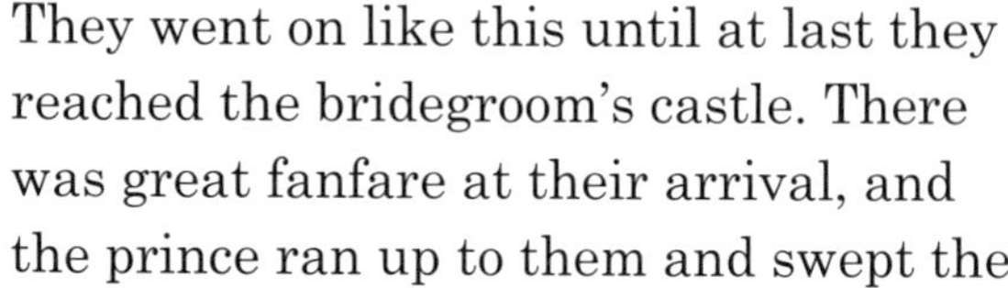

The next morning, as she and Little Conrad passed through the gate, the princess said to the horse, "Oh, poor Falada, there you hang."

the spot. But Falada saw all this happen, and remembered it.

The waiting maid mounted Falada, and the princess rode the lesser horse. They went on like this until at last they reached the bridegroom's castle. There was great fanfare at their arrival, and the prince ran up to them and swept the waiting maid off her horse, thinking she was his bride-to-be. He led her up the stairs, while the real princess had to stay behind. But the old king was looking out the window, and saw how fine she was, how gentle and beautiful. So he went to the royal chambers and asked the bride about her companion left in the courtyard, and who she was. "I took her along for the ride to keep me company. Give the girl some work to do so that she doesn't stand around idle." But the king had no work for her and could only think to offer, "There is a lad who looks after the geese. Perhaps she can help him." This boy was named Little

Conrad. And so the true bride had to help him look after the geese.

After a short time, the false bride said to the prince, "My dear prince, I have a favor to ask you." "Gladly," he replied. She went on, "Call the knacker and have him cut off the head of the horse I arrived on. It really annoyed me on the journey here." Of course in reality she was afraid that the horse might tell how she had mistreated her mistress. Now things had gone so far that the faithful Falada was actually slated to die. When the true princess learned of this, she secretly offered the knacker a gold coin in return for a favor. At the edge of town there was a great big dark gate through which she had to pass with the geese every morning and evening, and she asked him to nail Falada's head near the gate so that she could see it each time she passed through. The knacker promised to do this, cut off the horse's head, and nailed it near the great big gate.

Early the next morning, as she and Little Conrad passed through the gate, the princess said, "Oh, poor Falada, there you hang." And the head responded, "Oh, poor maiden queen, there you go. If your mother only knew, her poor heart would burst in two." She trudged away from the town in silence, and they drove the geese into the open fields. When they reached the meadow, the princess sat on the grass and let down her hair, which was as pure as gold. Little Conrad was taken by its sparkling luster, and tried to pull some of it out for himself, but then she said:

"Blow, wind, blow! Oh woe is me!
Take Little Conrad's hat with thee,
Let it fly and give him chase,
Till I've combed and braided my hair
And put it up, tidy and fair."

Suddenly a stiff wind rose up and plucked Little Conrad's hat right off his head, sending it flying across the countryside and him running after it. By the time he returned, the princess had finished combing her hair and putting it back up so neatly that he could not grab it. Little Conrad was upset and wouldn't speak to her, and so they watched over the geese in silence until it was evening, when they went home.

The next morning, when they passed through the great dark gate, the princess said, "Oh, poor Falada, there you hang." And the head responded, "Oh, poor maiden queen, there you go. If your mother only knew, her poor heart would burst in two."

"Blow, wind, blow!" she said. "Take Little Conrad's hat. Let it fly and give him chase, till I've combed and braided my hair."

Once on the meadow, she sat down and began to brush her hair again. Little Conrad ran over and tried to grab it, so she quickly said:

"Blow, wind, blow! Oh woe is me!
Take Little Conrad's hat with thee,
Let it fly and give him chase,
Till I've combed and braided my hair
And put it up, tidy and fair."

And the wind blew and swept the hat so far from his head that Little Conrad had to run after it. By the time he returned, the princess had finished brushing her hair and putting it back up, and not a hair was left that he could grab. So they kept on watching over the geese until evening came.

Once they were home that night, Little Conrad went before the old king and said, "I don't want to tend the geese anymore with that girl." "Why not, then?" asked the king. "Oh! She gets on my nerves all day long." The old king asked him to explain what had happened. Little Conrad said, "In the morning, when we walk through the dark gate with our flock, there's a horse's head on the wall, and she speaks to it, saying, 'Oh, poor Falada, there you hang.' And the head answers back, 'Oh, poor maiden queen, there you go. If your mother only knew, her poor heart would burst in two.'" And Little Conrad went on to tell him about what happened in the field when the wind came up and sent him running after his hat.

The old king told him to go out again the next day. When morning came, the king himself went and hid by the dark gate and listened as the girl spoke to Falada's head. Then he followed her into the fields, and hid behind a bush. There, with his own two eyes he saw how the goose girl and the goose boy drove their flock, and how after a while she sat down and undid her hair, which glistened in the sun. Then she said again:

"Blow, wind, blow! Oh woe is me!
Take Little Conrad's hat with thee,
Let it fly and give him chase,
Till I've combed and braided my hair
And put it up, tidy and fair."

And a gust of wind came and blew Little Conrad's hat away, making him run far afield after it, while the princess quietly combed and braided her hair. After the king had seen everything, he slipped away unnoticed.

When the goose girl returned that evening, he took her aside and asked her why she had done these things. "This I

The princess crawled into the iron stove and began to pour her heart out: "Here I sit, all alone, when really I'm a princess."

cannot tell you. Nor can I tell anyone else the reason for my woe. For I have sworn an oath under Heaven, since otherwise I would have lost my life." He insisted she tell him, but he could get nothing further from her. Finally he said, "If you refuse to tell me anything, then why don't you go tell the iron stove about your woes." And with that, he left.

She crawled into the iron stove, and began to weep and lament and pour her heart out: "Here I sit, all alone in the world, when really I'm a princess. A deceitful waiting maid forced me under pain of death to give up my fine clothes, and took my rightful place next to the prince, leaving me to toil away as the goose girl. If my mother only knew, her poor heart would burst in two." But the old king had been lurking near the stovepipe, and took in every word she said. He then asked her to come out of the stove, and he had her dressed in her regal clothes. She looked beautiful, like a miracle. The king summoned his son, and revealed to him that he had the wrong bride: She was just a waiting maid. Standing in front of him now was the real bride, who not long before was the lowly goose girl.

The young king was overjoyed to see how beautiful and virtuous she was, and a great feast was called for, and the court and all their good friends were invited. The groom sat at the head of the table, with the princess at one side and the waiting maid at the

other. The waiting maid was bedazzled by the princess's shiny jewelry, and did not recognize her in her finery.

Once they had eaten and drunk plenty, and were in a merry mood, the old king gave the waiting maid a riddle to solve: What would a woman be worth, he asked her, who had deceived King So-and-So in such-and-such a way—and here he recounted the whole story to her. "What judgment should befall her?" he asked, and the false bride answered, "She deserves nothing more than to be stripped naked and put into a barrel lined with sharp nails. And two white horses should be harnessed to it to drag her up and down the streets until she's dead." "That is you!" declared the old king. "You have just pronounced your sentence with your own words, and that is what shall be done to you." When the sentence had been carried out, the young prince married his one true bride, and they ruled the kingdom from that day on in peace and happiness.

The Twelve Dancing Princesses

Each night under cover of darkness and in the realm of dreams, twelve sisters sneak out to go dancing, and no one knows where they escape to or how they get there. The only trace of their romantic escapades is their worn-out shoes. This tale revels in fantasy, with trees of silver and gold, a castle teeming with music and merriment, and not one prince charming—who is perpetually cast in fairy tales as difficult to find—but twelve, with no apparent shortage in sight. Although court dancing was typically a display of gentility and manners, in this tale the princesses' dancing is a transgression. It proves too much for the king to bear, and he vows to stop it by granting anyone who solves the mystery one of his daughters to marry and his kingdom when he dies. The Grimms adapted their story from a tale from Münster, Germany. According to historians, in the story's four-hundred-year history, five hundred versions have been recorded in Central Europe, although the tale has not been widely found elsewhere. Folklorists Iona and Peter Opie note that the tale's bejeweled forest resembles one in the more than two-thousand-year-old *Epic of Gilgamesh*.—ND

Watercolors by Kay Nielsen, Danish, 1913

They stood in the midst of a magnificent tree-lined path where all the leaves were made of pure silver, and were shimmering and glinting.

Once there was a king who had twelve daughters, each more beautiful than the last. They slept together in one large room where their beds were lined up in a row. In the evenings, after they were all tucked in, the king would shut the door and lock it tight. But when he came back each morning to unlock the door, he would find that his daughters' shoes had been worn through from dancing, and no one understood how this could be happening. So the king let it be known that whoever found out where his daughters went dancing at night could choose one of them as his bride, and become king upon the king's death. But if anyone who came forward failed to solve the mystery after three days and three nights, he would lose his life.

Before long, a prince came forward and took on the dangerous challenge. He was well received, and in the evening he was shown to a room just outside the princesses' bedchamber. There a bed was set up for him, and he was told to watch closely to see where the girls went dancing. And to prevent them from doing anything in secret, or from leaving their bedchamber to go elsewhere, the king left their door open. But the prince's eyelids were like lead, and soon he fell fast asleep. When he awoke the next morning, all twelve girls had been out dancing, and their shoes stood there tattered, with holes in their soles. And so it went on like this for the second and third nights, and thereafter he was mercilessly beheaded. Still, more princes kept coming, all volunteering to take on the risky test, and they all lost their lives.

Now one day it so happened that a poor soldier, whose wounds kept him from ever serving again, was headed to the town where the king held court. On his way, an old woman approached him and asked where he was going. "I don't really know," he answered, adding in jest, "I'd almost like to try finding out where the king's daughters are dancing their shoes to pieces, and become king myself." "That isn't so difficult," said the old woman. "Just avoid drinking the wine they bring you in the evening, and then pretend you're fast asleep." Then she gave him a special cape and said, "When you drape this over your shoulders, you'll be invisible and able to follow the girls unnoticed."

As soon as the soldier heard this good advice, he became serious about the matter. He took heart and went before the king to put himself forward as a suitor. He was as graciously received as the others, and given regal clothing to wear. At bedtime he was led to his room, and as he prepared to go to bed, the eldest daughter brought him a glass of wine. But he had fastened a sponge under his chin, and he let the wine flow into it, without swallowing one drop. Then he lay down, and after a little while began to make snoring sounds, as if in the deepest sleep. The twelve princesses heard him, and giggled. The eldest said, “Here’s another one who’ll lose his life.” Then they got out of bed, opened their wardrobes, trunks, and boxes, and took out their most splendid clothes. They got ready in front of their looking glasses, and frolicked around with glee about going dancing. But the youngest one said, “I don’t know. You are all so happy, but I have a strange feeling. I think something awful might happen to us.” “You silly goose,” said the eldest. “Always afraid of something. Have you forgotten how many princes have already come and tried in vain? I didn’t even really need to give the sleeping potion to this one. That oaf wouldn’t wake up if a tree fell on him.”

When they were all ready to go, they went to check on the soldier. His eyes were closed and he did not stir one bit, so they thought they were safe. Then the eldest went to her bed and tapped on it, whereupon it sank straight down into the ground. One after the other they followed her down through the opening. The soldier, who had seen everything, waited just long enough, then put on his special cape and climbed down behind the youngest princess. But on the stairs he stepped on the hem of her dress, and she said, frightened, “What’s that? Who’s holding my dress?” “Don’t be ridiculous,” said the eldest. “You must have just snagged it on a nail.”

They went all the way down to the bottom until they stood in the midst of a magnificent tree-lined path. All the leaves were made of pure silver, and were shimmering and glinting. The soldier thought, “I should take a piece back with me to show the king.” So he snapped off a branch, and a loud crack shot through the woods. Again the youngest sister cried out, “Something’s not right. Didn’t you all hear that noise?” But the eldest sister merely

The soldier sneaked onto the boat with the youngest sister, whose prince remarked, "I don't know why, but the boat is much heavier today."

said, "That's just a welcome salute from our princes, whose wait will soon be over."

They then came to another boulevard of trees, with leaves of gold, and then at last to another, where the leaves were all brilliant diamonds. He broke off a branch from each kind of tree, making a loud crack each time. And each time the youngest sister jumped, but her eldest sister kept insisting that the noise was from a welcome salute. They kept walking and came to a large lake where twelve boats were moored. In each of them sat a handsome prince who had been waiting for one of the twelve princesses, and each prince took one princess on board his boat. The soldier sneaked onto the boat with the youngest sister, whose prince remarked, "I don't know why, but the boat is so much heavier today. I'm having to row with all my might just to get it moving." "How can that be?" answered the youngest sister. "It must be because of this warm weather that's also making me feel so hot."

On the far side of the lake there was a beautiful castle lit up with candles, and merry music from drums and trumpets rang out. They rowed the rest of the way and went inside, and each of the princes danced with his favorite princess. Our soldier danced along too, secretly and unseen, and whenever one of the sisters was handed a glass of wine he drank it dry, so that by the time it reached her lips it was empty. The youngest was very disturbed by this, but the eldest silenced her every complaint. They danced on until three o'clock in the morning, at which point their shoes were worn through and they had to stop. The princes rowed them

They went inside the beautiful castle, and each of the princes danced with his favorite princess. Our soldier danced too, secretly and unseen.

back, and this time the soldier sat in the first boat with the eldest sister. The princesses said their goodbyes at the shore and promised to return the next night.

When they reached the stairs, the soldier dashed out in front and scurried up to his bed, where he resumed his snoring. As the tired twelve tiptoed slowly back into their room, they could all hear him, and said, "This one won't do us any harm." They took off their evening gowns and put them away, lined up their shoes with holes in their soles under their beds, and lay down to sleep. In the morning, the soldier chose not to say one word, preferring instead to witness the unusual ritual again. And so he went along the second and third nights, when everything was as before, and each time the girls danced until their shoes fell apart. And on the third night he brought a wineglass back with him as proof of what he had seen.

When the hour had come for the soldier to answer to the king, he gathered up the three branches and the wineglass, and went before him. The girls, meanwhile, stood behind their door and listened to what he had to say. The king put forward the question, "Where have my twelve daughters been dancing their shoes to tatters at night?" And the soldier answered, "With twelve princes in an underground castle," and then gave a full account of what he had seen, revealing the evidence he'd brought back.

The king summoned his daughters and asked them whether the soldier was telling the truth. They saw that their secret had been given away and that lying would not help, so they admitted to everything. With that, the king asked which of his daughters the soldier wished to marry. He answered, "I'm not as young as I once was, and so I will choose your eldest." The very same day their wedding was held, and the soldier was promised the kingdom upon the king's death. But the other princes had to swear off seeing the remaining sisters for as many days as the number of nights they had danced with the twelve dancing princesses.

The Star Coins

Although very brief, this introspective tale has enjoyed great popularity for its touching story and its beautiful final image of coins falling from the sky. The story is simple but poignant: After the death of her parents, an impoverished girl goes into the world on her own. She meets other suffering souls and gives away everything she owns until the heavens come to her rescue and reward her selflessness with a shower of coins that fall like stars from the sky. Stars have inspired storytelling for millennia, from the constellations of Greek mythology to nursery rhymes such as "Twinkle, Twinkle, Little Star." In this tale, however, the stars are not part of a map of the night sky, but instead reflect the girl's beneficent and luminous inner morality. Folklorist Hans-Jörg Uther has noted that the Grimms carefully chose their title to conjure the long history of heavenly bodies in folklore and evoke the association of shooting stars with the heroine's good fortune. The soulful motif of a celestial shower of coins has resonated strongly with audiences and been a favorite of illustrators. The Grimms adapted their version from a tale in an eighteenth-century book by German writer Jean Paul.—ND

Color lithograph by Viktor P. Mohn, German, 1882

As she stood there with nothing left, suddenly the stars began to fall from the sky. They were shiny coins of pure silver.

There once was a little girl whose father and mother had both died. She was so poor that she no longer had a roof over her head, nor even a bed to sleep in. Finally she had nothing left but the clothes on her back, and a piece of bread in her hand that some kindhearted soul had given her. But she was still a good and caring girl.

Left all alone in the world, she put her trust in a kind and loving God and set out across the fields. On her way she met a poor man who asked, "Oh, please give me something to eat. I am so hungry." So she handed him the whole piece of bread, saying, "May God bless this for you," and walked on. Then came a child, who pleaded, "My head is aching with cold. Please give me something I can cover it with." So she removed her hat and gave it away. After she had walked farther on, a second child rushed up, who was freezing cold without a vest, and she gave that child her own. Still farther, yet another lost child begged for a skirt, and our girl gave hers away as well.

Finally, just as darkness fell, she entered the forest. Once more a poor child came begging, this time asking for a shirt. The kind girl thought, "The night is dark; no one will see me. I can safely give away my shirt." And she took it off and gave it away too. As she stood there with nothing left at all, suddenly the stars began to fall from the sky. Showering down around her, they proved to be hard, shiny coins of pure silver. And having just given away the shirt off her back, she suddenly found herself wearing another, this one of the very finest linen. So she gathered up the silver coins in it, and was rich and generous all the days of her life.

Snow White and Rose Red

Sibling rivalry peppers many of the Grimms' tales, but in this story of two loving sisters, the girls complement one another right down to their picturesque names: Snow White (no relation to the tale "Snow White") and Rose Red. Self-sufficient and kindhearted, they live harmoniously with their widowed mother and a new friend, a talking bear. With the coming of spring, the bear returns to his habitat, while the sisters have a series of unpleasant encounters with a cantankerous dwarf. The girls repeatedly help the combative dwarf out of life-threatening situations despite his shameless mistreatment of them. Their thoughtfulness is rewarded when the bear puts an end to the crabby creature once and for all and turns into a handsome prince who, fortunately for the second sister, has a brother. The Grimms adapted the tale from Karoline Stahl's *Fairy Tales, Fables, and Stories for Children* from 1818, adding the bear. Wilhelm Grimm rewrote the story over many years, ultimately creating an adventure story laced with moral lessons amid the dwarf's spirited outbursts. Historian Jack Zipes speculates that the story resonated with Wilhelm because its central theme of a productive and uncompetitive partnership between two siblings mirrored his relationship with his brother, Jacob.—ND

Tempera drawings by Gustaf Tenggren, Swedish-American, 1955

here was once a poor widow who lived a secluded life in a little cottage. In front of the cottage was a garden where two rosebushes grew: One bush had white petals, and the other red. She had two daughters who were so like the roses that one was called Snow White, and the other Rose Red. They were good, loyal children, and as diligent and resourceful as any two children in the world have ever been. Snow White was the gentler and shyer of the two. Rose Red preferred to run around in the fields and chase flowers and butterflies, while Snow White stayed at home with her mother, and helped her around the house or read to her in quiet moments. The two girls loved one another so dearly that they always held hands when they went out together, and whenever Snow White said, "We won't ever leave each other," Rose Red would answer, "Not as long as we live," and their mother would add, "Whatever one of you has, you must always share it with the other."

They would often go into the woods on their own and gather red berries, and the animals never did them any harm. In fact, they trusted the girls, and would draw very close to them: The little rabbit would eat cabbage out of their hands; the deer would graze right by their side; the stag would bound merrily past; and the birds would stay still in the branches and sing their favorite songs.

Nor did any mishap ever visit the girls. If they were out in the woods too late and night set in, they would simply lie down close to one another on the mossy ground and sleep until morning. Their mother knew this, and was never worried. One such time, when the red of dawn woke them from their night in the woods, they saw a beautiful child in a shining white dress seated not far from their little campsite. It stood up, gave them a friendly smile, and walked off into the trees without saying a word. As they looked around, they realized they had slept on the edge of a ravine. Had they taken just two more steps in the darkness the night before, they would have fallen in. Their mother told them the child must have been the guardian angel who watches over children.

Snow White and Rose Red kept their mother's cottage so spotless that it was

The widow had two daughters who were so like the two rosebushes that one was called Snow White, and the other Rose Red.

pleasing to the eye to look inside. In the summer Rose Red took care of the house, and each morning she would put a little bouquet by her mother's bed before she awoke, and in it a rose from each of the two bushes. In the winter Snow White would light the fire and hang the kettle on the hook above it. The pot was made of brass yet shone like gold, so finely was it polished. In the evenings, as snowflakes fell, their mother would say, "Snow White, go and bolt the door." Then they would sit by the fire, and their mother would take out her glasses and read from a big book of tales. The two girls would sit and listen while they spun wool. Next to them on the floor lay a little lamb, and behind them on its perch sat a little white dove with its head tucked under its wing.

One evening, as they sat cozily together, someone knocked urgently on the door. "Quickly, Rose Red," said her mother. "Open the door. It must be a wayfarer looking for shelter." Rose Red got up and unlocked the bolt, thinking some poor man would be at the door. Instead, it was a bear! He stretched his big head inside, and Rose Red screamed and jumped back, frightened. The little lamb gave out a nervous bleat, the dove beat its wings wildly, and Snow White hid behind her mother's bed. But the bear began to speak, and said, "Please don't be afraid. I won't harm you. I'm half frozen

They would often go into the woods on their own and gather red berries, and the animals trusted them and would draw very close.

"Don't be afraid. I won't harm you," said the bear. "I'm half frozen and just want to warm up in here for a while."

and I just want to warm up in here for a while." "Oh, you poor bear!" replied the mother. "Come lie down by the fire, but be careful not to burn your fur." Then she called to the girls, "Snow White, Rose Red, come out! The bear says he won't hurt you, and I believe him." So the two girls came out from hiding, and bit by bit the little lamb and the dove came closer to the big beast, no longer afraid. "Listen, children," said the bear. "Brush some of that snow out of my fur." And they got a broom and swept his fur free of snow. He lay down by the fire and gave a contented and cozy little rumble.

Before long, they were all on familiar terms, and the girls grew more carefree in playing around with their clumsy guest. They tousled his hair, put their feet up on his big back and rolled him back and forth, and prodded and flicked him with a switch from a hazel tree. When he rumbled, they would just laugh. The bear enjoyed all the attention, and only if they got a little too rough would he cry out: "Oh, children, please let me live! Snow White, Rose Red, stop! You might be mauling your own suitor." When finally it was time to sleep, and the girls had gone

to their beds, the mother said to the bear, "For heaven's sake, you're welcome to stay here and lie by the fire. That way you'll be safe from the dreadful weather outside." At dawn the girls let him outside, and he trotted off through the snow into the woods. From then on he would come every evening at the same hour, lie down by the fire, and let the children play with him as much as they pleased. They grew so accustomed to having him there that they never locked the door for the night until the big brown guest arrived.

When spring came and everything turned green, the bear went to Snow White one morning and told her, "Now the time has come for me to leave, and I can't come back until the summer's over." "But where are you going, dear bear?" Snow White asked. "I must go back into the woods," he said, "and protect my treasure from the wicked dwarfs. During the winter, when the ground is frozen hard, they stay beneath it and can't get out. But now that the sun is thawing the soil, they'll soon burrow through and look for things to steal. Whatever falls into their greedy little hands ends up in

The dwarf's beard was caught in the tree trunk, and the little man was jumping up and down like a dog on a leash.

their caves and is rarely seen again." Snow White became very sad at his departure, and when she unlocked the door for him, and he made his way outside, he got caught on the door latch, and it tore off a piece of his fur. For an instant, Snow White thought she'd seen something shimmer brilliantly, like gold, underneath his fur, but she could not be sure. The bear bounded off and disappeared among the trees.

Some time later, their mother sent the girls into the woods to gather kindling. There they came across a felled tree lying on the ground, and saw something hopping up and down in the grass by the trunk. At first they couldn't tell what it was, but as they came closer, they saw it was a dwarf with an old, wrinkled face and a snow-white beard that was longer than he was tall. The end of the beard was caught in a cleft in the tree trunk, and the little man was jumping up and down like a dog on a leash, unable to get out of his bind. He fixed his fiery red eyes on the girls and shouted at them, "What are you doing standing there? Can't you come over and help me?" "What have you done there, little one?" asked Rose Red. "You silly goose, with your nosy questions," he

retorted. "I was trying to split the tree to get some smaller wood for the kitchen. Big logs burn my modest portions of food right up, since dwarfs' needs are small and we don't gobble everything up like you greedy folk. I'd already gotten the wedge in nicely, and everything would have gone just fine, except the abominable wood was too smooth and the wedge sprang right out again, and the tree snapped shut on my beard! I couldn't get it out in time. Now it's stuck in there, and I can't get away. Oh—are you two weaklings laughing at me? Well, I'll tell you what: You're one nasty lot!"

The girls tried as hard as they could, but they could not pull the beard out; it was clenched too tightly. "I'm going to run and get some help," said Rose Red. "You crazy goat's head!" snarled the dwarf. "Who needs more people? The two of you are already too many for my taste. Don't you have a better idea?" "Don't be so impatient," said Snow White. "I think I can come up with something." She took a pair of scissors out of her pocket, and snipped off the end of the beard. As soon as the dwarf was freed, he picked up a sack filled with gold that he'd hidden among the roots of the tree, and grumbled, "My, you people are really rough around the edges. Chopping off a piece of my handsome beard! For crying out loud!" And with that he swung the sack over his shoulder and went off without so much as another glance at the stunned girls.

One day, some months later, the girls went fishing for their supper. As they neared the stream, they saw something that looked like a big grasshopper hopping near the water, as if it wanted to jump in. They ran closer and realized it was the dwarf. "What are you doing?" asked Rose Red. "Are you trying to jump into the water?" "I'm certainly not such a fool," the dwarf shouted. "Don't you see? This abominable fish wants to pull me in." The little fellow had been sitting on the bank fishing, and unfortunately the wind had come and twisted his beard into the fishing line. Just then, a big fish took the bait, but the dwarf was not strong enough to reel it in, so now the fish had the upper hand, and was pulling the dwarf in. He held onto the grass and the rushes, but this did not help much. As the fish thrashed, the dwarf had to follow, and was in constant danger of plunging into the water. The girls had arrived just in time. They took hold of him and tried to

There was nothing left to do but cut the beard. The dwarf screamed, "Is that your notion of manners, you misfits?"

The girls grabbed the dwarf and pulled until the eagle flew off. Then the dwarf shrieked, "Couldn't you have been more gentle with me?

loosen his beard from the fishing line, but to no avail. Beard and line were terribly entwined. There was nothing left to do but to get out the scissors and cut the beard, losing a piece of it in the process. When the dwarf saw this, he screamed at the girls, "Is that your notion of manners, you misfits? To mar a man's face? It wasn't enough that you clipped off the end before; now you've cut off the best part! I can't let myself be seen like this among the other dwarfs. May you lose the soles of your shoes on the walk home!" And with that he picked up a sack filled with pearls that he'd hidden in the reeds, and without another word he carried it away and disappeared behind a rock.

Some time later, their mother sent the girls to town to buy some needles and thread, and ribbons and bows. The way led them across a heath where enormous boulders were scattered. There they saw a large bird soaring overhead, and it began to circle above them slowly, and then to fly lower and lower until finally it dove down not far from one of the boulders. Just then they heard an awful, piercing scream. They ran toward it and saw with horror that the eagle had seized their old friend, the dwarf, and was ready to fly away with him. The compassionate girls grabbed the little fellow tightly and pulled on him to try to keep him down until the eagle finally flew off without its prey. As the dwarf recovered from his shock, he lambasted them again in a piercing shriek: "Couldn't you have been more gentle with me? You've torn my fine tunic! It's in tatters and has holes all over. You bumbling, clumsy riffraff!" And with that he picked up a sack filled with precious stones, and slipped back under the boulders into his lair. The girls, already quite accustomed to his thanklessness, went on their way and ran their errands in town.

On their way home they returned across the heath and surprised the dwarf, who had emptied his sack of precious stones onto a clear spot on the ground, not expecting anyone to walk by at such a late hour. The evening sun shone down on the stones, and they shimmered and sparkled so gloriously and colorfully that the children stopped in their tracks and gazed at them. "What are you doing standing there with your mouths agape?" shouted the dwarf, whose ashen face turned scarlet red with rage. It seemed he was about to continue his cursing, when they heard a

loud growl, and a bear came running out of the woods. The dwarf jumped up, terrified, but he could not take cover in time. The bear was already upon him. He cried out, his heart racing with fear, "Dear Mr. Bear, please spare me! I'll give you all my treasure. See the lovely precious stones lying there? Spare me my life! What do you want with a skinny little fellow like me? You wouldn't even notice me between your teeth. But those two godless girls: Take them! What tender morsels in your mouth they'd be, plump as the finest quail. For heaven's sake, eat them!" The bear didn't pay any attention to his words, and with one swing of his massive paw, he swatted down the evil little creature. And there the dwarf lay, still.

The girls had fled from the scene, but the bear called after them, "Snow White! Rose Red! Don't be afraid. Wait for me. I'll come with you." They recognized his voice and happily waited for him. As he neared them, his furry coat began to fall away, and there stood a handsome man, dressed all in gold. "I am a prince," he said. "But I was put under a spell by that wicked

"Snow White! Rose Red! Don't be afraid," the bear said. His furry coat began to fall away, and there stood a handsome prince.

dwarf who ran off with my treasure. I was to remain a wild bear running through the woods, and only his death could free me. Now he has gotten what he deserved."

And so Snow White married the prince, and Rose Red married his brother, and they shared the many treasures that the dwarf had hidden in his underground lair. Their old mother lived for many more years in peace and contentment with her daughters. She had taken the two rosebushes to her new home, and planted them right outside her window, and each year they bore the most lovely roses. One had white petals, and the other red.

The Hare and the Hedgehog

In this legendary tale, two different animals challenge each other to a race. At first it looks like it will be a straightforward showdown between a fast hare and a slower, ill-fated hedgehog. We quickly learn, however, that winning the race requires a range of skills—luckily for the hedgehog, ones that don't require breaking a sweat. Knowing he is the weaker contender, the hedgehog decides to outsmart his haughty opponent by enlisting his wife as a body double, a classic stunt that has been used in magic tricks, capers, and espionage for as long as people have wanted to fool one another. What the hedgehog lacks in speed, he makes up for with his wits. The ancient theme of mismatched competitors appears in tales in many cultures, for instance in Aesop's fable "The Tortoise and the Hare." The story was first published in 1840 in Low German (Plattdeutsch) by writer Wilhelm Christian Schröder, who adapted it from oral versions circulating in northwestern Germany. In 1843, for their fifth edition, the Grimms included the popular tale in its original Low German. Set outside Buxtehude, Germany, near Hamburg, the story made the thousand-year-old town famous.—ND

Hand-colored lithographs by Gustav Süs, German, 1855

OPPOSITE *The hedgehog was standing at his front door, gazing out into the morning breeze and crooning a little tune to himself.*

This story, children, might sound like a pack of lies, but as a matter of fact it's all true. My grandfather—who loved telling me this story—always used to say, "It must be true, my boys, otherwise no one would tell it." In any case, this is how it goes: One Sunday morning around harvest time, just as the buckwheat was flowering, the sun was shining brightly in the sky, and a warm morning breeze was blowing through the grain stalks. The larks were singing in the air, the bees were buzzing through the buckwheat, and the people were on their way to church in their Sunday finest. All creation was happy and content, including the hedgehog.

Now, the hedgehog was standing at his front door with arms folded, gazing out into the morning breeze and crooning a little tune to himself, as well or as poorly as a hedgehog possibly could sing on a cheery Sunday morning. As he sang half out loud, it occurred to him that this was a good time to stroll through the fields and check on his turnips, while his wife washed and dressed their youngsters. There were turnip fields very close to his house, and since he and his hedgehog family liked to eat turnips rather often, he considered them his own. No sooner said than done: The hedgehog closed the front door behind him and made his way out to the fields. He was not very far from home and was just about to pass by the blackthorn bushes into the turnip field when he came across the hare, out on

RIGHT *He thought it was a good time to check on his turnips, while his wife washed and dressed their youngsters.*

OPPOSITE *The hedgehog bade the hare a friendly "good morning." But the hare, who was horribly stuck-up, did not return the greeting.*

BELOW *The hedgehog's wife cried, "Have you lost your mind? Why would you possibly want to run a race against the hare?"*

similar business; that is, he was looking after his cabbages. As he caught sight of the hare, he bade him a friendly "good morning." But the hare, who in his own way was a rather fine gentleman but, frankly, horribly stuck-up about it, did not return the hedgehog's greeting. Instead, making his face into a haughty sneer, he said, "How is it that you're out in the fields so early in the morning?" "I'm taking a walk," said the hedgehog. "A walk?" the hare scoffed. "I was under the impression you had better things to do with those legs of yours."

This wisecrack annoyed the hedgehog terribly. He could take just about anything, but he drew the line at a jab about his legs, which had been crooked since birth. "I think you're imagining things," the hedgehog replied, "if you're implying that you can do more with your legs than I." "Of course I can," claimed the hare. "We just might have to put that to the test," said the hedgehog. "I'll bet that if we had a race, I'd run right by you." "That's ridiculous. You with your crooked legs!" jeered the hare. "As far as I'm concerned, go right ahead if you're so set on it. What will you wager?" "One French gold coin and a bottle of brandy," replied the hedgehog. "I accept!" said the hare. "Let's shake on it, and then we can get started right away." "There's no hurry," said the hedgehog. "I still haven't eaten yet. Let me first go home and have some breakfast, and I'll meet you back at this very spot in half an hour."

The hare agreed, and with that the hedgehog left. On his way home he thought, "The hare is going to rely on his long legs, but I'll still get him at his own game. He may be a fine fellow, but he's a fool! And he's going to pay." Once he was back home, he said to his wife, "Wife, get

yourself dressed right away. You have to come to the fields with me." "What's going on?" she asked. "I've bet a French gold coin and a bottle of brandy with the hare. We are going to race, and you have to be there." "Oh, my God, husband!" she cried. "Are you crazy? Have you lost your mind? Why would you possibly want to run a race against the hare?" "Pipe down, wife," the hedgehog said. "That's my business. Don't go poking around in a man's affairs. Let's go! Get yourself dressed and come along with me." What should Mrs. Hedgehog do? She had to go along with him whether she liked it or not.

On their way over, the hedgehog said to his wife, "Now listen to what I have to say. Do you see that long field? That's where we're going to run the race. The hare will run in one of the furrows, I'll run in the one next to it, and we'll start up at the top. Now all you have to do is stay put down there at the end of my furrow, and when you see the hare come along, you simply call out to him: 'Here I am already.'" They got to the field and the hedgehog showed his wife her spot, then went uphill to the starting point. When he reached the top, the hare was already there. "Can we get started?" he asked. "Yes, indeed," answered the hedgehog. "Let's go!" And with that each runner lined up in his furrow. Then the hare counted out, "Ready, set...go!" and tore off down the field like a tornado. But the hedgehog ran only about three steps, then ducked down into his furrow and sat waiting.

As the hare reached the bottom of the field, barreling at full speed, the hedgehog's wife called out at him, "Here I am already!" The hare stopped short in astonishment. He was sure it was the hedgehog himself calling to him, since as you and everyone well know, the hedgehog's wife looks just like Mr. Hedgehog. Rattled, the hare thought to himself, "They're trying to make a monkey out of me." He called out, "We're doing this again! One more lap!" And he took off once more like a tornado, with his big ears pressed back against his head. The hedgehog's wife, though, stayed calmly in her spot. When the hare reached the top of the field, the hedgehog called out to him, "Here I am already!" The hare was infuriated and screamed, "Let's run again! One more lap!" "No trouble," replied the hedgehog. "We can run as many laps as you like." And so the hare ran the race seventy-three times.

As the hare reached the bottom of the field, barreling at full speed, the hedgehog's wife called out at him, "Here I am already!"

Mr. Hedgehog took his prize, and they went home together in good cheer. Since then no hare has dared to race against the hedgehog.

And each time the hedgehogs, in their own way, kept up with him. Whenever the hare reached the top or the bottom of the field, the hedgehog or his wife would shout, "Here I am already!"

But on the seventy-fourth go-round, the hare did not make it to the end of the course. In the middle of the field he fell dead to the ground, blood flowing from his mouth. Mr. Hedgehog took his prize, the French gold coin and bottle of brandy, and called for his wife to come out from the furrow. They went home together in good cheer, and if they have not died by now, then they must still be alive. And that's how it happened, there on the Buxtehude Heath, that the hedgehog ran the hare into the ground. Since then no hare has dared to race against the Buxtehude hedgehog.

The moral of the story is, first of all, it should never occur to any of us to make fun of a humble person, no matter how great we think we are, even if that someone is only a hedgehog. And second of all, it's better when you are wooing a young lady to choose one who is your equal, and who—as we've learned—is your spitting image too. That is to say, if you are a hedgehog, well then, you should make sure your wife is a hedgehog too.

Puss 'n Boots

This story of an irrepressibly classy cat and his humble master has won the hearts of readers and listeners for over three hundred years. A miller's youngest son receives a single cat as his meager inheritance. Little does he know that this cat is special. He talks, wears fancy boots, and knows how to rub elbows with royalty. He is also smart enough to realize that his well-being depends on his master's. Puss 'n Boots becomes the quintessential behind-the-scenes producer, boldly orchestrating his owner's social climb from miller's son to landed gentry. While animal-helper stories have been found in the ancient cultures of Europe, Asia, Africa, and the Americas, versions of this feline tale first emerged in Italy during the Renaissance. The Grimms included a variation from Hesse, Germany, in their first edition, but they removed it from subsequent editions after critics deemed it too similar to the well-known seventeenth-century French version by Charles Perrault. The story is included here because the Grimms' publication of the tale continued its broad circulation, which influenced many artists and storytellers. Their version also contains, as historians have observed, enough differences in the retelling to warrant our appreciation and, above all, enjoyment.—ND

Color lithographs by Herbert Leupin, Swiss, 1946

miller had three sons, a mill, a donkey, and a cat. The sons had to work the mill, the donkey had to bring in the grain and afterward haul away the flour, and the cat's job was to chase away the mice. When the miller died, his sons divided up the inheritance: The eldest got the mill, the middle son got the donkey, and the youngest the cat, since there was nothing more for him to inherit. He was saddened by this, and said to himself, "I really got the short end of the stick. My eldest brother can make grain, and my other brother can ride his donkey. What on Earth am I supposed to do with this cat? Skin him and make myself a pair of fur gloves? That's about it."

"Now listen," the cat weighed in, having understood everything. "You don't need to kill me off for a pair of lousy gloves from my fur. Just have some boots made for me instead, and let me go out and be seen among the people. I promise it will lead to great things for you." The miller's son was bewildered to hear the cat speak like this. But just at that moment a shoemaker came walking by, and so he called him in and had the cat fitted for some boots. When these were finished, the cat put them right on. Then he grabbed a sack, filled it partway with grain, looped a cord through the top to make a drawstring, tossed the bag over his shoulder, and strode right out the door on two feet, just like a human.

In those days, there was a king ruling the land who delighted in feasting on partridges. But the king was distressed because there was not a partridge to be found. The forest was full of them, but they are easily frightened and the hunters could not get near enough to them. Now, the cat knew this, but was convinced he had a better way to get them. Once in the woods, he put his bag on the ground, opened it up wide and spread the grain around in it. Then he buried the cord in the grass, taking the end with him into the bushes. There he hid, lurking and lying in wait. Soon the partridges waddled up, found the grain, and one after the other hopped into the bag. When enough of them were inside, he yanked the rope tight, then ran right over and wrung the birds' necks. Then he tossed the bag again

The cat lay in wait. Soon the partridges hopped into the bag. He yanked the rope tight and set out for the king's castle.

over his shoulder and set out for the king's castle.

"Halt! Where do you think you're going?" demanded the guard. "To see the king," answered the cat boldly. "Ha! Are you crazy? A cat to see the king?" "Let him go in," said another guard. "The king is bored these days, and maybe this cat can amuse him with his purring and playing." When the cat went before the king, he bowed low and said, "My Lord, the Count"—and here he rattled off a long and terribly impressive-sounding name—"sends Your Majesty his highest regard and offers you these partridges, which he just caught in his snares." The king was astonished at the sight of the beautiful, plump birds, and could hardly contain his excitement. He ordered the cat to take as much gold from the royal treasury as he could carry away in the bag, saying, "Bring that to your master, and thank him a thousand times over for his gift."

The poor miller's son had been sitting at home by his window, head in his hands. He thought he had just thrown away his very last coins for the cat's boots and wondered what good this crazy idea could possibly do him. Just then the cat pranced in, dropped the heavy bag from his shoulder, untied it, and poured the gold pieces out in front of the miller's son. "See what you've got in return for these boots? The king himself says hello and thanks you kindly." The miller's son was overjoyed at his newfound wealth, but dumbfounded at how the cat had gotten his paws on it. But

OPPOSITE *The king ordered the cat to take as much gold from the royal treasury as he could carry away in the bag.*

BELOW *When the king heard this, he sent one of his entourage racing back to the castle to fetch some of his own clothes.*

our feline fellow told him the whole story while pulling off his boots, and added, "You have enough gold now, but this is not the end of your good fortune. Tomorrow I'll put my boots on again and make you richer still. After all, I told the king that you are a count."

The next day, as promised, the cat went out hunting again, well heeled in his boots, and brought the king a fine fat catch. And so it went on for days on end, and each day the cat brought home more gold. He soon became so beloved by the king that he could come and go as he pleased and wander through the castle wherever he chose. Once he was in the royal kitchen, warming himself by the fire, when the coachman came in cursing, "Oh, how I'd like to throw the king and princess to the dogs! All I wanted was to go to the tavern for a beer and a few games of cards, and instead I have to drive them around the lake now." When the cat heard this, he sneaked home and told his master, "If you really want to be a count, and be really rich, then come with me to the lake for a swim." The miller's son didn't know what to say, but followed the cat to the lake anyway. He took his clothes off until he was stark naked, and then jumped into the water. But the cat took his clothes away and hid them, and was barely finished when the king's carriage came rolling by. The cat immediately began to make a fuss. "Oh! Most beloved and gracious king! My lord was bathing here when a thief came and stole his clothes from the bank. The count is still in the water and cannot get out. But if he stays in any longer, he'll catch cold and die!" When the king heard this, he made his carriage stop, and sent one of his entourage racing back to the castle to fetch some of his own clothes. Soon the "count" found himself putting on resplendent attire. And since the king was already fond of him

PAGES 282–283 *The king invited the count into the coach. The princess did not need any convincing, since she thought she might fancy him.*

because of the flocks of partridges he believed the count had given him, he invited the count into the royal coach. The princess did not need any convincing either, since the count was young and handsome and she thought she might fancy him.

In the meantime the cat had raced ahead and come to a large meadow where over a hundred people were making hay. "Who does this field belong to, people?" he asked. "The great sorcerer," they replied. "Now listen," the cat continued. "The king is about to ride by. When he asks who owns this field, you must answer, 'The count.' And if you don't do this, you will all meet your maker!" With that, the cat went on farther, and soon he came to a field of grain so large that no one could see the end of it. There were over two hundred people reaping the harvest. "Who does this grain belong to, people?" he asked. "The great sorcerer," they replied. "Listen, the king will ride by shortly. When he asks who owns this grain, you must answer, 'The count.' And if you don't do this, you will all meet your maker!" Finally the cat came upon a magnificent forest, where more than three hundred people were chopping down great oak trees for lumber. The cat asked again, "Who does this forest belong to, people?" "The sorcerer," they said. "Listen, the king will ride by shortly. When he asks who owns this forest, you must answer, 'The count.' And if you don't do this, you will all meet your maker!"

The cat continued on his way, and the people followed him with their eyes as he left. Because he looked so peculiar, striding along in his boots like a man, they were truly afraid of him. Soon he came to the sorcerer's castle and boldly walked right inside and up to its owner. The sorcerer looked at him with disdain and asked him what he wanted. The cat bowed low before him and said, "I have been told that you are able to change yourself into any animal you want. Now, I can believe this as far as dogs, foxes, or wolves are concerned. But what about an elephant? That seems to me quite impossible, and so I've come to see it with my own eyes." The sorcerer replied proudly, "That's a mere trifle for me," and in an instant he was an elephant. "Impressive. But what about a lion?" "Nothing to it," said the sorcerer, and became a lion right in front of the cat.

The cat pretended to be startled and cried, "Unbelievable! Impossible! I would never have even dreamed of such a thing.

"The king will ride by shortly," said the cat to the people. "When he asks who owns this grain, you must answer, 'The count.'"

But it would be more astonishing than anything else if you could make yourself into a very small animal. Say, the size of a mouse. You can obviously do more than any other sorcerer in the world, but I bet this is beyond even your reach." The sorcerer was flattered by these sweet words and said, "But of course, my dear little cat. I can do that too," and he scurried around the room as a mouse. But the cat was right behind him from his very first step, caught him in one swift pounce, and gobbled him right down.

OPPOSITE *The cat asked, "What about an elephant?" The sorcerer replied, "That's a mere trifle for me," and in an instant was an elephant.*

BELOW *The sorcerer scurried around the room as a mouse, but the cat caught him in one swift pounce and gobbled him right down.*

Meanwhile the king had continued on his tour with the princess and the count, and they came to the broad meadow. "Who does this hay belong to?" asked the king. "The count," the people called out, just as the cat had ordered. "You have quite a nice piece of land, Count," said the king. Then they came upon the vast field of grain. "Who does this grain belong to, people?" "The count." "Oh, dear Count! What great, splendid estates indeed!" And then on to the forest they went. "People, who does all this wood belong to?" "The count." The king was even more baffled and said, "You must be a very wealthy man, Count. I don't believe even I have such an abundant forest."

Then finally they came upon the castle, where the cat stood waiting at the top of the staircase. When the cat saw the carriage stop below, he leapt down and opened its door, saying, "Your Majesty, you have arrived at the castle of my master, the count, who will be delighted for the rest of his days by the honor of your visit." The king climbed down and was impressed by the grand building, which was almost as large and beautiful as his own castle. The count led the princess on his arm up the stairs into the hall, which glimmered with gold and precious stones. There she was promised to the count, who became king when her father died, with Puss 'n Boots as his prime minister.

The Golden Key

Because many fairy tales were originally shared orally, it is not always possible to tell what the Brothers Grimm changed or added. However, in this tale about a boy who discovers a treasure chest and its key, we get a glimpse of their editorial decision making. They added the story, which originated in Hesse, Germany, to their second edition in 1815, and it remained the final story in every edition thereafter. This tells us that the Grimms saw it as a meaningful summation, a key to understanding fairy tales. Folklorist Hans-Jörg Uther reminds us that just as this tale leaves the ending for us to imagine, all fairy tales evolve with each retelling, in both words and pictures, without end. They are interactive, and absorb the languages and cultures they pass through. The finale to the Grimms' collection is also a fitting finale to our book, which pairs the original tales with a variety of artistic interpretations, emphasizing the vital roles played by both the storyteller and the audience in the ongoing, vibrant life of the tales. The ending of the final tale seems to say, "You, too, are a part of the process. Take it from here." —ND

Luckily the key fit. And now we'll have to wait until he has unlocked it and raised the lid to discover the wonderful things inside.

ne winter when a deep snow lay upon the ground, a poor boy had to go out to fetch wood with his sled. Once he'd gathered the wood and loaded it up, he was so frozen with cold that he decided to make a fire to warm himself a little before going home. He began to scrape away the snow, and as he cleared a patch of earth he found a little golden key. He thought for a moment, and figured that where there's a key, there must also be a lock. So he dug around in the hard soil until he found a little iron box. "If only the key fits!" he thought. "There are sure to be precious treasures inside the box." He looked and looked, but couldn't find a keyhole. At last he found one so small he could hardly see it. He tried the key, and luckily it fit. He began turning it in the keyhole. And now we'll just have to wait until he has unlocked it all the way and raised the lid. Then we'll discover what wonderful things are tucked away inside.

Artists' Biographies

by Noel Daniel

Hanns Anker

(German, 1873–1950)

The book cover (page 14, top left) and the color lithographs of "Cinderella" (pages 103–110) are from Aschenbrödel *(Cinderella), published by A. Molling & Comp., Hannover, Germany, circa 1910.*

German artist Hanns Anker was known for his work in painting, set design, illustration, and graphic art. Schooled in his hometown, Berlin, at the Academy of Arts and the former School of Arts and Crafts, he also studied in Paris under Jean-Paul Laurens at the Académie Julian, whose alumni include, among others, Jean Arp, Marcel Duchamp, Jacques-Henri Lartigue, Henri Matisse, and Kay Nielsen. In addition to illustrating books for children and teens, Anker also produced portfolios of his drawings, and, at the turn of the twentieth century, published an influential treatise on painting and graphic design.

In the history of children's books, Anker is primarily known for the fairy tales he published in the 1910s and 1920s, copies of which are exceedingly rare today. In *Cinderella* he illustrated the original tale faithfully, eschewing overdecoration of the scenes for a clear and simple style. Yet he loosened his restraint for the frames, embellishing each image with an Art Nouveau design that looks as if it could be used for jewelry, interior furnishings, glass, or wallpaper. While the decorations are unrelated to the story's content, they instantly modernize the book design. *Cinderella* allowed Anker to meld the decorative forms of Art Nouveau with the Grimms' tale. For example, the illustrations of Cinderella's gowns show handsome Art Nouveau fabric designs. Anker's illustrations not only beautifully interpret the tale with a new twist, they are also striking examples of the new tendencies in book illustration that arose from the decorative-art movements that swept across Europe in the early twentieth century.

L. Leslie Brooke

(British, 1862–1940)

The watercolors and drawings of "The Golden Goose" (pages 214–221) are from The Golden Goose Book, *published by Frederick Warne & Co., London, 1905.*

Born in Birkenhead, England, Leonard Leslie Brooke was one of the most successful British illustrators of the early twentieth century, along with Randolph Caldecott, Kate Greenaway, Beatrix Potter, and Arthur Rackham, delighting audiences with his humorous, whimsical illustrations. His illustrations of "The Golden Goose," in which a lowly simpleton becomes a hero by tickling the funny bone of a princess previously unable to laugh, beautifully encapsulate his playful irreverence and touching charm. Brooke even sneaks a joke book, *The Boke of Joke* [sic], into one of his illustrations, on page 218, which the king is evidently using to try to make his daughter laugh. In this one detail we see how far children's books had come in England by the turn of the twentieth century. Just half a century earlier, the joke book's frivolous contents would have been considered unwholesome for children and substituted with genteel morality tales. Even the suitability of fairy tales was heavily

PAGE **292** *"Sleeping Beauty," from Heinrich Lefler and Joseph Urban's fairy-tale calendar, 1905.*

debated, as was whether children should be permitted to read for recreation and enjoyment. But Brooke came of age as an illustrator when the straitlaced and prim children's books of the Victorian era were a thing of the past. It was a time, according to historian Julia Briggs, rife with subversive parodies of the now unfashionable and square morality tales. The plurality of meaning within the Grimms' tales—from naughty to nice—was now being fully explored by their illustrators.

A prodigious artist from an early age, Brooke graduated from the Royal Academy of Arts in London, and first came to prominence upon the successful publication of *Nursery Rhyme Book* in 1897. The book's editor, Andrew Lang, was an important Scottish collector of folklore and myth who released twelve volumes of popular fairy tales, starting with *The Blue Fairy Book* in 1889. Brooke became a prodigy of the publisher Frederick Warne, whose successful children's books helped bring the children's book industry to prominence in England. (Warne published the first books of Brooke's contemporary Walter Crane, and published Beatrix Potter's Peter Rabbit stories for forty years.) Brooke also wrote and illustrated popular books of verse, including *Johnny Crow's Garden* (1903) and *Johnny Crow's Party* (1907), which were part of the trend of nonsense books that flourished at the time.

Walter Crane
(British, 1845–1915)
The book cover (page 11, top left) and the color engravings of "The Frog Prince" (pages 23–30) are from The Frog Prince, *published by George Routledge and Sons, London, 1874.*

Walter Crane was a British artist and designer who influenced generations of illustrators well into the twentieth century with his innovative children's books. Harnessing the design principles of the Arts and Crafts movement, Crane embraced children's books for their potential to advance the art of book design. He was a master of his craft and a relentless experimenter, intermingling text, decoration, and image to recast children's books as aesthetically unified and carefully planned.

A native of Liverpool, Crane apprenticed with the well-known engraver William James Linton. By twenty, he had produced his first toy books of nursery rhymes with Edmund Evans, a master printer at the cutting edge of color technology. Their immediate success confirmed the public's appetite for high-quality, affordable children's books. They proceeded with a string of nearly forty publications in a Pre-Raphaelite style, beginning with *The Frog Prince* and including *Cinderella* (1873), *Beauty and the Beast* (1874), *Jack and the Beanstalk* (1875), and *Little Red Riding Hood* (1875). In his lifetime, Crane would illustrate scores of books for children and adults, including the classic 1882 book *Household Stories from the Collection of the Brothers Grimm*, with a translation by his sister Lucy Crane.

While Crane illustrated books throughout his life, his prolific output of exquisitely designed and inexpensive children's books between 1865 and 1875 most dramatically changed the way books were conceived and produced for children. A devoted proponent of the Arts and Crafts movement with William Morris, Crane spearheaded a generation of artists whose ideas about book design were as influential as their illustrations, and with the dramatic advances in publishing in the UK, he was able to put his ideas to the test. For Crane, according to historian Susan E. Meyer, the entire bookmaking process encapsulated larger ideas about the role of high-quality decorative arts in everyday life—ideas that were the ideological backbone of the Arts and Crafts movement, and later an important part of Art Nouveau and Art Deco.

As both a designer and an artist, Crane drew inspiration from many different sources, including from the intricate handcraft of medieval illuminated books, Japanese color woodblock printing, early Italian Renaissance painters, and the avant-garde Pre-Raphaelites. As historian William Feaver has noted, the scene around the dinner table in "The Frog Prince" (pages 26–27) reflects this medley of influences, from the suggestion of Botticelli in the princess to Neoclassicism in the furnishings to the sideboard's blue-and-white Japanese-style plates. Indeed, Crane was active in other areas of the decorative arts, including wallpaper and tapestry design, stained glass, and textiles. Crane also founded the Art Workers Guild of 1884. Other notable books illustrated by Crane include Oscar Wilde's *The Happy Prince and Other Tales* (1888) and his acclaimed *The Faerie Queene* (1895–1897) by Edmund Spenser.

George Cruikshank

(British, 1792–1878)

The color lithograph of "The Shoemaker and the Elves" (page 161) is a reprint of an 1823 black-and-white illustration by Cruikshank from the book Grimms' Fairy Tales to Which Is Added Grimms' Goblins, *published by Worthington Co., New York, 1888.*

A native of London, George Cruikshank is remembered as the most gifted illustrator of nineteenth-century England. An ebullient talent and witty caricaturist, Cruikshank created thousands upon thousands of cartoons that deftly handled a variety of themes, from politics to theater to social commentary. At a time when social and political caricatures were widely circulated, Cruikshank's many images were both popular and influential. By the 1820s he began illustrating books, leaving an indelible mark on the history of book illustration when he drew images for the first English translation of the Grimms' fairy tales, a two-volume publication entitled *German Popular Stories* (1823–1826).

Featuring twenty-two lively, humorous illustrations, the book was an instant phenomenon and proved a watershed moment in the history of illustrated books. It was one of the very first illustrated books of the Grimms' tales published anywhere in the world (the first illustrated edition was published in Amsterdam in 1820). It may be puzzling to readers today that fewer than two dozen wallet-sized black-and-white images announced the beginning of a boom in book illustration. Yet to many readers and artists, the thoughtful, high-octane spirit of Cruikshank's illustrations unlocked the potential of uniting text and image. The images were entertaining and dynamic, and not only illustrated the stories, but added fresh dimensions to their interpretation. According to historians, it was through Cruikshank that the Brothers Grimm recognized the power of illustrating the tales and their broader appeal as entertainment. The illustration of "The Shoemaker and the Elves" in *German Popular Stories* was reportedly one of Cruikshank's favorites.

This particular image is from an 1899 reprint of the popular 1882 book *Household Stories from the Collection of the Brothers Grimm*, illustrated by Walter Crane, to which were added color versions of Cruikshank's illustrations from his *German Popular Stories*. The new book *Grimms' Fairy Tales to Which Is Added Grimms' Goblins* was an original publishing idea, joining two beloved illustrators, and testifies to the continued popularity of Cruikshank's illustrations seventy-five years after they were created. They also speak to the publisher's desire to render the dynamism of Cruikshank's images in color as modern printing technology advanced. Over Cruikshank's lifetime, he illustrated more than eight hundred publications and was the first to illustrate Charles Dickens's books.

Elsa Dittmann

(Austrian, ca. 1905–unknown)

The silhouettes of "Little Brother and Little Sister" (page 38), "Hansel and Gretel" (page 58), "Cinderella" (page 100), "Snow White" (page 188), "Rumpelstiltskin" (page 203), "The Goose Girl" (page 228), and "Snow White and Red Rose" (page 250) are from Dittmann's book of silhouettes, Aus Grimms Märchen (From the Grimms' Fairy Tales)*, published by Konegen Verlag, Vienna, 1925.*

Austrian painter, illustrator, and silhouette artist Elsa Dittmann was adept at rendering both interior and exterior tableaux in her accomplished paper cutting. She attended the Art School for Women and Girls in her hometown of Vienna from 1920 to 1923. The school had been founded in 1897 by women artists as a private, alternative facility for women who were not allowed to matriculate at the Academy of Fine Arts, as was common throughout Europe at the time. For two years thereafter Dittmann continued her studies at Vienna's School for Arts and Crafts. In 1925, the year she finished her training, she was commissioned to illustrate twenty of the Grimms' fairy tales for the compilation *From the Grimms' Fairy Tales*, and her medium of choice was paper cutting.

Paper cutting had been used to illustrate the Grimms' tales since the mid-1850s. Popular among both men and women, it was a visual art that resonated with a broad audience. Silhouettes had been a fixture within popular culture in Europe since the 1750s, and creating them was a pastime of royalty and the leisure class, as well as folk artists, some of whom traveled from town to town entertaining customers by whipping up portraits on the spot. Fashionable and affordable, silhouettes of loved ones were ubiquitous mementos.

In the wake of this trend, some artists began to experiment with paper cuts to illustrate literary works, and as straightforward silhouettes receded in popularity with the rise of photography and photographic portraiture, paper cuts became more sophisticated, including multiple characters, backgrounds, and complex decorative elements. Some artists, according to historian Marianne Bernhard, even used other technologies in addition to scissors (or small knives) to produce the desired effect, such as lithography or woodcutting. But Dittmann's work was different. The final page of her book of the Grimms' fairy tales shows a silhouette of an elegant pair of sharp scissors cocked open, ready to take a snip. These scissors, placed next to the German word for paper cutting, *Scherenschnitte* ("scissor cuts"), tell us that Dittmann, who was returning to paper cutting well after its eighteenth- and nineteenth-century heyday, was a purist, and a close look at her work confirms her approach. She used only paper and scissors to make the images, recalling the centuries of handcraft that had defined the accessible art, a gesture that honored the appeal of fairy tales across all strata of society.

OPPOSITE *"Rapunzel," from Heinrich Lefler and Joseph Urban's fairy-tale calendar, 1905.*

Fedor Flinzer

(German, 1832–1911)

The images of "Little Brother and Little Sister" (pages 41–46) are details from a single-page color lithograph from the book Märchenpracht und Fabelscherz, Freut der Kinder junges Herz (A Parade of Tales and Fun Fables to Warm the Child's Heart)*, illustrated by Josef Emil Dolleschal, Fedor Flinzer, Gottfried Franz, Heinrich Merté, and Carl Offterdinger, published by Wilhelm Nitzschke Verlag, Stuttgart, 1881.*

German artist Fedor Flinzer was a prolific and well-known children's book illustrator who contributed artwork to hundreds of projects. Married to a niece of composer and conductor Richard Wagner, Flinzer made a name for himself as one of the most influential drawing instructors in Germany, and garnered an international reputation when he published his instructional book on drawing in 1876. An alumnus of the Dresden Academy of Fine Arts, Flinzer was beloved for his anthropomorphic and lively illustrations of animals, which are gloriously exemplified in Julius Lohmeyer's *König Nobel* (*King Nobel*) in 1886.

Flinzer's illustrations of the Grimms' fairy tales are representative of an exciting moment in children's book publishing in Germany at the end of the nineteenth century when books became large and multicolored. His colorful, beautifully executed lithographs on dense paper perfectly suited the oversize children's books being published at this time. However, while many of his contemporaries favored tightly detailed black-and-white engravings in which an architectural element, such as a castle with many rooms, framed interconnecting scenes, Flinzer shifted away from the visual vestiges of feudal power to embrace a more natural motif of intertwining branches to link progressive scenes.

Wanda Gág

(American, 1893–1946)

The drawings of "The Fisherman and His Wife" (pages 72–83) are from the book Tales from Grimm, *published by Coward-McCann, Inc., 1936.*

Award-winning American illustrator Wanda Gág released her first book in 1928, the best-selling children's classic *Millions of Cats*, which has been in print ever since. Active at a time when very few high-quality picture books by American authors existed, she is celebrated as one of the first truly great American illustrators of children's books. Gág's parents, artists themselves, were first-generation German-Bohemian immigrants. Gág was the eldest of seven children and grew up in New Ulm, Minnesota. Growing up in a predominantly German-American Midwestern town, she was surrounded by the German language, according to biographer Sara Keller, and was introduced to the Grimms' tales as a girl. After her father's death, when she was fifteen, her family turned to welfare to survive. When she was twenty-three, her mother died, and a year later, in 1917, the young artist received a coveted scholarship to the Art Students League in New York City, a school through which many artists have passed, including Georgia O'Keeffe, Jackson Pollock, Norman Rockwell, and Mark Rothko.

Gág's folk-art aesthetic and warm, expressive style appealed to a readership hungry for new material. In the first decades of the twentieth century, the most popular picture books for children were coming from Europe, where the traditions of illustration, design, printing, and art training were deeply entrenched. As historian Susan E. Meyer has noted, because these books were not yet protected by U.S. copyrights, American publishers simply reprinted them. However, as American print technology and distribution were fortified after World War I, the children's book market expanded, and American publishers were on the hunt for homegrown talent. After art school, Gág, an accomplished lithographer, began exhibiting her work, which drew the attention of a children's book editor and an invitation to publish. After the success of *Millions of Cats*, Gág continued to publish original stories, and between 1936 and 1946, she illustrated and translated three volumes of the Grimms' fairy tales in homage to their influence on her career. Sadly, Gág's promising career was cut short by cancer, from which she died at age fifty-three.

A talented painter, illustrator, and engraver, German artist Rudolf Geißler devoted most of his career to illustrating the Grimms' fairy tales. He studied art in his hometown of Nuremberg, then in Leipzig, and later in Dresden under the tutelage of legendary nineteenth-century illustrator Ludwig Richter. Illustrated broadsides such as Geißler's of "The Bremen Town Musicians" were important predecessors to the comic strip and were themselves descendants of serial woodcuts, which scholars typically date to as early as the thirteenth century.

Geißler created illustrations for one of the most important and successful publishers of inexpensive broadsides, Braun & Schneider in Munich. For fifty years beginning in 1848, Braun & Schneider published illustrated broadsides called the Münchener Bilderbogen (Munich Broadsides) in a range of styles, from protocartoons to elaborate and highly detailed illustrations. Unlike their competitors, they hired fine artists like Geißler to do them. Braun & Schneider used a woodcut technique to print the broadsides, and Geißler, a talented engraver, was well suited for the process.

Rudolf Geißler

(German, 1834–1906)

The illustrations of "The Bremen Town Musicians" (pages 138–143) are from the hand-colored broadside Die Bremer Stadtmusikanten *(*The Bremen Town Musicians*), number 1045, book 44, of the Münchener Bilderbogen series, published by Braun & Schneider, Munich, 1892.*

Fanny and Cécile Hensel

(German, 1857–1891 and 1858–1926)

The book cover (page 11, top right) and the silhouettes of "The Frog Prince" (page 20) and "Rumpelstiltskin" (page 200) are from Ins Märchenland *(*Into the Fairy-Tale Land*), published by B. Behr's Verlag, Berlin and Leipzig, 1879.*

Sisters Fanny and Cécile Hensel were grand-nieces of the German composer and performer Felix Mendelssohn. According to the German Silhouette Society, it was Fanny and Cécile's aunt Luise Hensel (a poet, religious teacher, and one-time love interest of Clemens Brentano) who first introduced them to paper cutting. Their paper cutting was a hobby and they published little, but their intricate and sophisticated style shows that they mastered the medium despite never receiving a formal art education. In 1879, a few years before they both married, they created *Into the Fairy-Tale Land*, a small book featuring twelve elegant silhouettes of the Grimms' fairy tales, each accompanied by a brief text. Please see the Elsa Dittmann entry for more on the history of paper cutting.

Divica Landrová
(Czech, 1908–1982)
The color images of "Little Red Riding Hood" (pages 126–135) are from the book Rotkäppchen (Little Red Riding Hood)*, designed by J. A. Novotný, with German text by Lotte Elsnerová, and published by Artia, Prague, 1959.*

Czech artist Divica Landrová was an illustrator, graphic designer, and painter who lived and worked in Prague. In 1929 she graduated from Prague's School of Applied Arts, and during her formative years as an artist, she traveled to France, Yugoslavia, and Germany. By the 1940s, she was illustrating children's books. According to the *Lexikon der Kinder- und Jugendliteratur* (*Lexicon of Children's and Young Adult Literature*), it was a time of tremendous interest in children's literature in her country, and the first decades of the twentieth century saw an impressive rise in the number of public libraries, publishers, and magazines dedicated to the subject. Children's literature continued to flourish between the world wars, and every possible kind of literature for children was released, from adventure and detective tales, to fairy tales and folklore, to magical tales, moral tales, and poetry. It was against this background that Landrová first entered the art world, where she remained active for the next twenty years.

By the 1950s, Landrová was collaborating on animated films of modern fairy tales, including the color film *Kde je Míša* (*Where Is Misa*) in 1954. Landrová continued to illustrate children's books through the 1950s and early 1960s, publishing two books in German, *Rotkäppchen* (*Little Red Riding Hood*) in 1959 and *Aschenbrödel* (*Cinderella*) in 1960. In *Little Red Riding Hood*, featured in this book, Landrová sets silhouettes against layers of white and gray, a move that demonstrates the influence of early animated film. Although documentation of Landrová's activities is scarce, she appears to have been inspired by the innovative silhouette films of acclaimed German animator Lotte Reiniger, who made over forty films between 1919 and 1980.

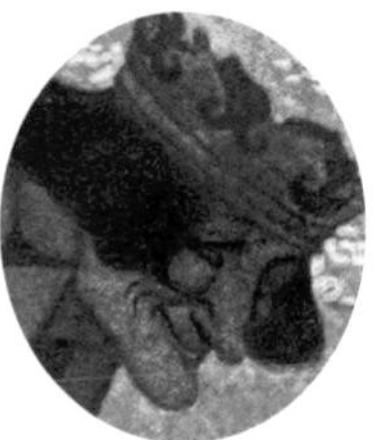

Heinrich Lefler and Joseph Urban
(Austrian, 1863–1919, and Austrian-American, 1872–1933)
The color halftone prints of "Sleeping Beauty" (page 292), "Rapunzel" (page 299), "The Goose Girl"

(page 304), "Swan, hold fast" (page 311; an adaptation of "The Golden Goose") and "Snow White" (page 317) are details from Lefler and Urban's 1905 calendar featuring illustrations of the work of the Brothers Grimm, Hans Christian Andersen, Ludwig Bechstein, and the poet Ludwig Fulda, published by Munk, Vienna, 1904.

Austrian artists Heinrich Lefler and Joseph Urban were two of the most important figures to emerge from Vienna's thriving Art Nouveau scene at the turn of the twentieth century. Lefler studied at the Academy of Fine Arts in Vienna and Munich and worked as a book illustrator, set and costume designer, and artistic adviser for opera and theater. Urban was a well-respected and prolific illustrator, set designer, and architect who also studied at the Academy of Fine Arts in Vienna. Both were among a group of important Viennese artists who rejected conservative trends in art in favor of the burgeoning international Art Nouveau style. In 1900 Lefler and Urban founded a collective of artists called the Hagenbund.

That same year Gustav Mahler appointed Lefler head set designer of the Vienna Court Opera (now the Vienna State Opera). Three years later Lefler took on a similar role at the world-renowned Vienna Burgtheater. He also held a professorship at the Academy of Fine Arts in Vienna, beating out Gustav Klimt for the post. Urban migrated to the United States in 1911, first becoming the art director of the Boston Opera Company, then designing Ziegfeld Follies productions on Broadway, and from 1914 until his death in 1933 working as head set designer for the Metropolitan Opera. Nearly all of his architectural projects have been destroyed, including the 1920s Ziegfeld Theater. Notable surviving works include the Hearst Magazine Building (built in 1926–1927) and the main building of The New School (1929–1930), both in New York City. A loyal supporter of Urban, newspaper titan William Randolph Hearst hired him to be art director and set designer for many of Hearst's Hollywood movies.

Lefler and Urban collaborated on many projects during their time together in Vienna, including the illustrations for their 1905 fairy-tale calendar. Their ornate imagery melds their interest in architecture, interior design, and costume design with Romantic tropes that were popular in fairy-tale illustration at the end of the nineteenth century, such as medieval castles and chivalric princes.

Herbert Leupin

(Swiss, 1916–1999)

The book cover (page 17, top right) and the color lithographs of "Puss 'n Boots" (pages 279–284) are from Der gestiefelte Kater (Puss 'n Boots). *The color lithographs of "Sleeping Beauty" (pages 175–180) are from the book* Dornröschen (Sleeping Beauty)*, and the color lithographs of "Mother Holle" (pages 116–121) are from the book* Frau Holle (Mother Holle)*. Published by Globi Verlag, Zurich, 1946, 1948, and 1949, respectively.*

Herbert Leupin was an award-winning poster artist from Switzerland who also published a series of illustrated books of the Grimms' fairy tales. Leupin produced one thousand posters over a forty-year period beginning in the 1930s, ranging in style from humorous to childlike to modern. Interested in art from an early age, Leupin studied graphic design at the Basel School of Applied Arts as a teenager, and then in Paris at the graphic-design school of Paul Colin, the renowned poster artist who helped launch Josephine Baker. The 1940s proved to be a prolific decade for Leupin, who, like some of his contemporaries, by this time was working in a Surrealist style that came to be known as magical realism.

Leupin's love of anthropomorphizing animals in his advertising campaigns caught the eye of publishers, and between 1944 and 1949 he was commissioned to illustrate six of the Grimms' fairy tales. By the 1950s, Leupin had transitioned from lithography to the new process of offset printing. While the new faster technology was unable to reproduce the hyperrealism he favored, it enabled a less labor-intensive process and fostered improvisation, changing advertising worldwide. It was at this time that Leupin embraced cartoonlike characters that could express the humor he sought. His clients included Coca-Cola, Eptinger, Suze, Agfa, Ford, and the famous chocolatier Milka, whose mascot, a white cow, Leupin famously covered in purple spots in 1952; it has been in use ever since.

Heinrich Leutemann

(German, 1824–1905)

The color lithograph of "The Wolf and the Seven Little Goats" (page 35) is from the book Märchen-Wundergarten (Wonder Garden of Fairy Tales)*, which includes illustrations by Carl Offterdinger, E. Klimsch, and Heinrich Leutemann, published by Wilhelm Effenberger, Stuttgart, 1893.*

German artist Heinrich Leutemann was a tireless and popular nineteenth-century illustrator, watercolorist, and painter known for his books and broadsides of animals and his self-penned children's books. A graduate of the Academy of Arts in his hometown of Leipzig, Leutemann came of age as an artist when the first zoos were opening to the public and when the popularity of shows and books featuring exotic animals surged. Throughout his career, he illustrated a wide range of material, from educational books, to zoological and ethnological anthologies, to books about antiquity. Leutemann also created many animal illustrations for the multifold enterprises of his friend Carl Hagenbeck, the famous animal trainer and trader. Evidently encouraged by Leutemann, in 1907 in Hamburg Hagenbeck opened the world's first cage-free zoo, which is still in existence. The name Hagenbeck might also be familiar to circus lovers: He had recently sold his circus to an American who renamed it the Hagenbeck-Wallace Circus, which ultimately became the second-most-successful circus in America, after Ringling Bros. and Barnum & Bailey.

Books about animals became exceedingly popular in both Europe and the United States at this time, and Leutemann's were voraciously consumed. In Leutemann's fairy-tale illustrations, the animals are often given human characteristics, which was common at the time. In "The Wolf and the Seven Little Goats," for example, Leutemann dressed the mother goat in clothes, accentuating the Grimms' original text, where the goats live like a human family in a cottage, able to converse and show emotion. Although Leutemann anthropomorphizes his fairy-tale animals, the animals are still faithfully and skillfully rendered in their natural form, even under the warm glow of domestic life.

OPPOSITE *"The Goose Girl," from Heinrich Lefler and Joseph Urban's fairy-tale calendar, 1905.*

Heinrich Merté

(German, 1838–1917)

The images of "Hansel and Gretel" (pages 60–65) are from a single-page color lithograph from the book Märchenpracht und Fabelscherz, Freut der Kinder junges Herz *(*A Parade of Tales and Fun Fables to Warm the Child's Heart*), illustrated by Josef Emil Dolleschal, Fedor Flinzer, Gottfried Franz, Heinrich Merté, and Carl Offterdinger, published by Wilhelm Nitzschke Verlag, Stuttgart, 1881.*

Born in Darmstadt and later a resident of Munich, German painter Heinrich Merté was part of a generation of highly trained artists who created large-scale color illustrations for popular fairy-tale books. For Merté and others of his generation who sought careers as professional artists, the first step was attending an art academy. The nineteenth century saw a boom in the establishment of rigorous art academies across Europe, inspired by the French model. Most major cities had one, including Stuttgart, where Merté studied.

These art academies were steeped in technique and tradition, highly valuing subjects drawn from history, religious tales, myth, and literature. Yet invariably these institutions were also hotbeds of debate about how art should be made and which subjects were superior. Over the course of his lifetime, Merté witnessed profound rifts within the academic tradition as an emerging avant-garde movement challenged the formality of academic art. At the very same time that Merté painted idealized nudes against a dreamlike landscape, Édouard Manet shocked viewers with a controversial, bold version of the same subject in *The Luncheon on the Grass* (1862–1863), the first warning shot of changes to come within academic art. Merté was but one year older than innovator Paul Cézanne and two years older than Impressionist Claude Monet, who would soon champion the subjectivity of visual perception in painting.

Yet while Impressionism and subsequent avant-garde movements roiled the art world and ultimately made way for twentieth-century Modernism, fairy tales remained an electric current of inspiration for even diametrically opposed artists. While the thrill of rendering fairy tales in real-world landscapes appealed to Romantic academic painters such as Merté, the tales' rich psychological terrain and imaginative allure inspired Impressionists such as the famous German painter Max Slevogt (1868–1932), who illustrated the Grimms' tales again and again over his lifetime. By the 1920s, as most avant-gardists were avoiding clear representational forms, Surrealists were creating enigmatic fantasy worlds, no doubt drawing inspiration from the wealth of fairy-tale illustrations—which have one foot in the real world and one foot in fantasy—that had been created over the past hundred years.

Viktor Paul Mohn

(German, 1842–1911)

The color lithograph of "The Star Coins" (page 249) are from Mohn's Märchen-Strauß für Kind und Haus *(*Fairy-Tale Bouquet for Child and Home*), published by Georg Stilke, Berlin, 1882.*

Viktor Paul Mohn was a German painter, illustrator, and professor of art who studied first at the Dresden Academy of Fine Arts and then under the famous artist Ludwig Richter. Mohn's most influential book for children was his 1882 *Fairy-Tale Bouquet for Child and Home*, the first book of the Grimms' fairy tales ever to be printed entirely in color, a sign of things to come for children's books. Mohn's book features ten tales interlaced with full-page color images, decorative frames, large ornate headings, and double-page spreads, a publishing rarity at the time. The book also includes several text areas designed to look like three-dimensional scrolls (not featured in this book), creating the illusion that a reader can peel them back to step through the book's pages into a fairy-tale world. While the book was groundbreaking in its design, Mohn's tableaux testify to the past's continued allure for artists in the nineteenth century's final decades. As historian Regina Freyberger has noted, his idyllic castles, Romantic landscapes, and lush forests are reminders of this era's fascination with the real-life evidence of a medieval past, even as society raced toward modernization. Indeed, fairy tales, castles, and real life collided in Mohn's lifetime when King Ludwig II of Bavaria, nicknamed the Fairy-Tale King, built the elaborate neo-Gothic castle Neuschwanstein on the site of medieval ruins. This castle, built from 1869 to 1892, would inspire Disneyland's Sleeping Beauty Castle, built decades later and half a world away in California.

Mohn's book was not only a technical milestone, but it also presaged the future of children's books in its ambitious synthesis of text and image. Perhaps even more interestingly, *Fairy-Tale Bouquet for Child and Home* creates a participatory reading experience for children. Its large lettering, continuous imagery, and three-dimensional-scroll effect invite children to engage with the book. One can easily imagine a child actively exploring the images while listening to an adult's reading of the text. The scroll effect, in particular, suggests not a distant fairy-tale world, but an immersive fantasy world right behind the page that one could easily pass into, like in *Alice in Wonderland* (1865) and, later, *The Chronicles of Narnia* (1950–1956). Although they have very different styles, Mohn's experiments in intermingling text and image echo those of his British contemporary Walter Crane, whose work is also featured in this book.

Kay Nielsen

(Danish, 1886–1957)

The book cover (page 15, top right) and the watercolors with ink of "Sleeping Beauty" (page 2), "Hansel and Gretel" (page 8), "The Fisherman and His Wife" (page 16), "The Goose Girl" (page 13), "Rumpelstiltskin" (page 204), and "The Three Feathers" (page 210) are from Hansel and Gretel and Other Stories by the Brothers Grimm, *published by Doran, New York, 1925. The watercolors with ink and gilt of "The Twelve Dancing Princesses" (pages 241 and 244) are from the book* In Powder and Crinoline, *published by Hodder & Stoughton, London, 1913.*

Danish artist Kay Nielsen remains one of the most fascinating and beloved illustrators of the early twentieth century. Born in Copenhagen, Nielsen was exposed to art early through his parents; his mother was a popular dancer and actress, and his father was the director of Copenhagen's Dagmar Theater. Nielsen was a precocious illustrator and left for Paris in 1904 to study at the Académie Julian. Several years later he moved to London, where he enjoyed a period of swift and steady productivity in book illustration and stage design. In 1914 he published a collection of Scandinavian folktales entitled *East of the Sun and West of the Moon*, the first of a string of richly produced gift books that later included *Hans Christian Andersen's Fairy Tales* (1924) and *Hansel and Gretel and Other Stories by the Brothers Grimm* (1925).

Nielsen's strikingly beautiful and decorative style in pen, ink, and watercolor set him apart; he applied his watercolor densely, building layers of rich blues, reds, golds, and greens. But it was his blend of fantastical landscapes and uncanny characters that made him unique. An array of influences informed Nielsen's style, including Rococo, Japanese woodcuts, Arabic art, Art Nouveau, and Art Deco. Compelled in particular by the robust culture of book design in Art Nouveau and Art Deco, Nielsen experimented vigorously with decorative elements such as elaborate frames, endpapers, and filigree patterns. Although Nielsen won success and recognition in publishing's boom years prior to World War I, he watched his opportunities shrivel as the postwar tide retreated sharply from fantasy and expensive book production, which was no longer economically viable for publishers.

On a job invitation in 1936, Nielsen headed to the burgeoning mecca of modern fantasy, Hollywood. At first, it seemed like a perfect fit. He was hired to work on Disney's ambitious animation feature film *Fantasia* (1940), which incidentally was the movie that inspired Maurice Sendak of *Where the Wild Things Are* fame to become an illustrator. Nielsen designed the phantasmagoric segment "Night on Bald Mountain" for the film, and shortly thereafter started work on *The Little Mermaid*, but the film was aborted. Nielsen never again regained steady employment. After a hopeful but ill-fated stint at chicken farming, he spent the last years of his life painting a few murals for schools and churches in Los Angeles, where, sadly, he eventually died penniless and in obscurity, only to be rediscovered years later.

Dora Polster

(German, 1884–1958)

The illustrations of "The Wolf and the Seven Little Goats" (page 37), "Little Brother and Little Sister" (page 47), "Rapunzel" (page 48), "Cinderella" (page 105), "The Bremen Town Musicians" (page 136), "Sleeping Beauty" (page 170), "Snow White" (page 182), "Rumpelstiltskin" (page 205), and "Jorinda and Joringel" (pages 222 and 226) are from the book Deutsche Märchen gesammelt durch die Brüder Grimm (German Fairy Tales Collected by the Brothers Grimm)*, published by Langewiesche-Brandt, Ebenhausen bei München, Germany, 1911.*

Dora Polster was born in Magdeburg, Germany, and excelled from an early age as a painter, watercolorist, graphic designer, and illustrator. In 1911 Polster was commissioned to illustrate a book of Grimms' fairy tales. She chose to create images that resembles silhouettes, but which are in fact brush drawings.

Polster's many images in black and the occasional cornflower blue show her versatility as a an artist, and also the influence of Art Nouveau in her preference for ornamentation and a flat frieze style, such as in the opening images for this book's "Rapunzel" (page 48), "Sleeping Beauty" (page 170), and "Jorinda and Joringel" (page 222). While silhouettes of the Grimms' fairy tales were often published in books with scant text, the book to which Polster contributed her illustrations was more ambitious: Her images are incorporated directly into the pages alongside the text of the tales. Polster moved in literary as well as painterly circles in Munich, according to historian Ottilie Thiemann-Stoedtner, and among her acquaintances was the celebrated poet Rainer Maria Rilke. She was married to the writer Hans Brandenburg, whose work she also illustrated.

Arthur Rackham

(British, 1867–1939)

The watercolor with pen and ink of "Jorinda and Joringel" (page 225) and the silhouette of "The Bremen Town Musicians" (page 140) are from the book The Fairy Tales of the Brothers Grimm, *translated by Mrs. Edgar Lucas, published by Constable, London, 1909. The silhouettes of "Sleeping Beauty" (pages 1, 18, 172–174, 178, 181, 320) and "Cinderella" (page 319) are from the books* Sleeping Beauty *and* Cinderella, *adapted by C. S. Evans from the Grimms' fairy tales, published by William Heinemann, London, 1919 and 1920, respectively.*

British illustrator Arthur Rackham was a fabulously successful book illustrator in the first part of the twentieth century. He received critical acclaim and a devoted following in his lifetime, and is revered as one of the bright lights in the illustrious first decades of twentieth-century book publishing. Although Rackham had already illustrated a number of books, he burst onto the publishing scene in 1900 with the popular publication of *Fairy Tales of the Brothers Grimm*, variations of which he would publish over many years. Five years later he illustrated Washington Irving's *Rip Van Winkle* to rave reviews. These successes were followed in 1909 by another version of the Grimm book, with new illustrations, a remarkable forty of which were in color. It is from this publication that the watercolor of "Jorinda and Joringel" (page 225) and the silhouette of "The Bremen Town Musicians" (page 140) are drawn. Rackham's illustrated version of *Gulliver's Travels* by Jonathan Swift followed that same year.

By this point, his reputation as the foremost illustrator in the English-speaking world was assured, and he exerted considerable influence on his contemporaries. Rackham himself is said to have drawn inspiration from fifteenth-century German artist Albrecht Dürer, among others. From elves to witches to giants, Rackham's illustrations did not shy from the dark corners of fairy-tale forests or the eerie beauty of magical landscapes. The gnarled, mysterious trees; grimacing archetypes; and earthy hues of mustard, browns, and muted reds caught the imaginations of decades of readers and led to commercial success, even to the consternation of some disapproving adults who thought his gothic style might be too vexing to children. Highly sought after, Rackham illustrated many of the greats of the burgeoning field of children's literature, including J. M. Barrie's *Peter Pan in Kensington Gardens* (1906), Lewis Carroll's *Alice's Adventures in Wonderland* (1907), plays by Shakespeare, and Charles Dickens's *A Christmas Carol* (1915). In the 1920s Rackham illustrated two extended adaptations by C. S. Evans, *Sleeping Beauty* and *Cinderella*, all in silhouettes. Selections from these works are included in this book.

Rackham's career as a book illustrator dovetailed with the emergence of the halftone printing process, which rendered exceptional detail and the full tonal range of an image, and suited his detailed and dramatic imagery impeccably. His imitators, of which there were many, eventually passed into mature styles of their own, but for generations of readers, Rackham's prolific pen and individual style loomed large, as indelible as the stories themselves.

Käthe Reine
(German, 1894–1976)
The book cover (page 17, top left) and the silhouettes of "The Brave Little Tailor" (page 84), "Cinderella" (page 112), "Mother Holle" (page 114), "Little Red Riding Hood" (page 124), "Snow White" (page 193), and "The Star Coins" (page 246) are from Grimms Märchen *(*Grimms' Fairy Tales*), published by Volksverein-Verlag, Mönchengladbach, Germany, 1925.*

Artist Käthe Reine was one of the most important silhouette artists in Europe between the two world wars. She grew up in Rostock, Germany, and spent most of her life there. A talented artist from a young age, Reine ventured to Düsseldorf in the mid-1910s to further her art education. Although women were not yet allowed admission to Düsseldorf's prestigious Art Academy, she did attend the city's School of Applied Arts, honing her talent as a painter, watercolorist, and silhouette artist. In the difficult economic climate following World War I, Reine made use of her training in applied art by working at a fashion house, creating designs for home furnishings.

It was during this time that two large books of Reine's accomplished silhouettes were published: a collection of the Grimms' fairy tales in 1925 and a book of tales by Hans Christian Andersen one year later. These books cemented her place as one of the most important silhouette artists of fairy tales of her generation. During the Nazi occupation in Germany, however, Reine struggled to find outlets to publish her silhouettes, since the Nazis had banned the magazines that had previously published them. After World War II she found sporadic work in her hometown of Rostock in the newly formed communist East Germany. According to the Rostock Women's Initiative, although Reine never fully found firm footing amid the changing artistic preferences of the new government, she continued to paint for the rest of her life.

Oswald Sickert
(German-British, 1828–1885)
The illustrations of "Tom Thumb's Travels" (pages 164–169) are from the hand-colored broadside Der kleine Däumerling *(*Tom Thumb*), number 64, book 3, of the Münchener Bilderbogen series, published by Braun & Schneider, Munich, 1851.*

German-British painter and illustrator Oswald Sickert was born into an artistic family in a small town outside of Hamburg, Germany. He received his art education first at the Copenhagen Academy and then in Munich and Paris before he emigrated in 1868 to London, where he ultimately achieved success in the English school of painting. Early in his career, in 1851, just three years into Braun & Schneider's ambitious venture to hire

OPPOSITE *Illustration from the fairy tale "Swan, hold fast" ("*Schwan, kleb an,*" 1847, by German writer Ludwig Bechstein, adapted from the Grimms' "The Golden Goose"), from Heinrich Lefler and Joseph Urban's fairy-tale calendar, 1905.*

highly trained artists to illustrate inexpensive broadsides for a broad public, the Munich-based publishers commissioned Sickert to illustrate the Grimms' tale "Tom Thumb's Travels."

As a serious artist with a bright future who had been schooled in the academic tradition, Sickert was perfect for the task. However, for this fairy-tale project, he relaxed his style and imbued his illustrations of the mischievous Tom Thumb with a humorous touch that makes these images very different from the landscape oil paintings he became known for. In this broadside he embraced the dramatic appeal of the diminutive little boy, showing him scrambling up the back of a bewildered woman, catching his breath while sitting on a sausage, and singing mightily on the dinner table, all creative additions to the story of Sickert's own invention. His son Walter Richard Sickert (1860–1942) would become one of England's finest Impressionist painters.

Jessie Willcox Smith

(American, 1863–1935)

The oil and charcoal painting of "The Goose Girl" (page 235) is from A Child's Book of Stories *by Penrhyn W. Coussens, published by Duffield & Company, New York, 1911.*

Known for her idyllic, gentle images of childhood, artist Jessie Willcox Smith was one of the leading American illustrators of the early twentieth century. Her natural talent and persistence, combined with a perfect storm of artistic and social developments, led to a flourishing career and popular recognition when few other women illustrators achieved prominence. Active for more than four decades, she illustrated nearly two hundred magazine covers; more than sixty books, including Louisa May Alcott's *Little Women* (1915) and Charles Kingsley's *The Water-Babies* (1916); and numerous calendars and posters.

Smith first enrolled in art school in 1884 at a time when more and more art institutes in the United States were providing equal opportunities for women. By 1885 she had been accepted to the country's oldest art academy, the prestigious Pennsylvania Academy of the Fine Arts in Philadelphia, where she studied with preeminent painter Thomas Eakins. Yet, according to biographer Edward Nudelman, it wasn't until nearly ten years later, when she took classes from Howard Pyle, the most famous living illustrator in America and a talented teacher, that she discovered her own style.

Under Pyle's enthusiastic tutelage, Smith—along with Maxfield Parrish, N. C. Wyeth, and others—became part of an influential movement to elevate the quality of illustrated books in America, and to dispel the prejudice against illustration as a fine art. Improvements in printing, the rise of magazines—and thus jobs for artists—and a growing children's book market helped advance their mission. Smith contributed illustrations to many magazines during her lifetime, such as *Ladies' Home Journal*, *Scribner's*, and *St. Nicholas*, but to none more than *Good Housekeeping*, whose covers she illustrated every month from 1918 to 1933. Smith was also a talented painter. She worked fluently in oil and preferred painting by natural light, the luminous effect of which can be seen in "The Goose Girl." As historian Michael Patrick Hearn has noted, her oil paintings resemble those of Impressionist Mary Cassatt, another pioneering woman artist of this era who was also a student at the Academy of the Fine Arts in Philadelphia.

Otto Speckter
(German, 1807–1871)
The images of "Rapunzel" (pages 51–57) are from the hand-colored broadside Rapunzel, *originally released as number 216, book 9, of the Münchener Bilderbogen series, published by Braun & Schneider, Munich, 1857.*

Born in Hamburg, German artist Otto Speckter was a versatile and imaginative lithographer and book illustrator. In children's literature, he is especially well known for his animal illustrations, but he was also skilled at creating inventive single-page engravings like that of "Rapunzel," where he embedded beautifully detailed scenes into an architectural frame such as a castle. Speckter's framing devices often reflected the medieval and Gothic architecture that existed in many European towns of his day. While other artists used this technique also, Speckter's architecture stands out for being both familiar and accessible, and his human figures are especially expressive. The images are full of delightful details available to careful viewers, and were important contributions to the Münchener Bilderbogen, Braun & Schneider's popular broadside series, in the 1850s and 1860s.

In the history of illustration, Speckter's dense, ornate engravings represent one trend of a mainstream publishing industry that was rapidly expanding in the late nineteenth century. On the other side of the spectrum was the simpler protocomic style seen in Rudolf Geißler's illustrations of "The Bremen Town Musicians" (pages 138–143) and Oswald Sickert's images of "Tom Thumb's Travels" (pages 164–169). Academically trained artists like Speckter, Geißler, and Sickert often switched from one style to the other, familiar with both traditions: The protocomic style, for example, can be traced back for centuries in popular woodcuts and tapestries, while, according to historian Regina Freyberger, the carefully plotted interweaving imagery of the more ornate style echoes the parabolic style of medieval and Renaissance religious painting and stained glass.

In Speckter's day, both styles were very popular and reached a broad audience through the inexpensive Bilderbogen series, whose mission was to bring great images by great artists to the people. These two different styles together represent the state of fairy-tale illustration in the late-nineteenth-century industrializing world. The protocartoon style forecasts cartoon strips and comic books, while Speckter's style shown here is an approach steeped in tradition and training. At the close of the nineteenth century, these two styles of illustration—the high art of the past and the people's art of the future—coalesced momentarily and easily around the Grimms' tales.

Gustav Süs
(German, 1823–1881)
The book cover (page 10, top left) and the hand-colored lithographs of "The Hare and the Hedgehog" (pages 268–274) are from Het Wettloopen tüschen den Haasen un den Swinegel up der Buxtehuder Heid (The Race Between the Hare and the Hedgehog on the Buxtehude Heath)*, published by Arnz & Comp., Düsseldorf, Germany, 1855.*

German artist Gustav Süs was born eleven years after the Brothers Grimm first published their fairy tales, and his life spans the great burst of activity in children's book illustration that followed in their wake. As a young artist, Süs studied painting in the Grimms' hometown of Kassel at the Academy of Art and then later in Frankfurt am Main. He wrote as well as contributed illustrations to more than forty books and is considered one of the most important illustrators of children's books featuring animals in the nineteenth century. While many of his contemporaries embraced Romanticism, Süs focused primarily on illustrating animals in a warm, anthropomorphic style that foreshadowed their portrayal in children's books of the late nineteenth century and throughout the twentieth century. He often created secret, private worlds inhabited by unique animal personalities, yet featuring the familiar domestic trappings of the human world. It was a style that did not catch on in his day, and that all but died out in the nineteenth century's second half, only to later reemerge with great success among twentieth-century illustrators such as the British artist Beatrix Potter, author of the many best-selling Peter Rabbit books.

In "The Hare and the Hedgehog," his exquisite line drawings are made even more lifelike by color, which, according to Regina Freyberger, was applied by hand, likely by women and children in workshops as was often done in the days before color printing. He also wrote his own fairy tales, a practice that was in its infancy among illustrators, and that would bloom in the late nineteenth century and throughout the twentieth in the sophisticated literary endeavors of Ludwig Bechstein, Erich Kästner, and legions of writers and illustrators worldwide who have penned their own tales.

Gustaf Tenggren

(Swedish-American, 1896–1970)

The tempera drawings of "The Devil with the Three Golden Hairs" (pages 146–157) and "Snow White and Rose Red" (pages 253–265) are from the books Tenggren's The Giant with the Three Golden Hairs *and* Tenggren's Snow White and Rose Red, *respectively, both published by Simon and Schuster, New York, 1955.*

The long and diverse career of Swedish-American artist Gustaf Tenggren took him from the golden age of illustration (circa 1890 to 1920) deep into the heart of the first animated feature films produced in Hollywood, and on to a successful career illustrating best-selling children's books in the United States. Born in 1896 in the small town of Magra in western Sweden, Tenggren was recognized early for his talent, and he received a scholarship to study at the Valand School of Fine Arts in Gothenburg. In 1917, he was hired to illustrate the popular annual of Scandinavian folktales *Bland tomtar och troll* (*Among Gnomes and Trolls*), succeeding Swedish legend John Bauer. By the early 1920s Tenggren made his way to New York City, where he began publishing a string of children's books, including *The Grimms' Fairy Tales* (1922) and *Mother Goose* (1929), and receiving lucrative commercial jobs.

Tenggren's richly detailed style recalls the earlier heyday of European shining stars of children's book illustration, notably Arthur Rackham and Kay Nielsen. It was this style that the Walt Disney Company sought to evoke in its first animated feature film, *Snow White and the Seven Dwarfs*, and in 1936 Disney hired Tenggren as an art director. For the next three years, he worked on Disney animations including *Pinocchio* (1940), *Fantasia* (1940), and *Bambi* (1942), all in all contributing to seven Disney films before leaving in 1939. Tenggren's departure from Disney marked a dramatic shift in his drawing style. Although he had originally been hired for his Rackham-esque European style, he made a 180-degree turn and embraced a simpler, straightforward approach that shaped the rest of his career. He joined the new mass-market publishing venture Little Golden Books in 1942, the series' inaugural year. He would contribute nearly twenty books over the next twenty years to the series, beginning with *The Poky Little Puppy* (1942), of which more than fifteen million copies have been sold. It was during this time that he drew the illustrations for the series' *Tenggren's The Giant with the Three Golden Hairs* and *Tenggren's Snow White and Rose Red.* Based on the sheer volume of millions-selling titles Tenggren has contributed to, he is, according to some historians, the best-selling Swedish artist of all time. Tenggren remained prolific well into the 1940s and 1950s, illustrating a slew of books for children and youth.

Joseph Urban
(Austrian-American, 1872–1933)
See Heinrich Lefler

Franz Wacik
(Austrian, 1883–1938)
The color halftone prints and the silhouettes of "The Brave Little Tailor" (pages 87–98) are from Das tapfere Schneiderlein (The Brave Little Tailor)*, published by Gerlach & Wiedling, Vienna, 1915.*

In 1911 Austrian artist Franz Wacik was twenty-eight when he joined the legendary Art Nouveau collective the Viennese Secession, which had been founded in 1897. The Secessionists profoundly shaped his artistic endeavors for the rest of his life, and he remained a member until his death twenty-seven years later. The diversity of Wacik's interests, which included poster design, graphic art, book illustration and design, stage design, and frescoes, reflects the Secessionists' wide range of engagement in applied art. Born in Vienna, Wacik studied at that city's School for Arts and Crafts with Alfred Roller, one of the founding members of the Vienna Secessionists along with Gustav Klimt, and later at Vienna's Academy of Fine Arts, where he studied painting with Art Nouveau great Heinrich Lefler, who is also featured in this book.

Wacik found his artistic home in book illustration early, and created images for the fairy tales of the Brothers Grimm and Hans Christian Andersen, as well as for the books of E. T. A. Hoffmann, Hugo von Hofmannsthal, and others. An accomplished humorist, Wacik also created hundreds of political cartoons for the satirical Viennese magazine *Die Muskete* (*The Musket*). He had his first exhibition in 1910 at the Secession building, where nine years later he exhibited his witty illustrations for his *The Brave Little Tailor*, featured in this book. By 1929 Wacik, like others, was experimenting with animated short films, and he created an animation of *The Brave Little Tailor*. Walt Disney, too, had been experimenting with the medium since the early 1920s, and in 1937 took inspiration from the Brothers Grimm and released America's first color animated feature film, the enormously popular *Snow White and the Seven Dwarfs*, which marked the beginning of Disney's classic cartoon series that is still very much alive today.

Wanda Zeigner-Ebel
(German, unknown)
The book cover (page 14, top right) and the color lithographs of "Snow White" (pages 184–199) are from Sneewittchen *(*Snow White*), published by Gerhard Stalling, Oldenburg, Germany, 1920.*

German artist Wanda Zeigner-Ebel illustrated two books of fairy tales in the 1920s, *Snow White* and *Andersens Märchen* (*Hans Christian Andersen's Fairy Tales*). Zeigner-Ebel was part of a new wave of artists commissioned to illustrate single-tale books as the children's book market in Europe continued to expand and full-color books became more affordable to print and to purchase. Like the pioneering British illustrator Walter Crane before her, Zeigner-Ebel blended text and image in an unequivocally modern approach to bookmaking whose roots reached back to the Arts and Crafts movement. While scant biographical information is available about Zeigner-Ebel, her illustrations hint at her method and purpose. Gone is any suggestion of the medieval past that seduced Romantic artists in the nineteenth century. Instead, a decidedly naive folk style is celebrated. She saturates clothes, nature, and the pages' borders with colorful patterns and earthy decoration resembling Russian folk art. This is particularly evident in the scene of Snow White surrounded by the dwarfs, who are as simply and warmly depicted as Russian nesting dolls (pages 190–191). The influence of the period's burgeoning Russian folk art is also apparent in the interior decoration of the dwarfs' home, in which the little men are depicted as resourceful folk artists who have lovingly decorated their immediate environment.

If, in general, the Brothers Grimm believed that fairy tales were expressions of cultural identity, then Zeigner-Ebel's rendering of "Snow White" in the folk-art style of Russian peasants is astute: Seen in the context of her time, it speaks to the increasingly global circulation of artistic influence. Not only were the Grimms' tales influencing cultures beyond the German-speaking world, but German artists were absorbing artistic trends of other countries to in turn illustrate these classic German tales.

OPPOSITE *"Snow White," from Heinrich Lefler and Joseph Urban's fairy-tale calendar, 1905.*

Translator's Note

Once upon a time I counted thousands of deutsche marks in a Dresdner Bank vault with a colleague who spoke in heavy Saxon dialect; deciphered medieval German texts in rare-books rooms; and performed Schubert lieder in places as different as Moscow and Montana. These experiences stretched and challenged me, and the German literary, theatrical, and musical culture came to exercise an unexpected grip.

The Grimms occupy an iconic place in that canon, of course. Yet initially I had little sense how best to unpack these stories for today's English-speaking readers—and listeners. I leaned on my training: countless hours of living with the language, and theatrical instincts I'd honed for years. In my mind I saw fantastic animated films as I worked through these stories. They were dark, complex, and arcing versions, not the Disney films associated with the material. There is no denying the unforgiving morality or the harshness of daily life one finds in the tales. But even more striking, finally, was the full range of emotion, especially the comedy and delight of the characters and their antics.

I faced a balancing act between adherence to the original structure, and freedom with the abundant choices of English. I tried to use clear "camera angles" and to dose in narrative color as a sensory highlight. Noel Daniel and I disciplined ourselves to hold fast to the original, despite my urges to tread off the path into the magical woods. I sincerely hope readers will feel that our efforts resulted in a fresh and enjoyable translation reflecting the depth and wonder of these magnificent tales, which offer something for all ages.

Matthew R. Price
New York City

Note on the 1857 edition of *Children's and Household Tales* by the Brothers Grimm

The fairy-tale collection of the brothers Jacob (1785–1863) and Wilhelm Grimm (1786–1859) is known and cherished worldwide. But it is often forgotten that the Brothers Grimm can be counted amongst the finest humanities scholars of the nineteenth century: They also published extensive studies on legal, historical, mythological, and linguistic topics, including a comprehensive German dictionary, on which they began working in 1838. They even understood their devotion to folk literature, its fairy tales, songs, and fables, as a tribute to archaeology. So, when they first published their fairy-tale collection *Kinder- und Hausmärchen* (*Children's and Household Tales*) in 1812, they did not have a young readership in mind. However, their scientific approach, evident in the text-only layout of the book as well as the vast annotations given to each fairy tale, did not correspond to the common perception of fairy tales as entertaining children's literature. Moreover, the brutal and erotic content of some of the fairy tales was not thought suitable for a young readership. The German poet Achim von Arnim told the Brothers Grimm as much when *Kinder- und Hausmärchen* was first published, and even though the Brothers Grimm did not agree with their friend, Wilhelm Grimm revised the collected fairy tales so that the book became suitable for children. Thus, over the course of forty-five years and seven editions, up to the last one in 1857, the fairy-tale collection of the Brothers Grimm was transformed from a scientific archaeological collection of folk literature to a genuine children's book. The 1857 edition is the basis of this book.

Dr. Regina Freyberger
Art Historian
Munich, Germany

— INDEX —

Index

—IMAGE CREDITS—

Image Credits by Source

© Laura Barrett (see Image Credits by Artist for page numbers)
Photographs 2010 by the Brüder Grimm-Gesellschaft, Kassel, Germany (14, 103, 104, 106–107, 109, 110)
© Collection of Herbert Leupin, Switzerland (116–122, 175–177, 179, 180, 279–287)
The Collection of Kendra and Allan Daniel; photography by Gavin Ashworth (2, 8, 13, 16, 204, 210, 235, 244)
© **1911, 1928, 1981 Langewiesche-Brandt KG**, Ebenhausen bei München, Germany (37, 47, 48, 105, 136, 170, 182, 222, 226)
The Los Angeles Public Library (1, 15, 140, 172–174, 178, 181, 225, 295, 300, 307, 312, 316, 319, 320)
The Library of Congress [LOC] (31, 39, 51–57, 102, 137–139, 141–143, 164–169, 211, 213, 229, 237, 245, 251)
The Cotsen Children's Library, Department of Rare Books and Special Collections, Princeton University Library (292)
The Collection of Dr. Regina Freyberger (35, 86–99)
Random House Inc. (146–157: from *Tenggren's The Giant with the Three Golden Hairs* (adapted from the Brothers Grimm) by Gustaf Tenggren; and pages 253–265: from *Tenggren's Snow White and Rose Red* by Gustaf Tenggren. Both copyright © 1955 by Artists and Writers Guild Inc. and Random House Inc. Used by permission of Golden Books, an imprint of Random House Children's Books, a division of Random House Inc.)
The University of Minnesota, Children's Literature Research Collections (72–83)
The Victoria Albert Museum, London, UK/The Bridgeman Art Library (241)

Unless otherwise noted, the remaining images come from private collections.

Image Credits by Artist

HA Hanns Anker: 103, 104, 106–107, 109, 110
LB Laura Barrett, contemporary illustrator: 6, 21, 22, 28, 32, 33, 36, 49, 59, 70, 71, 85, 101, 108, 113, 115, 123, 125, 144, 145, 158, 159, 162, 163, 171, 201, 205, 206–209, 212, 223, 227, 231, 232, 236, 238, 239, 243, 248, 266, 267, 275–277, 288–291
LLB L. Leslie Brooke: 214–221
WC Walter Crane: 23–27, 29, 30
GC George Cruikshank: 161
ED Elsa Dittmann: 38, 58, 100, 188, 203, 228, 250
FF Fedor Flinzer: 41–46
WG Wanda Gág: 72–83
RG Rudolf Geißler: 138, 139, 141–143t
FCH Fanny and Cécile Hensel: 20, 200
DL Divica Landrová: 126–135
LU Heinrich Lefler and Joseph Urban: 292, 299, 304, 311, 316
HL Herbert Leupin: 116–122, 175–177, 179, 180, 279–287
HLM Heinrich Leutemann: 35
HM Heinrich Merté: 60–69
VM Viktor P. Mohn: 247, 249
KN Kay Nielsen: 2, 8, 13, 16, 204, 210, 241, 244
DP Dora Polster: 37, 47, 48, 105, 136, 170, 182, 222, 226
AR Arthur Rackham: 1, 18, 140, 172–174, 178, 181, 225, 319, 320
KR Käthe Reine: 84, 112, 114, 124, 193, 246
OS Oswald Sickert: 164–169
JWS Jessie Willcox Smith: 235
OS Otto Speckter: 51–57
GS Gustav Süs: 268–274
GT Gustaf Tenggren: 146–157, 253–265
FW Franz Wacik: 86–99
WZE Wanda Zeigner-Ebel: 183–186, 190–191, 194–199

Key: t: top; b: bottom

Silhouette Credits by Page Number

Please see center column for the key to the artists' initials; LOC is the Library of Congress. All white-on-gold silhouettes in the book are black-on-white in the original.

Page **1**: AR. *Introduction*: **6**: LB. *The Tales*: **18**: AR. *The Frog Prince*: **20**: FCH. **21, 22, 28**: LB. **31**: LOC. *The Wolf and the Seven Little Goats*: **32, 33, 36**: LB. **37**: DP. *Little Brother and Little Sister*: **38**: ED. **39**: LOC. **47**: DP. *Rapunzel*: **48**: DP. **49**: LB. *Hansel and Gretel*: **58**: ED. **59**: LB. *The Fisherman and His Wife*: **70, 71**: LB. *The Brave Little Tailor*: **84**: KR. **85**: LB. **86, 88, 93, 96, 99**: FW. *Cinderella*: **100**: ED. **101**: LB. **102**: LOC. **105**: DP. **108**: LB. **112**: KR. **113**: LB. *Mother Holle*: **114**: KR. **115, 123**: LB. *Little Red Riding Hood*: **124**: KR. **125**: LB. *The Bremen Town Musicians*: **136**: DP. **137**: LOC. **140**: AR. **143b**: LOC. *The Devil with the Three Golden Hairs*: **144, 145**: LB. *The Shoemaker and the Elves*: **158, 159**: LB. *Tom Thumb's Travels*: **162, 163**: LB. *Sleeping Beauty*: **170**: DP. **171**: LB. **172–174, 178, 181**: AR. *Snow White*: **182**: DP. **183**: WZE. **188**: ED. **193**: KR. *Rumpelstiltskin*: **200**: FCH. **201**: LB. **203**: ED. **205**: LB. *The Three Feathers*: **206–209**: LB. **211**: LOC. *The Golden Goose*: **212**: LB. **213**: LOC. *Jorinda and Joringel*: **222**: DP. **223**: LB. **226**: DP. **227**: LB. *The Goose Girl*: **228**: ED. **229**: LOC. **231, 232, 236**: LB. **237**: LOC. *The Twelve Dancing Princesses*: **238, 239, 243**: LB. **245**: LOC. *The Star Coins*: **246**: KR. **247**: VM. **248**: LB. *Snow White and Rose Red*: **250**: ED. **251**: LOC. *The Hare and the Hedgehog*: **266, 267, 275**: LB. *Puss 'n Boots*: **276, 277**: LB. *The Golden Key*: **288–291**: LB. Appendix: **319, 320**: AR.

Any credit omissions are unintentional, and appropriate credit will be given in future editions if holders of copyright contact the publisher.

About the Participants

TASCHEN editor Noel Daniel's recent books are *Magic 1400s–1950s* and *The Circus 1870s–1950s*. After graduating from Princeton University with a degree in German languages and literature, she studied media history in Berlin on a Fulbright Scholarship. She received a master's in London and was the director of a photography art gallery before becoming a book editor in 2002. She lives in Los Angeles.

Matthew R. Price has translated for leading theaters and publications in Germany and the United States. He graduated from Princeton University with highest honors in history, then studied German literature in Berlin on a DAAD Fellowship, eventually receiving his master's in opera and theater from the University of the Arts Berlin. He has since earned an MBA from Columbia University and lives in New York City.

Acknowledgments

From the Editor
I would especially like to thank my husband and collaborator, Andy Disl, one of the art directors at TASCHEN and the designer of this book, for lending this book his special touch. I would also like to give special thanks to the publisher Benedikt Taschen for his very generous support of the book and his helpful ideas to improve it.

I would like to thank Matthew Price, whom I first met twenty years ago in German class, for his intelligence, theatrical eye, and the unique touch he brought to the tales. With forty years combined experience speaking German, it was an absolute joy to delve into these tales with him. I invited Matthew to translate these stories because I felt his deep knowledge of theater history and the German language would bring alive the performative spirit of these stories and convey not only the pleasure of the original tales, but of storytelling itself.

Many thanks also to Dr. Regina Freyberger, author of the first comprehensive academic history of Grimms' fairy tale illustrations *Märchenbilder—Bildermärchen: Illustrations of the Grimms' Fairy Tales 1819–1945* (2009), who generously read my texts and offered helpful feedback and support. Special thanks also to the illustrator Laura Barrett, who so elegantly created new images to match the spirit of the vintage silhouettes. The translator would like to give special thanks to Timothy Dickinson for his historical guidance and watchful eye.

Many thanks also to:
Doug Adrianson, Alex and Bruce Bacon, Tyler and Wilson Bacon, Madeline Bryant, Tanja da Silva, Sara Duke, Kendra and Allan Daniel, Margery and Tom Daniel, Perry Daniel, Colin Enriquez, Sherri Feldman, Deborah Foley, Craig Gaines, Charles Greene, Harald Hellmann, Jessica Hoffmann, Andrea L. Immel, Sybille Jagusch, Victoria and Tom Kennedy, Florian Kobler, Monika Kohlberger, Bernhard Lauer, Charles R. Leupin, Dave Martinez, Andrea Mayer, Jörn Münkner, Kathrin Murr, Jennifer Patrick, AnnaLee Pauls, the Price family, Niklas Rahmlow, Emma Roberts, Jessica Sappenfield, Fran Seegull, Bernhard Schmitz, Sharon Shay Sloan, the Vieregg family, Steffen Wedepohl, Monika Wiedenmann.

Imprint

To stay informed about upcoming TASCHEN titles, please request our magazine at www.taschen.com/magazine or write to TASCHEN, Hohenzollernring 53, D-50672 Cologne, Germany; contact@taschen.com; Fax: +49-221-254919. We will be happy to send you a free copy of our magazine, which is filled with information about all of our books.

Design: Sense/Net Art Direction, Andy Disl and Birgit Eichwede, Cologne www.sense-net.net
Art Direction: Andy Disl and Noel Daniel, Los Angeles
Editorial coordination: Kathrin Murr, Cologne
Production coordination: Horst Neuzner, Cologne

Printed in China
ISBN 978-3-8365-2672-2

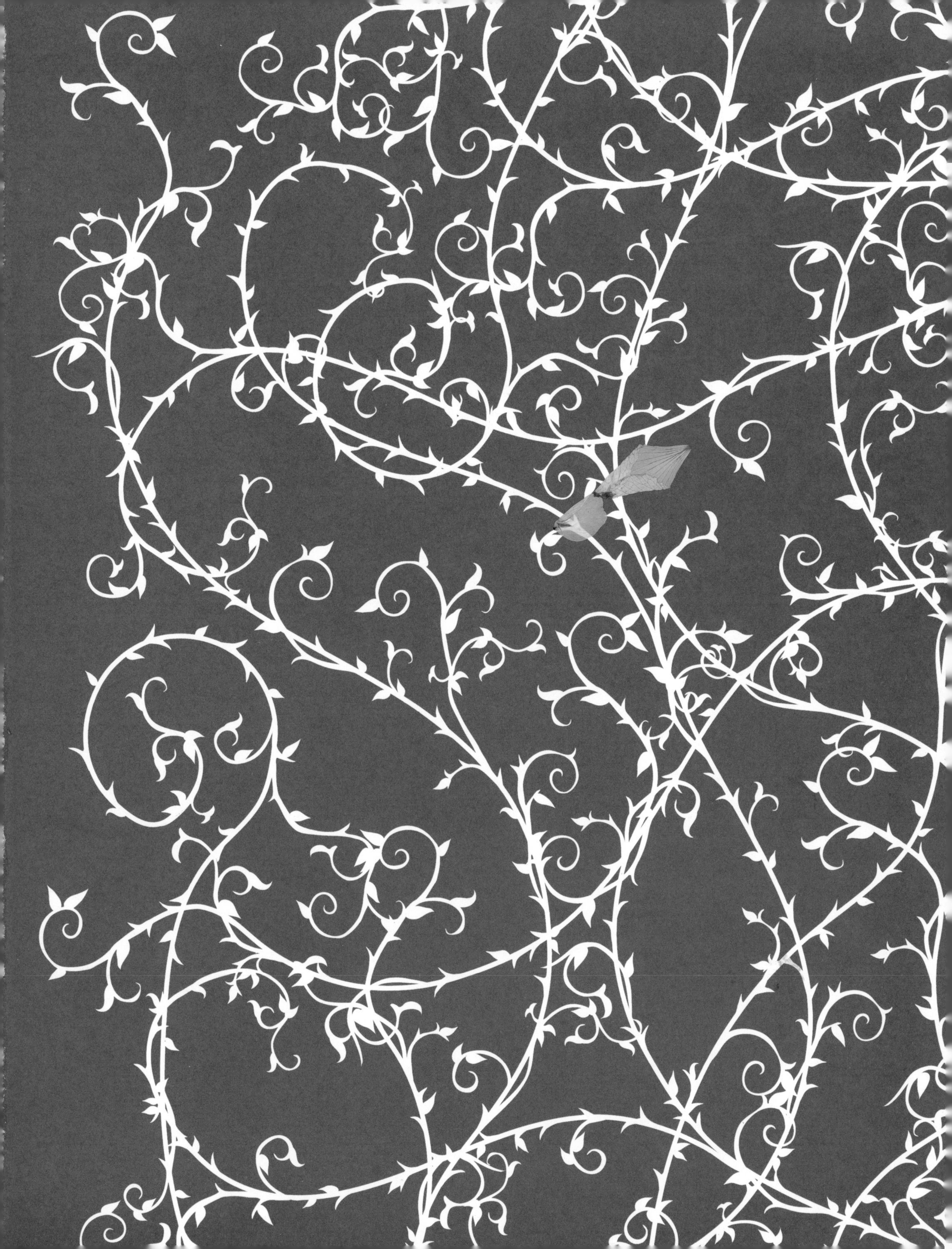

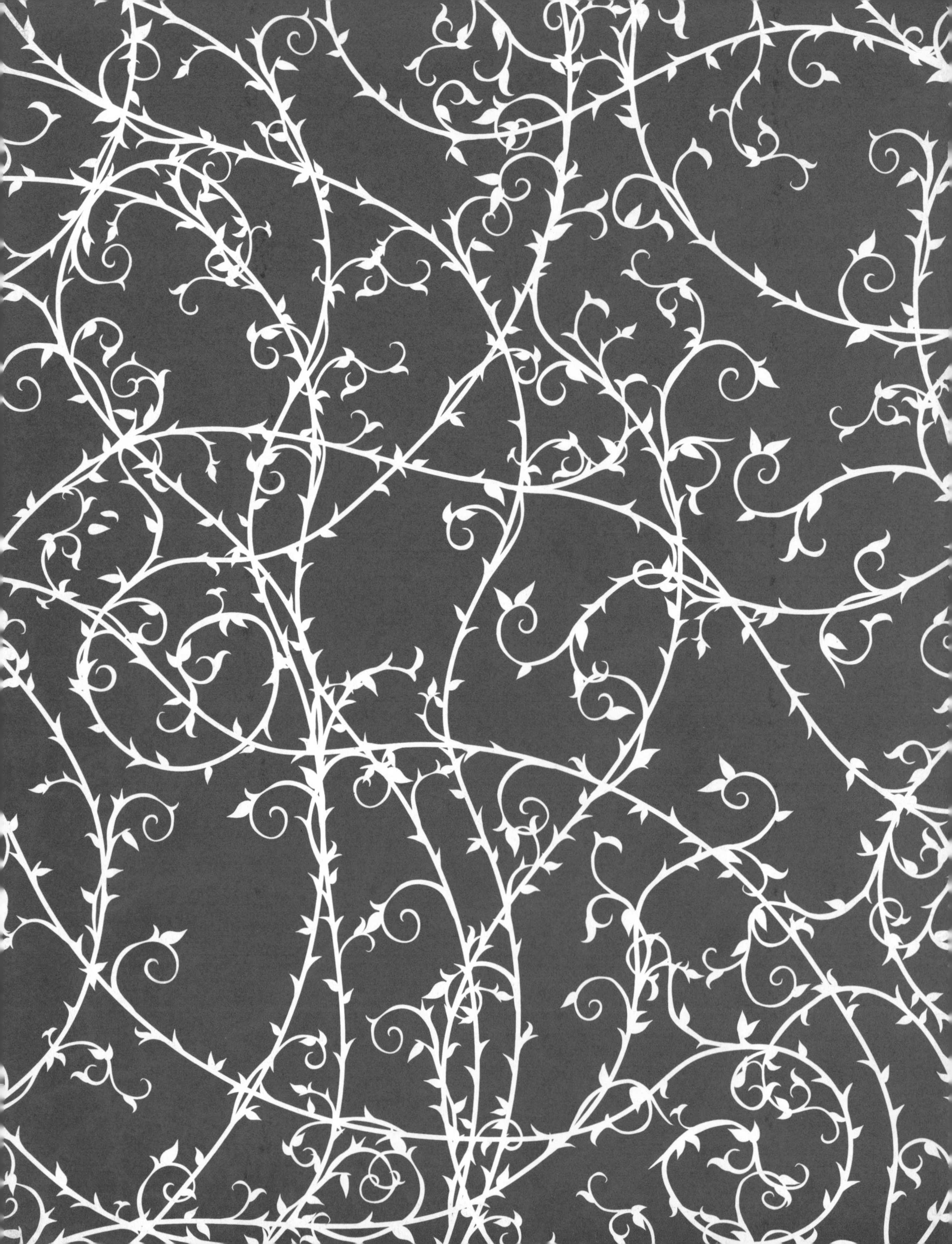